A Very Corporate Affair
Affair
Book 3

D A Latham

D A Latham

ISBN: 1492170607
ISBN-13: 978-1492170600

DEDICATION

To my dearest darling Allan

CONTENTS

ACKNOWLEDGMENTS

With thanks to;

Andrea Mills

Trystan Lutey

Penny Harrison

Tomme Darlington

Michael Harte

Becca Elliot

Jaqui Martin

Gail Hayward

and

Claire Plant

Chapter 1

"Elle, are you alright?" Ms Pearson's voice sounded distant. She looked concerned as I sat reeling at the revelations of the last hour of my life.

"Why did Ivan instruct you to reveal the content of his will while he's still alive?" was all I could manage.

"Because he wanted you to look after the companies, knowing you are either doing it for him, or doing it for yourself. Don't let the other directors push through any decisions," she replied. It made sense, with Ivan missing, his companies needed protecting from other, less altruistic directors. I would have looked after them for him, but he had needed me to understand that if the worst should happen, I would need to learn to control the other board members for myself.

"Anything else?" I prayed that there were no further revelations.

"No, not at this stage. I suggest you take leave of absence for now, and I hope for all our sakes that this situation is resolved quickly." Ms Pearson looked sympathetic.

"Yes....yes, so do I...." My voice faltered as I struggled to keep control. I stood to leave, and, even in my dreamlike state, remembered to shake her hand, before heading out to the car.

"Where to next?" I asked Roger, "and who instructed you not to tell me about Ivan earlier?"

"I think you need to go to Retinski head office. Mr Ranenkiov asked me to bring you. Mrs Ballard asked me not to interrupt your mother's funeral with the news."

I remembered telling Jo about the funeral during our weekend in France. "Ok, Retinski it is." We headed off, and almost straightaway my phone rang. It was Oscar.

"Hi Elle. I understand you spoke to Darius. Has anything else happened?"

I raised the privacy screen. "Yes, I've been informed that I'm acting as managing director of his companies in his absence, and I've been told that he asked Ms Pearson to inform me that in the event of his death, all his estate goes to me." Oscar went quiet. "Are you still there?" I asked.

"Of course, I'm just....shocked. He's an extremely wealthy man. I'll sort his bank accounts so that you have access, including the company ones. If you need any help, you can always count on me, you do know that don't you?"

"Thanks. Have you spoken to Darius?"

"Yes, just got off the phone to him. The Russian government are insisting that they don't negotiate with terrorists, which, in itself, presents a bit of a problem."

"What sort of problem?"

"I have to set the terrorists up a numbered bank account in Switzerland so they can access the ransom, otherwise I have no way of getting the money into Russia secretly, that is, without the Russian government finding out."

"So where's the problem?"

"They're peasant revolutionaries, with no way of getting to Switzerland."

"I see. How big a bag would be needed for that amount of cash?"

"It's not that simple. There'd be nothing to stop them taking the cash, and keeping the hostages, or worse, killing them."

I thought about it. "Retinski must have money inside Russia, especially given that Ivan inherited Vlad's estate. Let me talk to Ranenkiov."

7

"Be careful who you trust, there's going to be a lot of people with a vested interest in Ivan not coming back." *Like you Oscar?*

"Of course. I'm just on my way to Retinski now. I'll come and see you later on, when I know more."

"Ok. I'll be home tonight."

I cut the call, and sank into the seat, my mind racing with all the various pieces of information. I thought of what lay ahead, and quickly scrolled through the app store on my phone to download a Russian to English translator application. It wouldn't be ideal, but there was no way I'd be able to hire a proper translator quickly enough. When we arrived at the tower, I headed straight up to Retinski Headquarters.

Walking into Ivan's office was difficult, and slammed it home to me that this really had happened. The room felt empty and void without his electric presence. I switched on his screen, and found that it needed a password. I tried the names Bella and Tania first, with no luck. I typed in my name, and the screen sprang to life, confirming that I had indeed been on his mind. Before I could check the emails, there was a knock on the door. I opened it to find Mr Ranenkiov looking grave.

"Welcome to Retinski, Ms Reynolds, we have been advised of Ivan's wishes that you assume the position of managing director. Have you managed to find out any news?"

"Not much as yet. I need to know the cash position of Retinski in Russia, in case we have to pay a ransom quickly. I also need to meet the other directors."

"Certainly, please come this way, everyone is in the boardroom." I closed down Ivan's emails, and followed him out. We walked down the corridor, and into a large room, dominated by an enormous oak table, with ten men seated around it. Mr Ranenkiov showed me to the seat at the head of the table, before sitting in the chair beside me. I surreptitiously switched on the app, setting the phone beside me on the large chair. One man spoke in Russian to the man seated next to him, and a few people laughed. I glanced down to read the screen. ***Ivan must be judging the value of directors on how good their tits are.*** *sexist bastards.*

"I'd like to introduce myself, I'm Ms Reynolds, Mr Porenski's nominated acting managing director. Before you all introduce yourselves to me, I would like to make it clear that only English should be spoken in my presence please." A murmur rippled around the room. *Stuff 'em, I'm not sitting like a lemon while they all chat freely in a bloody foreign language.* I pressed 'record' on my iPhone.

Each man introduced himself to me in turn, outlining their position and area of responsibility. Every single one of them was Russian. "Does anyone have information on what the current situation is regarding Ivan's kidnapping?" I looked around the table expectantly. I figured at least one of them would have a link to the Russian government.

"It seems the group were held at gunpoint at the steps of the plane. We know they were taken onto a truck. We also know that a video message was sent directly to the Kremlin. It shows Ivan, and all ten guards alive, and held captive in a room. Their captors are demanding fifty million dollars for their release."

"Any political demands? Or is it purely money?"

"At this stage, just money. The Kremlin are saying publicly that they won't negotiate, however, they have put a negotiator in place, who has made contact with the kidnappers. He will try and keep them talking for as long as possible, to ensure the safety of the captives," said the finance director, a short, rather skinny man, with rather beady eyes, and a slightly beaky nose. I racked my brain to remember his name. "Oleg Marakov, finance director," he reminded me.

"Thank you Mr Marakov, is there fifty million on standby to pay these people?"

"Yes, but of course, we'd rather avoid paying it, if Russian authorities can rescue them by other means. Ivan is a prominent businessman, and as such, this is huge news throughout Russia. If the authorities can be seen to not capitulate to terrorists, it is so much better."

"Clearly. I'm sure the authorities don't want a spate of kidnappings arising from this, but my main concern is getting Ivan out unharmed. We all know what happened when the authorities tried to rescue hostages in other situations, and ended up killing half of them. I would like fifty million placed into a new, separate, bank account straightaway, just in case. Can you arrange that today please?" I fixed Marakov with a hard stare.

"Consider it done."

"Good. Now gentlemen, I will need you all to bring me up to speed on all the current companies, and any projects underway."

I was interrupted by a tall, rather imposing man, who I remembered had introduced himself as Andrei. "Is there a reason why you have been asked to become acting managing director, when you don't even know our company?" *Fair point.*

"I have been appointed to the board already. You have no director qualified in legal matters, so I was asked to join you as a non exec. Ivan appointed me as his nominated second in command, should this type of disaster occur. Please be aware that I will be sitting on this board when Ivan returns, so I would appreciate full disclosure from all of you."

Mr Ranenkiov spoke up. "Ms Reynolds is our lawyer from Pearson Hardwick, and due to her exemplary performance for our company, Ivan invited her to join us."

"The network of companies is rather complicated....." Oleg trailed off.

"I'm sure I can manage." I smiled at him to try and disarm him. He didn't smile back.

"Gentlemen, I would like a full list of the companies, their structure, and accounts for the last three years please, in English. I'll use this weekend to get up to speed, as I'm sure you can appreciate, this was rather sprung on me. Is there any other urgent business?"

Marakov looked sly. "Yes, we are about to vote through enhanced share options for the board. We are all in agreement, and it was only remaining for Ivan to cast the deciding vote. He had suggested it himself, so it was only a formality. He was planning to cut back on acquisitions, and use the cash to increase dividends and bonuses."

I gave him a hard stare. "I don't think this is the time or place for discussions like that. There will be no enhanced share options granted until Ivan returns, nor will there be any decisions about dividends or bonuses." There was a small murmur around the table. *Chancers.*

"Are you sure that going against the wishes of the board is a good idea? It would place you in a somewhat *difficult* position. It would be a disaster for the company if anything was to happen to our interim MD as well." *Threatening me now are you?* I ignored him.

"Now, if that's all, I suggest we all get on with sorting the information I'm going to need, and concentrate on getting Ivan back in one piece. I handed each man a business card with my mobile number and email address. "Any information or news on the situation in Russia, I would be grateful if you would contact me immediately." They all began to leave. Mr Ranenkiov followed me into Ivan's office, and sat down in front of the desk, facing me.

"You handled them very well. I think they thought you'd be a pushover. The share option thing was a crock of shit."

I smiled, "I know. I wasn't born yesterday, besides, I'm really hoping Ivan comes back in one piece, and I don't think he'd thank me for selling off bits of his company on the cheap. Now, is there anything that needs my immediate attention?"

"Not really. Just be aware that the other directors will begin jostling for position, should the worst happen."

"Do any of the other directors have direct links to the KGB?" I fixed Ranenkiov with a hard stare. He shifted in his seat slightly.

"I do, my brother in law works for them. To my knowledge, nobody else has a direct link, but saying that, corruption is common in Russia, and there's a lot at stake here."

"Am I the only one who actually wants him back alive and in one piece?" My mind was reeling from the realisation that there was nobody around me that I could truly trust. "What all of you seem to be unaware of, is that there is a plan in place in the event of Ivan's death. He dies, most of you lose your jobs. It's in everyone's interests that he comes back." *Yeah, tell that to the other backstabbers.*

Ranenkiov's eyes narrowed. "Have you seen the plans?"

"My boss drew them up for him. As you know, Ivan is the ultimate control freak, and that will extend after his death. The other directors should be careful what they wish for."

"You have my full support," he reassured me, "it would be a good idea for me to speak to the others, more privately, and remind them that Ivan would have made provision for this scenario. It would be far easier all round if we all worked together for the good of the company." He stood to leave. "Call on me anytime, I'll assist in whichever way I can. I'll also contact my brother in law, and see if there's any new information."

I thanked him, and reminded him to call me day or night as soon as I knew anything. I surreptitiously switched off the voice recording on my phone. As soon as I was alone, I switched Ivan's computer on. I scrolled through his emails, and saw the point the day before when he had stopped opening them. I clicked through, using google translate to switch them from Russian to English. I forwarded a few that contained reports through to my work email, and, satisfied that there was nothing of major importance to deal with, I closed down the email screen.

I clicked through the hard drive, finding mainly contracts and company reports. I sent some to my email to read through that evening, and changed the computer password before closing it down.

Ivan's secretary came in to introduce herself. She was a rather plain, dumpy woman in her late thirties called Galina. She seemed pleasant enough, although rather suspicious of me sitting in Ivan's office. I had seen her rather briefly before, so at least she knew I wasn't an imposter. She was genuinely upset at the news that Ivan had been kidnapped, and I noted, was the first member of his staff to express a modicum of emotion at the news. She went off to make a coffee, and my phone rang. It was Darius.

"Hi Elle, I just spoke to the Russian foreign secretary, and the negotiator they have in place. I have some news."

"Go on," I replied, thinking he sounded quite upbeat.

"Well, Ivan has British citizenship from when he claimed asylum here, so the Russian authorities are prepared to treat this differently from a domestic incident."

"What does that mean?"

"It means they will allow us to conduct a covert operation on their soil. Plus, here's the biggie, they'll even give us every assistance, provided we keep quiet about it, and assist them with their PR. they don't want to be seen to be allowing us in, if you see what I mean."

"Of course. I understand they don't want everyone of note suddenly kidnapped, and it would be embarrassing to have to admit that the British had to come and sort it out."

"The SAS have just set off for the Ural area. We have a decent idea of where the group are being held. They will do a recce, and hopefully get them out quickly, with no loss of life."

"Do we have a timeframe?" I fervently hoped it would be sooner rather than later.

"They want to do this quickly. Most kidnap negotiations are long and drawn out, so they won't be expecting anything yet. Russian forces tend to be clumsy and noisy, so sneaky arsed SAS men should be in and out before they even know what's happened."

"How risky is this?" I needed to know.

"There's always some risk Elle, but he's surrounded by his own guards. They are paid to take a bullet for him." He paused, "This is a major coup, being allowed to conduct a military operation on Russian soil. Our men are the best in the world at this type of thing. That's all the reassurance I can give you at the moment. Keep your phone with you at all times, and I'll call you the moment I know anything."

"Darius, thank you. It must have taken some doing to persuade the Kremlin to allow this."

"My pleasure. Listen, I have another call coming, so speak later." He cut the call. I sat back and thought about the conversation. I hadn't considered finding Darius and Oscar shagging to be a stroke of luck in my life before. Now it felt like enormous good fortune.

Galina returned with a cup of coffee, before asking if I required her for anything else that evening. I shook my head, and watched her leave. I was about to take a welcome sip of coffee, when the horrible, paranoid, thought struck me that I may well be a target now, and the only thing standing in the way of the other directors and ownership of Retinski, was me. I put down the cup, and made a mental note not to eat or drink anything there.

I headed down to my own office. Lewis was surprised to see me, but was busy with a client. I said hi to Laura, and sat down to deal with my emails. We had Steve Robbins' float on Wednesday, and he would be arriving at our offices at eleven to watch proceedings. I noticed that Matt had been assigned to sit with him, but I thought I would have to do my best to at least put in an appearance to reassure Steve that I hadn't forgotten him. Laura came in with an extremely welcome cup of tea. I swigged it gratefully. It was the first time I'd relaxed since ten that morning.

"How was the funeral?" She asked softly.

"Surreal, horrible. This has got to be the worst day of my life."

"Have you been to Retinski head office yet? Lewis told me that you are acting MD till Ivan's released."

"Yes, and I wasn't exactly welcomed with open arms. It felt like I was the only one who wanted Ivan back safe and well. They were too busy planning how to fill their boots. The only civilised one was Ranenkiov." Laura looked sympathetic.

"Anything I can do to help?"

"I may need to ask you to fetch me a Starbucks on Monday. I'm terrified to drink anything there, in case it's made with a polonium tea bag. I'm also going to need a Russian translator, one who's signed an NDA. I can't use google translate for legal documents, it's not accurate enough."

"That bad? Oh Jesus Elle, aren't you worried about what you've got yourself into?"

"Yeah, I am a bit. I'm sure it will all be over soon enough." *Bloody hope so.*

"I hope so for your sake. You really didn't deserve all this today. Well, if you need anything brought up on Monday, just call. I'll sort a translator first thing Monday morning."

I thanked Laura, and she gathered up her handbag and some shopping, and headed home. I glanced at the clock. It was nearly eight. The deli would be shut, and I was starving. I grabbed my handbag, and headed down in the lift. Roger was waiting outside for me. "Good evening Elle. Are you going home?"

"Please." I slid into the car gratefully.

"Jo suggested I take you to Sussex. It's more secure, and it'll stop the girls getting lonely."

I thought about it. I had a load of work to do, reading up on the companies. A fridge full of food, ready and waiting, sounded like heaven. "Are the security teams still guarding it?"

"Oh yes. It's 24/7 there, whether Ivan's present or not. It's the one place I can guarantee you'll be fine. I can arrange security at your flat if you want to stay in London though," he added hastily.

"Let me get my laptop, and we'll go to Sussex." We took just five minutes to get to my flat. I quickly grabbed my laptop, phone charger, and my book, and locked up. Within fifteen minutes I was back in the car, and heading South. On the way, I text Oscar to let him know where I was going, and sank into the seat. I was totally numb, both with shock, and anxiety at the tasks that lay ahead.

Oscar called to say he was on his way down too, and would come round the next day. I scrolled through the emails on my phone, reading one from Marakov to tell me the bank account had been set up, and the money transferred in. I hoped we wouldn't need to use it, but if a delaying tactic was needed, at least it was in place.

The girls greeted me enthusiastically when I arrived, dancing around my feet, looking for fuss. I petted them, before heading into the kitchen to find Jo. She looked shell-shocked, and had clearly been crying. She pushed a glass of wine towards me, and a plate of steaming chicken casserole.

While I was eating, she described the events of that morning, and the night before, when it had become apparent that the plane hadn't taken off. I found out that Nico was Ivan's head of security, and in his absence, Roger was in charge. "Have you heard anymore news?" She asked.

"Yes, at this stage it's confidential, but I'm hopeful. I just want him back in one piece Jo. His staff were bastards to me at headquarters today, and I feel out of my depth, and, and, " a sob broke free, and the dam burst. All the emotions of the day poured out in an unrelenting flow of tears. Jo handed me a square of kitchen roll, and I blew my nose. I had known I'd be fighting to keep everything safe for his return, what I hadn't considered was how bereft and scared I'd be for Ivan himself. I missed him.

"Those men should be ashamed of themselves, they should have been helping you, not behaving like the callous, greedy buggers that they are. Ivan will be appalled at them."

We were interrupted by my phone ringing again. I walked out onto the terrace to answer it. "Hi Darius, what's the news?"

"He's been located. Now, the terrorists are getting edgy with the negotiator over the money. Is there any in place yet? We need a distraction to keep them talking for another few hours."

"Yep, money's in place. Let me open my laptop and give you the account number." I went back into the kitchen, opened my laptop, and scrolled through to find the email Marakov had sent. I reeled off the account details to Darius.

"Perfect, this should make them relax somewhat. Bit of luck they'll all be toasting their success with vodka. I'll call as soon as there's news."

"Ok, thanks." I cut the call, and turned to Jo, "he's been located."

"Let's hope they can get him out in one piece," she replied.

Jo went home at around half ten, and I promised to let her know the moment there was any news. I put my phone on loud, and got into bed to begin reading the reports from the other directors. The two spaniels joined me, squashing their little bodies tightly up against mine, in a sort of doggy group hug.

I was too wired to sleep, so sat up till three in the morning, reading through the myriad complexities of Retinski. Eventually, my brain switched itself off, and I fell into a fitful doze.

I was woken early by my phone ringing. My brain immediately springing into action. "Morning Elle, just thought I'd let you know that a rescue operation is underway. I'll call you again the moment I have concrete news."

"Thanks Darius. Have you been up all night?"

"Caught a few hours on the couch in my office. This cooperation between our security services is a huge deal, so it's important that everyone gets it right.

"I bet. I'll speak to you soon I hope." We said our goodbyes, and he cut the call. I glanced at the bedside clock, it was half five. The two spaniels woke and stretched, before snuggling back to sleep. I had no chance of dozing off again, so got up and went down to the kitchen to make a coffee. I plugged my phone in to charge, and sat at the island with my laptop open, to carry on with the reports, although it was looking increasingly hopeful that I wouldn't need to understand the minutiae of the company quite so quickly. *Plan for the worst, hope for the best.* My mother's words popped into my head.

Time seemed to pass interminably slowly that morning, as often happens when waiting for news. I was too jumpy to concentrate on the profit and loss reports that I was trying to read, so gave up, and clicked through all the news websites instead, just in case anything was being reported. Even the Reuters news agency had nothing new to say on the matter.

I made another coffee and some toast, which I just picked at. The knot in my stomach had grown to epic proportions, twisting my insides into a painful lump of anxiety. The longer this went on, the more fearful I became, sure that something had gone wrong.

Jo arrived at nine, announcing that she had come to keep me company, and that she couldn't just sit at home watching the news.

"The rescue attempt is underway, I'm waiting for news." I said. "It started at half five this morning, so I'd expected to hear something by now." I didn't want to actually voice my concern that something had gone wrong, but inside, I was certain that it had. It should have all been over hours ago. Jo's eyes filled with tears, as the implication of what I'd just told her sank in. We both jumped when my phone began to ring. I ran outside to answer it.

"Hi Darius. What's the news?"

"He's out. They all are. Five terrorists dead. Sorry it took so long, but they didn't go in straightaway, as there were operational issues. He's aboard his jet heading to Moscow to refuel, so don't expect him to call you."

"Oh thank god he's safe. As long as I know he's ok, I can wait."

"Good, now the story is that Ivan's guards overpowered the terrorists and escaped. It must never come out how this really happened. You understand that?"

"Of course, my lips are sealed."

"Well, I know you're good at keeping secrets.....Ivan is being briefed on board the plane. Apparently he's in good health, and will give a brief press conference in Moscow while he waits for refuelling, so keep the news on, and you might see him for yourself."

"Will do, and Darius, thank you, and never, ever worry about my ability to keep a secret."

"Glad to help, enjoy your weekend."

I went back into the kitchen, "He's out," I yelled at Jo, "on his way to Moscow to refuel. Put the news on, because there should be a press conference. I've got a quick call to make, but yell if he appears." I went back out to the terrace and called Mr Ranenkiov. "It's Elle, I have news. Ivan's free."

There was a stunned silence for a moment. "That's fantastic. My brother in law said that something was happening at the top levels, but he wasn't privy to it, so couldn't get information."

"Apparently he's on his way to Moscow, and will give a press conference, so put your telly on. Also, can you call Marakov and get him to pull the ransom cash back to Retinski please. I'm hoping it wasn't touched."

"Consider it done. Can I ask though Elle, how you know all this?"

"That's confidential I'm afraid."

"I see, well, I don't know who your contacts are, but you must have some pretty powerful people behind you." I stayed silent. "I'll call Marakov, then the other directors. I'll call you back in a little while."

"Ok." I cut the call. Within 30 seconds it rang again. "Hi Oscar, have you heard the news?"

"Yes, just spoke to Darius. Great stuff. Can I come over?"

"Sure, I'll tell Roger to let you in. See you in a bit." I wandered back to the kitchen. "Would you tell Roger that Oscar's on his way over please? I'm gonna nip up and get dressed." Jo was beaming with happiness.

"Do you want some breakfast?"

"No thanks, I had toast earlier, and I'm sure Oscar would have eaten already. Do you know what Ivan's favourite dinner is? I want to cook for him tonight."

Jo thought for a moment. "He likes roast beef the most, I think. Tell you what, once I've seen this press conference, I'll nip to Waitrose and pick up everything you need for a roast."

"Great. He's probably gonna be worn out and sick of cabbage soup, so I'll spoil him a bit."

I ran upstairs, and threw on a pair of shorts and a T-shirt, and ran back down, just as Oscar arrived. "Hey, great news huh? Come and have a coffee while we wait for the news conference."

"You look exhausted Elle, I bet you didn't get a wink of sleep. Hey girls, how's my favourite spaniels?" He bent down to pick up both spaniels, one in each arm, and let them lick his face enthusiastically. I watched in fascination, shocked that he seemed to genuinely like them. I would never in a million years had Oscar down as liking animals. "Shall we see if we can watch your Daddy on the telly?" he crooned at them, smiling as their ears perked up at the word 'Daddy'.

We all went into the lounge, and I flicked on the big TV. Jo brought in cups of coffee, and Oscar played with the dogs while we waited. They seemed to adore him, rolling around at his command, and giving paw.

Chapter 2

Ivan looked a little tired, and his suit a bit crumpled at the press conference, which was in Russian, with subtitles. I drank in the sight of his beautiful face, not quite believing my own eyes that he was actually alive, free, and in one piece. He briefly described how his guards had waited for the ideal opportunity to overpower the terrorists utilising the superior training gained from their time in the Russian military.

He fielded a few questions from the journalists, before telling them that he would be heading straight back to London to get on with running Retinski Industries, even though he would have loved a few days holiday in his beloved Moscow. He told the reporters that it wouldn't put him off returning to Russia, *we'll see about that,* and he hoped that terrorists would think twice before attacking people, given that he had proven that Russian military training had made his guards almost invincible.

I saw Nico in the background, looking a little uncomfortable as Ivan spoke. He thanked everyone for their concern, and stood up, saying that his plane would be ready for take off in a few minutes.

As soon as the press conference was over, Jo announced that she was going to Waitrose. Oscar and I decided to take the girls out for a walk through the woods. We walked for a while in companionable silence, before Oscar spoke, "Are you feeling a bit better now?"

"Oh god, yes. I was in full meltdown last night, what with the funeral, the kidnapping, and the hassle I had at Retinski. I came back here and just cried. It all just felt like too much."

"It's what your life will be like with Ivan.... Complicated."

"So you keep telling me."

"You must be able to see it, I hate to think of you living in fear of your life." Oscar spoke softly, but with conviction. I thought about my paranoia the night before in the Retinski offices.

"I know. In a lot of ways I know you're right, but I need to stay the course. Part of my meltdown was the fear that I'd never see him again."

"Are you in love with him?"

I glanced up at Oscar, "Yes, I think so. I have feelings for him."

"I think so, means you're not. When you're in love, you know. It's irrefutable when it happens to you."

"Maybe I'm not an emotional person," I challenged. I was certain that my hesitation with Ivan was down to recent events, and not a lack of feelings for the man himself.

"That's not true Elle, you're quite normal emotionally," he paused, "when you look ahead, how do you see your future?"

I frowned as I thought about it. "Always on my own. I never had daydreams about husbands and babies, if that's what you're asking. It was always just me, with a good job, and a comfortable life. I like that Ivan breaks down my barriers, you know, by refusing to be fussed about my hang ups. He makes me feel normal."

"Didn't I do that for you?"

"No, I felt ashamed of being poor, and as I said before, you found me a bit distasteful. I never felt good enough, so it was almost as stressful being with you, as it is worrying that Ivan's mates being free and easy with the polonium. I can protect myself against them, I refused to eat or drink anything at Retinski yesterday. I can't protect my self esteem from being with a man who is more comfortable with male genitals than mine." I tried to choose my words carefully. "There are times that I wish I was with you, and I want to run into your arms and start again, when I realise I got a lot wrong about you, but then I worry that I'll never be enough for you." I stared at the ground, wondering what he'd say. He stayed quiet for a while.

Eventually he spoke. "I would change for you. I would treat you the way I should have treated you from the start. If you are truly in love with Ivan, then I'll just worship you from afar, but if you're not, or you're unsure, then as your friend, I'd urge you to get yourself away from him."

"You're a great friend," I said, not wanting to say more than that.

"I try to be."

The girls came racing back over, breaking the tension. We headed back to the house. I wanted to shower and change before Ivan returned, and Oscar said he had a builder coming to discuss some repairs to the castle.

Roger saw Oscar out, before informing me that Ivan would be landing in approximately four hours time at Gatwick. "It will take us approximately half an hour to get to the south terminal. I'm assuming you want to meet him?"

"Oh definitely, I'll be ready by three." I made a cup of tea, and checked through my emails. The other directors had each mailed their relief at the situation being resolved, their tone entirely different from the day before. *I bet they're cacking themselves.*

I watched the news conference again online, gazing at his beautiful face, trying to understand the feelings I had for him. I'd no sooner closed my laptop when Jo arrived back with bags of shopping. She busied herself preparing everything, waving off my offer of help. I worked out that we'd be home around half four, so she timed everything to be almost ready shortly after that.

I showered, did my hair, and applied some makeup, wanting to look my best. In the end I was ready by half two, and had to endure watching the clock for the last half hour before it was time to set off.

Roger took the Bentley, and we pulled directly into the private flight area of the south terminal, and were waved straight through the security gates. Ivan had been worldwide news, so I figured the staff at Gatwick weren't going to get picky about having his car ready and waiting.

I paced around the seating area while we waited, probably getting on Roger's nerves. Eventually I was rewarded by the sight of Ivan and his entourage striding through the walkway. He looked grim, and frankly rather angry. I hesitated, not wanting to throw myself into his arms until I was sure it would be welcomed. He fixed me with his laser stare as he strode towards me.

"Elle, thank you for coming to meet me. I have rather a lot to ask you on the way back to the house."

I stood rather uncertainly, before trotting along behind him to the car. He looked furious. We slid into the back of the Bentley, and set off. Ivan immediately raised the privacy screen.

"Did you send in the SAS?"

"Yes."

"How?"

"That's confidential. Are you not pleased to be home?" I was shocked by his anger, and his attitude.

"Of course I am, I'm just wondering what the fuck happened. One minute Marakov was negotiating, the next, men in black balaclavas burst in."

I frowned. "Marakov wasn't negotiating. What gave you that idea?"

"The terrorists said Marakov put fifty mill in an account for them."

"Oh yeah, I got him to do that, but he wasn't negotiating. He was too busy trying to persuade me to grant enhanced share options and bonuses to the board. If anything, he sounded as though he didn't want you back alive, none of them did. It's why I chose the route that I did."

"He would have dealt with it, I didn't need you rushing in to save me," he said sulkily.

I stared open mouthed. "Nobody was dealing with it Ivan. It seemed like I was the only person mildly concerned about you. I'll play you the recording so you can hear it for yourself. Now I'm sorry if I stepped out of line, but you know what? I had a bit of a shit time too. If I did the wrong thing, I can only apologise." A thick silence spread between us, and I stared out of the window, trying not to cry. It wasn't the ecstatic homecoming I'd expected.

Back at the house, Ivan made a fuss of the girls. "Are you cooking something?" He asked, sniffing.

"Yeah, a roast beef dinner," I said sulkily.

"I'm not hungry," he snapped. I went to the oven and switched it off. I gathered up my bag and laptop.

"I'll head back to London." I fully expected him to ask me not to.

"Ok." He strolled out of the kitchen, and went upstairs. *So rude.* I called Roger to ask if he would drive me to Derwent station. I didn't even want to put them out by asking for a lift home. Roger seemed puzzled, but did as I requested without comment. I was back home by seven.

I dumped my laptop in the flat, and whizzed round to the mart. When I got back I opened my laptop, and composed an email to Ivan, adding the recording.

From: Elle Reynolds
To: Ivan Porenski
Date: 30th June 2013
Subject: ungrateful git
Attachments: memo A4m 632KB, cache 14ce

Dear Ivan

I have no idea what your bad temper earlier was all about. All I can say in my defence is that I did what I thought was right at the time. I have attached a recording of my meeting at Retinski with the other board members. Also attached are all the emails that passed between us. I also need to advise you that I changed the password on your computer. It took me about ten seconds to figure it out, so it wasn't terribly secure. It's now Tania2013

I appreciate you have had a tough time, but I'd like to respectfully remind you that I buried my mother yesterday. I've not had a great time either, so I kind of expected a little understanding.

I was advised of your will and contingency plans by Ms Pearson. I would like you to change that please. I have come to realise that I cannot live in your world. I'm sorry.

I would like to resign the directorships too. I think a clean break is better for me. I have never been so terrified as I was in the Retinski offices, knowing your colleagues wanted me out of the way. I may have misjudged them, and it's a 'Russian' thing, but it's way too brutal for me.

I'm sorry to let you down, but I just can't do this.

Elle

I pressed send, and closed my laptop, before making myself a sandwich, and switching on the telly. I watched the news coverage about Ivan's 'courageous' escape, and glugged down a large glass of wine, while wondering why I was so shit at relationships.

By half nine, my eyelids were growing heavy, so I turned off the telly, and washed up my glass. I checked my emails, to find one from Ivan that simply said 'fine'. I dragged myself to bed, and lay in the darkness, sobbing like a baby. All the stress, emotion, and anxiety of the past couple of days poured out in a fit of uncontrollable tears, soaking my pillow. Eventually, I fell into an exhausted sleep

I slept in until nearly half seven the next morning, probably due to my lack of sleep the night before. I dragged myself out of bed, and made a coffee, before looking out over the river, and contemplating the day ahead. I decided to head over to the West End, and spend a self indulgent day mooching around the shops. With nobody demanding to know where I was, or what I was doing, I thought I'd better enjoy my new found liberation.

I showered and dressed, debating whether or not to leave my phone behind, in case I was tracked. I decided against it. I felt safer having it, and if Ivan started stalking me, I'd stop him through legal means.

It felt great to hop on the tube, and travel anonymously. I started off with Oxford street, looking in the shops I'd never dream of going into with either Ivan or Oscar. I found a couple of cute little tops in Zara, and a funky pair of shoes in Russell and Bromley. I scoured Topshop for casual clothes, and picked up a couple of bargains. I bought a pair of skinny jeans in Miss Selfridge, and even braved Abercrombie and Fitch to pick up a hoodie and a couple of vest tops.

I hauled all my purchases home on the tube, which was a bit of a pain, and got home around four. With no word from Ivan, I cleaned the flat thoroughly, did my laundry, and managed to sit down in time for Top Gear. For the first time in ages, I felt relaxed and normal.

I got straight back into my routine Monday morning, and was at my desk by half seven looking immaculate. I scrolled through my emails, and deleted the Retinski ones that I had forwarded to myself on Friday. I checked my schedule, and added myself back in every day. Laura had booked me out due to me being granted leave of absence, so I sorted it all out, and added Steve Robbins back in on Wednesday for his company float. I emailed Ms Pearson, and copied Lewis in, informing them that I wouldn't require the time off, and that I wouldn't be accepting Ivan's offer of non exec positions in his companies due to my personal safety being compromised. Approximately two minutes later Lewis appeared.

"Ok, what happened?"

"Long story. The other board members took exception to me being foisted on them, made it plain they weren't keen. Tried to get me to sign off some cheap share options, and when I said no, scared the beejeebus out of me."

"And what did Ivan say?"

"I don't think he believed me. I emailed the recording, but he was so angry with me for getting him rescued that he just dismissed me. Want to listen to it?" Lewis nodded, and I played it.

Afterwards, Lewis shook his head. "I'm not surprised you wanted to get out of there. I don't understand why he was angry with you though. I would've thought he'd have been angrier if you'd let his directors help themselves to shares at a knockdown price."

"I don't understand it either," I admitted, "I genuinely thought he'd be pleased that I managed to face down his board, and assist in getting him freed. He was livid about the whole thing though."

"Maybe it's a case of the male ego being dented," said Lewis, "he was probably embarrassed enough about being captured in the first place, without you being the one to sort out his escape."

"You're probably right. Doesn't excuse it though. That's why I turned up here Friday evening. It was the only place I felt safe enough to have a cup of tea."

"Jesus Elle. I wondered why you came back here. Oh well, best off out of it. Now, does this mean you're at a loose end today? Only I have a contract that needs writing up."

"Sure." Lewis went off to get the file, and email me the details. Five minutes later he was back. He ran through the list of requirements, and I made a start. I enjoyed the intricacy of contract work, and the intense concentration it needed. I worked my way through methodically, pausing only to sip the tea that Laura brought in.

I finished at midday, and sent it back over to Lewis, as well as printing out hard copies to add to the file. I grabbed my handbag, and dropped the file into Lewis on my way through to reception. He was busy on the phone, so just gave me the thumbs up.

Priti was on annual leave, so I bought a magazine to read while I had my lunch. I just finished my chicken wrap when my phone chirped with a text from James. Eagerly, I opened it,

arrive back Fri afternoon. Can't wait

I text back that I couldn't wait either. I was excited to see him, and glad that it was less than two weeks until our holiday. I needed some fun time, and some time without a boyfriend. Going straight from one mental billionaire to another had proved to be a bit of a mistake. I stuffed my magazine into my handbag, and cleared away my lunch tray, before heading back up to my office.

Laura was still at lunch, so I made a tea, and checked through my emails. To my surprise, there was one from Ivan.

From: Ivan Porenski
To: Elle Reynolds
Date: Monday 1st July 2013
Subject: sorry

Dearest Elle

I listened to that voice recording this morning, and I'm genuinely horrified at the double crossing bastards. I'm sorry you were subjected to that, and thank you for not giving in to them, and allowing them to plunder Retinski in my absence.

Ivan

I read it twice, debating whether or not I should reply. Ivan was still a client, so I decided I needed to respond.

From: Elle Reynolds
To: Ivan Porenski
Date: Monday 1st July 2013
Subject: re sorry

Ivan

You're welcome.

Elle

I pressed send, and got on with getting everything ready for the factory purchase completion the following day, organising our bill, which would be paid at the same time as completion. An hour later, I checked my emails, immediately seeing one from Ivan.

From: Ivan Porenski
To: Elle Reynolds
Date: Monday 1st July 2013
Subject: re re sorry

Elle

Would you like to come to dinner tonight? We need to talk.

Ivan

I replied straightaway.

From: Elle Reynolds
To: Ivan Porenski
Date: Monday 1st July 2013
Subject: re re re sorry

No thank you. I have nothing to say to you that I haven't already said. Unless you have a legal issue, please leave me alone.

Elle

I pressed send, and minimised the screen. The afternoon proved to be quite hectic. One of my colleagues, Peter, had been working on an extremely complex merger, which was scheduled to complete the next day. There had been a flurry of last minute caveats and issues raised by both parties, so it ended up being 'all hands on deck' to get new contracts ready. We all helped out, finally getting everything done by around nine. I grabbed my gym bag, and headed home.

I was puzzled to see Roger waiting for me outside. I thanked him, but explained that I wouldn't be needing him anymore. He looked surprised, but I didn't hang around to argue. Back home, I kicked off my heels, poured a glass of wine, and heated up a pasta carbonara. I had just started eating when there was a knock on the door. "Who is it?" I yelled.

"Oscar" I opened the door, and stood aside to let him in. Pushing my carbonara aside, I poured him a glass of wine. "You look better," he observed.

"I feel much better thanks. A couple of good night's sleep works wonders."

"Ivan came up to see me today. Wanted to know how come you now control the SAS. I told him that someone in a high place was simply returning a favour. I gather he was rather angry with you over the whole affair."

"Yes, but I've got no idea why. He was livid with me for interfering."

"He wanted his colleagues to step up to the plate, and move mountains to get him out. I think it must have been quite shocking to discover that the only person who actually gave a toss was you. He made all those men extremely wealthy, so it must have been terribly disappointing listening to them trying to grab a bit more, and ignoring his plight."

"They were all too busy figuring out ways of extracting as much out of Retinski as they could. While the cats away, as they say. Besides, did he tell you I resigned the non exec positions? Asked him to change his will too. There's no way I'm dealing with those people again. I was bloody terrified."

"So is it over with him?" Oscar looked hopeful.

"Yes. He took his anger out on me, and I really don't want to be a part of that world anymore. I came back here on public transport, with no bodyguards or staff, and finally felt like I could breathe again. This is where I belong."

"I'm really glad to hear it. I've been so worried about you. He's used to living with the dangers that surround him, but you're not. It would have taken a heavy toll on your peace of mind."

"Did you sort your building work?"

Oscar pulled a face. "Yes, well, sort of. I spend my life patching up that castle. There's always something that needs doing on a place that size and that old. Between my father and I, I think we've practically rebuilt the damn place. One of the castellations needed repointing. Unfortunately English heritage have to be consulted on every bit of work, and an uninformed busybody normally likes to put their two penneth worth in, which is usually wrong. I think I know better than them which type of lime mortar should be used, given that almost half the castle has been repointed in my lifetime." I could see the annoyance written all over his face, so I refilled his wine glass.

"Have another drink."

Oscar sipped his wine. "I have something I need to tell you."

"Go on."

"Ivan asked me to join his board as a non exec today."

"You are his banker, so it makes sense. Plus you're rich enough not to want to screw him for some of his money, pardon the pun."

Oscar smiled. "I think he's planning to fire the board. He was meeting Paul Lassiter this evening."

"I don't blame him. The only one with any savvy was Ranenkiov, the rest were just greedy and rather weak around that slimy finance director, who incidentally, I wouldn't trust one iota."

"My guess is that Ivan's changing the board to try and persuade you to stay."

"He already accepted my resignation. So it's too late for that. I do think changing some of the board members isn't a bad thing though."

"He'll try and get around you, mark my words, and if he doesn't, then he's a fool. You were the best and most loyal member of that team this weekend. I did point that out to him by the way."

I finished my wine, and announced that I needed my bed, as it was getting late. Oscar leaned in to kiss my cheek, but ended up lightly brushing my lips instead. "Night Elle, sleep well." He left, and I headed into my room. I lay in bed thinking about Oscar, and how normal and comfortable he was beginning to feel.

Chapter 3

I was in work early the next morning, just in case there were any further last minute issues to help Peter with. He seemed confident that it was all done and ready, so I made a drink, and switched on my screen. Straightway I saw the email from Ivan asking me to attend a breakfast meeting in Smollenskis at eight. I quickly replied that I'd be there, before attending to the other messages in my inbox.

I headed down at ten to, and arrived before Ivan. I ordered myself a latte, and sat and waited. I was quite nervous about seeing him again, after being the target of his bad temper on Saturday. I concentrated on remaining cool and focused. He arrived exactly on time, flanked by two guards. They sat at the table behind us, and Ivan ordered our breakfast, scowling slightly when I said I just wanted a slice of toast. "So you have some work to instruct me on?" I kept my face impassive as I asked.

"Yes, I have several things I need to discuss with you. I have fired Marakov, on the basis of his lie about the share options, among other things. If he challenges me in court, I may need to call you as a witness."

"That's fine. You still have the recording I sent?"

"Yes. I played it to him. I hope it's damning enough to prevent him taking legal action to challenge his dismissal. To be truthful, it's damning enough to give me good reason to fire the entire board, as not one of them lifted a finger to help you, or me for that matter. Only Ranenkiov caught on that you were the person he should be loyal to."

"Very true. So what's the work you wish to instruct me on?" I didn't want to sit around listening to Ivan whine about his staff. He either had work for me or he didn't.

"I want to keep you on the boards. I don't want to accept your resignation."

"Too late. I resigned, you emailed back 'fine', it's too late to change your mind, and it's not a question of more money. I won't do it for any price." I looked him in the eye as I said it. I needed to wean myself off him, starting with allowing him to keep getting round me.

"And if I change the board completely? Maybe let you have a say who's on it?"

"Nope."

"Elle, be reasonable. I shouldn't have reacted in the way I did on Saturday, but I did say sorry."

"You emailed 'sorry' regarding the other directors. Now, I felt my safety was compromised at Retinski on Friday. I was scared to even drink a coffee. You may think that's normal, but I don't. I will play no part in your business or personal interests. Do I make myself clear?"

He looked sulky, "So that's it? You're just gonna leave me?"

"Well, imagine if you put up with intense fear on the day of your mother's funeral, sat awake for a night, listened to others being not fussed if I was alive or not, then at the end of it, I treated you as though you were something on the bottom of my shoe. Would you go back for more? I forgave you for Dascha, gave you another chance, which you threw back in my face. So yes, that's it." I kept my voice low and controlled. "So is there any work you wish to instruct me on?"

He ignored me. "If you check your contract, you have a three month notice period if you resign. If you don't attend board meetings as requested, you will be in breach of contract."

"Ok, that's fine. I can ask Oscar to organise some security to accompany me while I'm in your offices. It's not a problem. I would hate to renege on a contract, and of course you're aware that if I was sued and lost, I would end up disbarred. Three months isn't a long time." I smiled sweetly at his scowling face. *You won't win here Ivan.*

"Elle, there's nothing wrong with my offices. Nobody's going to hurt you there," he was getting exasperated. "I don't want it to be like this between us. I'm not going to hurt your career, you know that."

"Riiight, so that's why you brought up my contract. That doesn't exactly make sense. You want to invoke a contractual arrangement to have me there for the next three months, which I'll be doing under duress, but you want me to know that you're still sweet, cuddly Ivan who wouldn't hurt me. Now, if you don't want me there under duress, don't threaten me with my contractual obligations."

"You know how I feel about you, how you feel about me, let's not throw that away." His voice took on a pleading tone.

"You put my life in danger twice, now I know you'd say that I can have security, but that's not the same as not putting me in that position in the first place. You don't love me Ivan, you love money. This is just an infatuation you have. A man who loved me would have been thrilled to see me on Saturday, not sulky because the wrong person rescued him, just like you were when I rescued Bella instead of Nico doing it."

"I have never knowingly put you in danger, well, ok, I knew about Dascha, but I had no idea the board would behave as they did."

"I'm talking about your behaviour on Saturday, being angry with me, being so cold towards me. I pulled in a big favour to get you out of there without it costing all that money."

"But you won't tell me who or why?"

"No, I can't, I gave my word." We sat glaring at each other for a moment. I decided it was pointless sitting and arguing. I stood to leave. "If you have no tasks for me, I'd better be getting back to work. I have a lot to do. Email me when I'm expected at the next meeting please, but be aware I go away on the 14th for a fortnight." I strode away before he could reply. I heard him curse behind me.

I went back up to my office, and began some contract work that was waiting for me. I didn't hear from Ivan anymore that day.

Wednesday saw Steve's company float on the AIM market. Matt had done a great job of getting institutional investors interested, and we sat in the meeting room with Steve, watching the market data on a screen. That afternoon, we began to get the figures in from Deloitte, and they confirmed that the offering had raised almost thirty million in cash. Steve was delighted, as expected. He approved of the board of directors Matt had helped him put in place, and all in all, had achieved every single one of his aims. We toasted his success with champagne, and he left us an extremely happy man.

In contrast, Thursday was a bit meh. The factory completion was so slow and troublesome, it felt like we were pulling teeth, the vendor's lawyers being so obstructive that morning, it prompted a furious exchange of emails from me, telling them to get their finger out. They then went out for a long, slow lunch (probably just to wind me up), and we finally completed at half three in the afternoon. I wanted to leave at five to go to Waitrose and do a big shop to fill up the fridge before James got home.

I wrapped up my work, and was trotting through reception, when I came face to face with Ivan. "I just came to see you."

"I'm just on my way out, is there a problem I'm needed for?"

"Out? Where?"

"Oh, only the supermarket. My flatmates back tomorrow, and I need to fill up the fridge, and the cupboards. I ate his soup collection."

"Can I join you? Then I can talk to you on the way round."

"You want to do supermarket shopping with me?" I was incredulous, "with your guards trailing along too?" He had the grace to look a bit sheepish.

"They can help pack and carry it. Come on." He fell into step beside me, and we headed down in the lift.

It was strange seeing Ivan pushing a trolley down the aisles. He seemed perfectly comfortable pootling along with me, and I had to admit, it was a lot easier than doing it on my own. I tried to pick out the type of things that James normally bought, plus the ingredients for the roast that he'd been craving. "Did you remember to take all that stuff out of the oven on Saturday?"

"Yeah, the girls and I polished it off. Thanks for thinking of making that for me."

"James said he'd make one for me. I can't wait. I've not had a roast since before he went away." I saw Ivan cringe slightly.

"I'm really sorry about that. I'm really sorry about all of it to be honest."

"No, you're just sorry that I'm not coming back to you, yet again." I picked up a bunch of flowers to decorate the flat, and put them in the trolley. Half an hour later, I was all done, and, after waving Ivan's credit card away at the checkout, all paid. Ivan pushed the trolley to the car, where the guards loaded it in. I slid into the back seat next to him. "You haven't done much talking."

"I'm not really sure what to say. I seem to always get it wrong with you, even when I'm trying not to." He looked anxious.

"Look, this is for the best. I'm doing you a favour, you can find a nice, dozy supermodel who won't be bright enough to realise how much danger she's in, and won't need you to change your board of directors. You won't miss me for long."

"Is that what you really think?"

"Pretty much."

"Will you just tell me the truth of how you feel, and we can drop all this bullshit."

"Ok, I feel that you would prefer me if I was deaf and mute, a bit weak, and a bit dozy. Then you can be master of the universe, and I can just gaze at you adoringly. Sadly, I don't fit into that description, and I hate this 'brutal Russian' crap. Right now, if I was forced to choose, I'd choose to be on my own for a while, without a boyfriend."

We arrived at the flat before Ivan could reply. His guards carried my shopping up, and left it on the island. I switched the coffee maker on, and started unpacking. He waited until his guards were done, before asking them to stay outside. He watched me put the shopping away, and waited until I was finished, and had made the coffees before he spoke. "It was your incredible intellect that attracted me to you. I told you that before. I like that you can keep up with me. I just don't like they way you make me feel...helpless, I'm used to being the strong, capable one, not the idiot who needs looking after."

"I don't think you're an idiot, and you certainly don't need me to look after you. I think you have that the wrong way round. I'm the one who's crying all the bloody time, and you're the one who never notices. Your answer is to try and bully me, which, incidentally, won't work."

"I've never bullied you."

I raised an eyebrow. "Breach of contract? You threaten a lawyer who owns no property with that, which, if I lost, would bankrupt me, and end my entire career. You don't think that's bullying? Sending me into Conde Nast as an insurance policy for a psychopath, telling me if I didn't, I'd be killed by the Russian mafia, that wasn't bullying? I've spent half the time I've been with you, terrified for my life. You have me watched, tracked, and guarded, yet you never bloody notice when I'm upset about it." My voice was getting louder and more indignant. "Look, I don't want to keep dissecting why we couldn't make this work, I just want you to accept that it's over, and let me move on." I stared into my coffee, not wanting to look at his beautiful face. "Tell me what happened in Russia?"

"We were walking out onto the Tarmac, ready to get on my plane, and were ambushed. We were completely surrounded. They herded us onto a truck, and drove us to a remote house, locked us in a room, and we sat and waited. One of them taunted us when the negotiator told him that the money was ready, said he'd draw it out, then shoot us anyway. We could hear them all laughing about it in another room." He sipped his coffee, and shifted on the stool. "The next thing that happened was a bit of a blur, these men just burst in wearing all black, and told me in English to go with them. We could hear gunshots in another part of the house. He led us out to a truck, and we were driven out of there and back to the plane. Only one of the rescuers accompanied us back to Moscow, to brief us as to what we should tell the press, the rest sort of melted away. I knew it had to be either you or Oscar behind it, and I doubted that Oscar would particularly want me back alive."

"Oscar was a better friend to you than any of your colleagues. He offered to put up your ransom money if the board wouldn't." Ivan looked shocked.

"Really? You surprise me there. It was probably just a ploy to make himself look good though."

"No idea. He offered straightaway. Didn't hesitate at all." I paused. "Were you scared?"

He shook his head. "Not really. They were only asking for fifty mill, so I knew we could pay them off. If they'd have killed me, then Putin would have razed their villages to the ground like he did the Chechens. I felt pretty safe, but annoyed that I was delayed, and missed the funeral. How did it go by the way?"

"It went."

"I'm sorry I wasn't there to support you."

"That wasn't your fault. It was probably better that you weren't there. I had to step back into my old self, and I don't like anyone seeing that."

"You know I wouldn't have minded."

"I minded though. That part of my life is finished now, over."

He looked sympathetic. "So, changing the subject, what are we having for dinner?"

"I was just gonna have a sandwich. I assumed you'd need to get back to the girls. I didn't get anything for tonight."

"Shall we eat out then? You can't just have a sandwich. Let me take you somewhere nice."

"No thanks, I want to make sure the flat's ready for James, and besides, we're over."

"You still see Oscar, despite splitting up with him, so why can't you let me take you out and feed you?"

I thought about it for a moment, "Oscar isn't predatory, he's always a gentleman, whatever his feelings. His good manners are very deeply ingrained I suppose. Plus he cares about me," I added, which made Ivan scowl.

"Have I got bad manners now as well? Anything else wrong with me?" He barked out the words, clearly annoyed.

I began to get angry. "This! This is what's wrong with you! Ivan, you are handsome, sexy, and I fell in love with you. I cried bloody buckets when you went missing, yet the moment I try and tell you how I feel, you bite my head off, and ignore all the things I've actually done to prove how I feel about you. Now I know full well I could go back to Oscar, and you know what? I didn't. Now that may not be enough for you, but to me, actions speak louder than words. You can say the words 'I love you', but your behaviour tells me otherwise. You didn't see me for nearly a week, yet you dismissed me like a servant on Saturday. THAT'S WHY IM LEAVING YOU." I was losing my rag. Ivan stared at me for a moment, as if he couldn't believe what he was hearing. I began to cry, my anger, frustration and sadness getting the better of me. Big, fat tears ran over my cheeks. I swiped them away quickly. I hated people seeing me cry, and I expected Ivan would get angry at my weakness.

"Poor girl, come, let me hold you." He pulled me into his arms, and held me tight. "I'm sorry I'm such a useless boyfriend, I don't mean to do these things to you, I'm just used to being a bit self centred." He kissed my cheek softly.

"A lot self centred," I said between sobs, "I told you I was terrified at Retinski, but you didn't listen, and tried to bully me into going back there. Sometimes, just sometimes, it's not all about you, it's about me, and how I feel."

"Baby, I'm sorry. I'm sorry I made you cry, and I'm sorry for being a self absorbed idiot. I just want to make you happy, and keep you safe." I pulled away from him, and stared at his beautiful, anxious face, trying to gauge whether he was telling the truth or not. He wiped his thumbs under my eyes, probably to remove the panda effect that must have formed. "I think we need some quiet time together, just having fun, without the worries of business, or boardrooms. Tell you what, why don't I rustle you up something to eat, and we can watch a film this evening?" *Oh you're good at getting round me, I'll give you that.*

I sniffed loudly. "I bought some cooked chicken, we can have that." I sat on the stool watching as he peeled and sliced some potatoes, before frying them. He looked very comfortable in my kitchen, almost as comfortable as James. We ended up having sautéed potatoes, cold chicken and sweetcorn. It was actually really nice, and I began to relax a little.

I scrolled through Netflix, and we chose a rom com. I stretched out on the sofa, and Ivan sat by my feet, rhythmically stroking my legs. "Don't you have to get back for the girls?"

"Not really, they have their team with them, and I've seen them quite a bit today. They'll be fine for an evening."

"They got really excited when they saw you on telly. They both sat and watched with their ears pricked up. They knew it was you."

"So Mrs Ballard said. I gave them quite a lot of roast beef, so I'm completely forgiven for going away."

"Bet you wish I was so easily pleased."

"Yep, although you do seem a little happier now you've eaten." He smiled hopefully, and reached up to rub my tummy.

"I don't bother to cook when I'm on my own, too much hassle and mess."

"It looks very clean and tidy in here. Do you have a cleaner?" I shook my head.

"Did it Sunday, and been keeping it neat all week. I didn't want James to walk into a pigsty. He's very clean and tidy, we both are really. I suppose that's why we get along so well. My mum's old flat was horrendous when I went over there on the day of the funeral. I had to send Roger down the shop for milk and tea, and also cleaning stuff. There wasn't a useable cup in the whole flat." I shuddered at the memory of the mould. Ivan pulled a face.

"Somehow that doesn't surprise me. He struck me as somewhat disorganised. Did many people go?"

"Yeah, it was packed. I got upset that the only flowers were the ones I'd organised, and Ray had a hangover, and hadn't bought a black tie, so went in a grubby shirt, and creased trousers. I had to shout and swear at him to get him to shower and shave, he wasn't going to bother." Ivan gave my ankle a little squeeze.

"At least you never have to go back there again."

"I have to go over soon and collect her ashes from the crematorium. I think I'll sprinkle them there though, in the garden of remembrance. It's nice there, and I haven't got anywhere else to put them. It's over in Eltham."

"I'll come with you for that instead then, support you on that day."

"I thought I'd do it after my holiday. The first Saturday after I get back."

"I'll keep that day free."

"Ok." I stretched, and yawned. "I'm gonna have to send you home, I'm shattered."

"Oh.....I thought I was staying the night. I want to cuddle you, make you feel cherished."

"Smooth, very smooth."

He looked a little affronted. "I mean it, I want to hold you, cuddle you, feel your skin next to mine. I've missed you horribly you know. I know you think I'm a big brute, but I'm not a cold or unfeeling person."

Some unknown emotion flashed over his eyes. I thought about it for a moment, I wanted him to stay, I'd missed him like crazy, but on the other hand we hadn't really resolved anything. "On one condition."

"Name it."

"We talk at the weekend, and you listen without getting cross."

"It's a deal." He helped me to my feet, and wrapped his arms round me, before kissing my lips ever-so-softly. I pulled away, and locked the front door, before he followed me into my bedroom. He stripped off quickly, and slid into bed, holding his arms open for me.

Laying naked next to him again felt wonderful, as if it was where I belonged. His strong hands caressed my back, while he pressed tiny kisses over my face and neck. I stroked his warm skin, feeling the firm muscles of his sculpted arms. His kisses moved to my lips, soft and chaste at first, changing to deeper, and needier. His tongue flicked across mine, igniting my libido. I could feel his erection pressing against my thigh. *What woman would waste that?*

I encouraged him to move on top of me, pulling him into position. He seemed a little reluctant at first, until I tugged him slightly, giving my permission. My legs had fallen open shamelessly, and I was wet and ready, turned on by his lush kisses and heady close proximity. He gently fed his cock into me, and paused, closing his eyes, as if he was trying to savour the sensation of being inside me.

After a heartbeat, he began to move slowly, continuing to kiss me, as he slid in and out at a leisurely pace. Tonight was about making love, rebuilding our connection. Keeping his rhythm, he moved his attention to my breasts, lapping and sucking at each nipple in turn, making me arch off the bed. As I called out at my climax, he kissed me, swallowing my cries of pleasure.

As my orgasm subsided, he pressed deep into me and let go. I felt him twitching, as he remained in place, kissing me, and sucking on my bottom lip. "You, my darling girl, are exquisite. I missed you so much."

"I missed you too," I said, "I was so scared I'd never see you again." He pulled out of me, and lay beside me, nuzzling my neck.

"This is nice, I like cuddling you. You always smell so lovely."

"Spose I dipped out on the duty free perfume this trip?"

He chuckled, "sadly you did. I'll make it up to you though." He wrapped his arm around me, and soon enough, his breathing became deeper and slower. I lay awake for a while, revelling in the feeling of his arms round me, and his body pressed against mine.

Chapter 4

I decided to skip the gym next morning. It didn't seem fair to boot Ivan out of bed at half five, throw a slice of toast at him, and send him on his way before six. I wasn't entirely sure what the correct etiquettes were when it came to boyfriends staying over, but I was certain he wouldn't be too impressed at me racing out the door at ten to six. I padded out to the kitchen, and made us both drinks, taking them back to the bedroom. I set his down on the bedside table beside him, and waited for the aroma to wake him up.

He looked the picture of male beauty while he was asleep. He had one hand tucked under his face, which looked relaxed and serene. His hair was tousled and messy, his dark curls flopping over his forehead. The total effect was slightly spoilt by a bit of drool at the corner of his full, sensual mouth, so I prodded him awake. I didn't want him dribbling on my pillow.

"Morning baby, there's some coffee for you there. Sleep well?"

"Good thanks, you get up early don't you? It's only quarter to six. Do I have to get out of your way?"

I shook my head. "No, I'm not going to the gym. Thought it'd be a bit rude to wake you up and boot you out. Would you like some toast?"

"No, it's too early to eat. I'll get something a bit later. I'm meeting Lassiter in Smollenskis for breakfast." Ivan sat up, and took a sip of his coffee. "Gives me time to make love to you again," he said, taking my hand, and guiding it under the covers to feel his erection.

An hour later, I made us fresh coffees, after the first ones were left to get stone cold. Ivan sat at the island to drink his, while I made myself some toast. "Paul's doing some executive search for me. I wish you'd change your mind about the non exec positions, at the very least, the Conde Nast one."

I thought about it. "I'd still sit on the Conde Nast board. I don't know why you don't approach some of their board to sit on Retinski, or even merge the two into one, it would kill two birds with one stone. They're well versed in heading up a vast multinational, plus you'd get to integrate the two companies far more effectively than having two boards."

He stared at me for a moment. "You are a bloody genius at times. That's actually a brilliant idea. Would you be prepared to be a part of something like that?" I thought about it, it would almost certainly mean delivering the Conde Nast work for Pearson Hardwick, give me all the kudos of a major non exec position on my CV, and a combined 'super board' was unlikely to be quite as heavily influenced by the Russian contingent. Plus, of course, Oscar would be there.

"Yes, I'd sit on a board like that." Ivan looked delighted. "How's your schedule today?"

"No meetings planned. I'll be helping the others out I should think, as most of my current projects have either completed, or are in progress."

"Good. I'm booking you today. We can sound out some of the directors of Conde Nast, and draw up a planned super board. Structure it the way we want. I want to look at cost savings that can be gained by fully merging Conde Nast and Retinski."

"I'd keep the names separate, but that's easy to do. Set up a huge umbrella company, and list all the others as subsidiaries, feeding revenue through to the parent company. I did a similar set up for Paul Lassiter's firm. Should save a fortune in both tax and admin."

"Sounds like a plan. Can you be ready by ten to eight? I want you to join me at this meeting with Paul, then we can head over to Vogue house. I'll need to book you Monday as well, for meetings with the American directors. I'll pull them over here this weekend."

"Ok." I cleared away our cups, and made sure everything was immaculate, ready for James. Ivan left to get ready at his own apartment, and I jumped into the shower.

He picked me up at ten to eight, and we drove over to Smollenskis. Paul was already there, sitting in a private booth, to one side of the restaurant. Ivan ordered our breakfasts, and I sat and listened while he outlined some of our plans to Paul, asking him to source an international finance director with particular expertise in Russian finance. Paul listened intently, before also suggesting looking at the Conde Nast board first, and aside from the finance director, using his company to fill any gaps. It was going to become a vast multinational company, so he advised Ivan to put at least twenty on the new board, listing out the areas of expertise that would need to be covered. I recorded the conversation on my iPhone, so I could make notes later. There was way too much information to memorise.

After my second latte, I excused myself to go to the ladies. I left my bag with Ivan, and tried not to take too long, as I didn't want to hold up the conversation. When I returned, Paul seemed to be looking at me rather strangely. I smiled back, and noticed he didn't seem to want to look me in the eye. Intrigued, I decided to listen to the recording I'd been making, as soon as possible. We finished our meeting, and Paul shook my hand. "Nice to see you again Elle, you be careful now."

"And you. Hopefully see you again soon." He nodded, still avoiding my puzzled gaze. My phone had been partially hidden by my bag, so I shoved it in, and trotted along behind Ivan, surreptitiously switching off the recording. We headed over to Vogue house, where the British directors were waiting for us.

I watched Ivan command the boardroom. He was confident and powerful, as he outlined his plans to form a closer integration between his companies. The other directors sat up a bit straighter at the prospect of joining a super board to oversee the management of a vast and varied conglomerate.

I observed the other directors, making copious notes, and watching the way they interacted with each other. Ivan asked each of them to submit a detailed CV to him, listing their areas of expertise and experience, so that he could make his choices. The directors not chosen for the umbrella company would remain in control of the operations of the Conde Nast brand, with extra areas of responsibility, and extra money to go with it. All in all, Ivan was dangling some juicy carrots. I could almost see the people round the table salivating at the prospect of promotion and higher pay and perks.

We headed back to Canary Wharf for a quick lunch, before Ivan had to return to his own office to organise the American directors meeting on Monday. "I'll zip up to my office, and do some research on the correct structure for this umbrella organisation." In truth, I was itching to listen to the recording to find out what had unnerved Paul Lassiter so much.

"Ok, can you come up to Retinski about threeish? We can discuss the other directors, form a clearer idea where we're going with this."

"Sure." He pecked my cheek before I got out of the lift at my floor. I went straight to my office, declining Laura's offer of a cup of tea. I closed the door, got my phone out of my bag and pressed 'play'.

I made notes up until the point at which I went to the ladies.
"I'm just going to the ladies, watch my bag please Ivan."
"Sure."
Pause.
"So you and her an item now?"
"She thinks so."
"You hate Golding that much?"
"Jammy bastard gets everything he wants. I enjoy rubbing his nose in the fact that I'm fucking her, and he isn't. I'll keep her out of his reach until he gets bored."
"What if he doesn't get bored?"
"He will. She's nothing that special. Bit prissy and Miss Perfect if you ask me. Not sure why Golding's so dopey over her."
"He thinks a lot of her. You still seeing that actress? I've forgotten her name."

"Penny Harrison? Yeah. She's one dirty bitch I tell you. Thankfully, lawyer girl isn't too clingy, and I get plenty of time to go over to Penny's place. Makes it easier to put up with the uptight and vanilla I'm getting at home these days.

Laughter.

"Maybe Elle'll get bored with you, if she's only getting vanilla."

"Nah. She's ecstatic just to be getting a bit of Russian sizemeat. She won't go anywhere."

"Shh, she's coming back."

Pause, chair scraping noise.

"That's better, now, where were we?"

I paused the recording, and sat trying to take it all in. I felt sick with the sheer humiliation of it. I pulled myself together, and emailed it to my work address, to make sure I didn't lose it, and pondered what to do for the best. I quickly googled Penny Harrison, and found out she was a model, turned actress, who had appeared on a couple of TV dramas. I clicked on images, and dozens of pictures of a sultry, brunette beauty filled the screen. She reminded me a little of Dascha. Straightaway, I was transported back to being the little, dowdy, brown mouse. Hearing the two of them laughing at me, and my lack of sexual experience, cut me to the quick, but rather than crumble, I made the decision not to cry over Ivan yet again, I'd cried over that man way too much. I'd move on, with my head held high. If I ever felt like wavering, I'd listen to that recording again.

I was jolted out of my reverie by my phone ringing. It was Paul. "Hi Elle, forgot to ask, did you get those books on reading body language?" *Where's he going with this?*

"Yes I did. Very interesting reads thanks. We should discuss them sometime."

"Can I ask you something?"

"Go ahead."

"Did you record all of our conversation this morning?" I remained silent. "So you did then. Have you listened to it?"

"Yes I have."

"I'm sorry. You needed to know."

"You did that on purpose didn't you? Drew that information out of him, knowing I was recording so I could make notes later."

"Like I said, you needed to know. Choices should always be informed ones." With that, he cut the call. *Now what do I do?* I glanced up at the clock. It was only two. I still had another hour before I needed to be at the Retinski offices. I called Oscar.

"Hi Oscar, got a bit of an issue, and I'd like some advice. Are you free now?"

"Not right now, I'm at the Lords. Is it urgent, or can it wait till later?"

"It can wait. Are you going to Sussex tonight?"

"No, in the morning. I'll be at a function here until about ten tonight."

"Ok, is it alright if I pop down in the morning?"

"Sure. Not too early though. I'll see you tomorrow."

I said my goodbyes, and ended the call. I made the decision to say and do nothing. I wasn't seeing Ivan that evening, due to James' return, and could probably avoid him all weekend if needed. It didn't solve the problem, but it did push it down the road for me to deal with another time.

I concentrated on getting the information ready for setting up the umbrella company, sending it up to the slimy ratbag's email address. I headed up at five to three, plastering my professional smile onto my face. Galina showed me into Ivan's office, where he was staring intently at something on his screen.

"Hey baby, thanks for getting that information over. Every single one of those directors we saw this morning has sent their CV's over already. They must be keen. I spoke to the Americans, they are arriving Monday morning, so we'll have the initial meeting here at ten."

"No problem." I pulled out my iPhone, and added it into my schedule. I took a file from my bag, "Here are the notes from our meeting with Paul this morning, with his recommendations." He didn't look away from his screen, so I placed the file on his desk, and sat down opposite.

He looked up. "Right, here's how I see it so far, on the board for the umbrella company will be myself, as managing director, you, as company secretary, and legal, Oscar, as our banker, Ranenkiov as HR director, Andrea Mills as director of administration, Andrei Orlov as sales and marketing director, Jacqueline Martin as director of information technology, and Vladimir Sutin as director of real estate and property. That still leaves me with at least another eight places to fill, most importantly a finance director. The Conde Nast one is a woman," he looked at his notes, "Gail Hayward. She seems efficient enough, but...." He trailed off. *Sexist bastard.*

"You don't need to make any decisions until you've met the Americans. There's no big rush. Anyway, it may take Paul a while to come up with the right people."

"Yes, of course. What do you think about appointing Oscar as chairman?"

"You'd have to sound him out about that, he might not want that much involvement, I mean, it's not like you two are great friends is it?"

Ivan shot me a look, "we're friends, why would you think otherwise?"

I just shrugged, and changed the subject. "What about Joan Lester?"

"I think she's best placed to continue as MD at Conde Nast. I don't want to completely strip them of their top management. She runs it very well. I saw that their advertising revenue has grown in the last three years. Quite some feat in this climate." I nodded in agreement. "I think then that we'll meet the Americans on Monday, then make our choices. I'll book Lassiter on Tuesday morning when we have a clear idea of the skills that this new board needs."

Outwardly, I was listening to him drone on. Inside I was trying to come to terms with his total lack of respect for me, and his contempt for our sex life. Suddenly, he didn't seem so pretty anymore. I noticed the unattractive sneer of his lips as he spoke of women in business, and the unpleasant way he chewed his biro when he was thinking. I was jolted back to the present when he asked me a question. I stared at him rather blankly. "I'm sorry, I didn't hear that."

"You're about a million miles away. Come back to the present." He clicked his fingers in front of my face, smiling as he did it. *Do that again lover boy, and you'll end up with broken fingers.*

"Yeah, I'm struggling to concentrate today."

"I noticed. Excited about seeing your friend I expect?"

"Yes, yes I am."

"Look, why don't we wrap up for today? I need to get back and see the girls, get them ready for the drive down to Sussex. You can get back and see your flatmate." *And you can spend the evening with Penny Bloody Harrison.*

"Great. I'll speak to you soon." I grabbed my handbag, and left. If he was perplexed that I didn't kiss him goodbye, he didn't say anything. In truth, I couldn't bear to be that close to him.

The lift couldn't come quick enough, and I breathed a sigh of relief when I stepped out of the tower. I needed to form a plan to extricate myself from him, without massively damaging my career. As I walked home, I thought about different ideas, including calling the headhunter who had approached me a few weeks back. Changing law firms might be a solution to the problem.

I stopped for some fresh milk, and had just finished paying, when Paul approached. *Oh great, just what I need.* "Hello Elle, have you got time for a quick coffee?"

"Umm, I was just on my way home."

"It won't take long." He took my elbow, and steered me into Costa, sitting me at a table, before going to get two lattes. He put mine down in front of me, and sat down. "I dropped a bit of a bomb on you today," he said.

"Yeah well, serves me right for listening I suppose."

"Have you spoken to him about it?" I shook my head. I didn't particularly want to dissect the grisly detail with Paul, who was, after all, a client. "Are you going to speak to him about it?"

"Oh yes. I don't ever plan on going within six feet of the man ever again. At some point, he might notice, but then again, he might not." I paused, "why does he hate Oscar so much?"

Paul shifted in his chair. "He doesn't hate him, he's jealous of him. If you notice, he tries to emulate him in a lot of ways, the immaculate suits, fancy restaurants, that type of thing. Oscar was born into it, it's all second nature to him, his 'normal' if you like. Ivan's hangups come from being the son of peasants, shot like cattle, and his arrival in the UK as a poverty stricken immigrant. He can never have what Oscar has, no matter how wealthy or knowledgeable he becomes. Oscar was born with a title, a bank and a castle."

"I can understand all that, what I don't get is why he was so vile about me. I can understand that I'm not his cup of tea, but why say all those terrible things?"

"I think that's more complicated. I suspect it's more to do with his own overblown ego than anything else." I looked quizzically at him, he went on; "He knows that in many ways, he can't compete with Golding, and has no real idea why you left him. I think he's assumed that if you walked away from Oscar Golding, you'll walk away from him too. It's human nature isn't it? To push someone away before they walk of their own accord. I also suspect he was trying to ensure that I wouldn't be interested."

"You sound as though you're trying to apologise for him. It doesn't explain Penny Harrison though."

"I'm not apologising. It must have been horrible listening to the man you love speaking about you like that. I just felt that I should explain it a little, as I figured you must be quite hurt about the whole thing." I nodded, not wanting to admit to Paul that I was, in fact, devastated. "As for Penny Harrison, I don't know if he is or isn't still seeing her. Again, that could be ego or bravado talking. He wanted to paint you in a certain light, and making out that you were dull in bed to the point of having to see someone else, well, that's all part of it, don't you think?"

"I don't know what to think to be honest Paul. Now, there is something I'd like to discuss confidentially with you."

"Go on."

"I'd like to discreetly look around at other law firms. I think it may be the only way to get away from Ivan and Retinski without anybody losing face."

"How do you think your boss would feel about that? Surely they'd rather support you, and keep you, rather than lose you, and probably Retinski as well?"

"I don't want to leave, I really love the firm I work for, but I don't want to be tainted by being 'the girl who lost the Retinski contract'."

"I see. I can certainly sound out a few people. You have a stellar reputation. Are you set on being in Canary Wharf? Or are you happy to go back into the city?"

"I'd prefer the city if possible. Then I'd be completely away from it all."

"I'll see what I can come up with."

"Thank you, I'd appreciate that, now, I don't want to be rude, but I really have to go." We said our goodbyes, and with a growing sense of anticipation, I headed home.

Chapter 5

I walked into the flat, to be greeted with the smell of roast beef in the oven. I dumped my handbag on the island and called out, "Hi, I'm home." James bounced out of the laundry room.

"ELLE! I'm so glad to see you. Feels like I've been away forever."

I stood staring at him. He looked like an entirely different person. "You look so different, great, but like a different person." He pulled me into an awkward hug.

"Still the same, just less hair. You look a bit thin. Have you not been eating properly?"

"Not really," I admitted. "Let me look at you." I stood back to get a better look. "James, you are seriously hot. I bet the ladies went nuts for you in America." He pulled a face.

"Not terribly keen on American women, whiny voices and all that. Now, first things first. Glass of wine? Dinner's going to be a little while, and we need to catch up." I watched him as he sorted the wine. His curly brown hair was cut fairly short, not clipper cut short, but enough to look tidy. His jaw was strong, quite sharp, and had a hint of a cleft on his chin. He looked tanned and fit, which seemed to make his twinkly blue eyes even more pronounced. In short, he was drop dead bloody gorgeous.

While our dinner was cooking, he told me all about his time in the States, the friends he'd made, and the work he'd done.

Reading between the lines, it sounded as though he'd been a bit lonely and homesick.

During dinner, I told him an edited version of leaving Oscar, my work at the factory, getting together with Ivan, losing mum, and finally, the events of earlier on. He listened to the recording, and cringed. "Penny Harrison's not a relation of yours I hope?" I asked. He shook his head.

"Sounds like it's been rather eventful. Seems like you need this holiday. Only a week to go, are you excited?"

"I truly can't wait. I bought a kindle, some new bikinis, and I brought a lovely sundress back from the south of France." I thought of all the beautiful clothes left behind at Ivan's houses, including my red ballgown and rubies, and felt a little sad. There was no way I was asking him for them though.

"Well, hopefully this holiday will make you forget all about that rotter. A bit of drinking and sunbathing will do you the world of good."

"Yep, you're right. By the way, did you call Janine?" I watched his face pink up slightly.

"Yeah, I called her. She's left Trystan, come back to the UK. Wants to meet up."

"How do you feel about that?" I felt a pang. *Jealousy?*

"I'm meeting her tomorrow. I've been in love with her since the moment I met her. I need to find out if I'm truly over her, whether or not I can move on."

"Hmm. Well, that was a stupendous roast. I think I've put all the weight back on that I lost while you were away." I patted my tummy.

"It's still early. Shall we go out for a drink? I've missed proper beer."

"Is that wise on top of wine? You know how you get, hangovers and all that. Plus you normally moan when I let you drink." I bumped his shoulder to let him know I was teasing. I quickly changed into jeans and a vest, and we set off down the river path to the Dog and Duck.

It turned out to be one of those rare, fun evenings, where people seem extra friendly, the drinks seem colder, and the sun doesn't seem to go in for ages. It almost felt like we were on holiday already. At half eleven, we were thrown out by the landlord, so that he could close up. I started when Roger stepped in front of me.

"Mr Porenski asked that I see you home safely."

"Mr Porenski can go fuck himself, or Penny fucking Harrison," I slurred, "and you can stop tracking my phone Roger, s'creepy. I'm not his girlfriend anymore." I could hear James laughing beside me. I didn't often swear.

"You appear to be rather well refreshed, let me assist you getting home." He stood his ground.

"The lady said no thank you," said James.

"Yep, that's me, the lady, the prissy, uptight lady." James and I both giggled.

"Don't forget you like vanilla," slurred James.

"And Russian sizemeat." We both howled with laughter, and staggered on, leaving a rather bemused Roger standing by his car.

"Think you might have let the cat out the bag." James slurred the words out.

"Don't care. He's a twat, not like you. You're ok."

"Glad to hear it....oof, shit, did you put that lamppost there?" James rubbed his forehead.

"Nah, was probably that twatty Ruskie. Lets blame him."

"Yeah. Bastard."

"Do you feel sick?" I was feeling pretty ropey.

"Yeah, a bit."

"His fault too." We both laughed, but we were both staggering, and I was trying not to get seasick, as the pavement had begun to sway.

Oh god, let me die now, I thought, as I tried to peel my eyes open. They felt as though lumps of lead were holding them closed. I rolled onto my side, thinking there might be less gravity holding them shut in that position. I opened them, only to stare into the shocked blue eyes of James, laying beside me, who had clearly just woken up too. I glanced down. We were both stark naked, and laying on top of the duvet in my room. *Shit shit shit. What the fuck have I done?*

In the absence of anything much to say to redeem the situation, I muttered, "morning."

"Morning...this is a...surprise." He moved to cover up his man parts.

"James, I'm really sorry, I don't remember...."

"Neither do I."

"Did we?"

"I don't know."

I closed my eyes, as if my mortification would be less if I pretended he wasn't there. When I opened them, he was still there, laying on his front. "I can't get up right this minute Elle." He said, blushing almost purple. I frowned, it taking me a moment to catch on.

"Oh, I geddit, yeah, I'll leave you to it. I'll go make us some coffee. I hopped off the bed, and pulled on my robe. James didn't take his eyes off me. I wandered out to the kitchen, seeing the trail of clothes leading from the front door to the bedroom. It was a total blank from walking away from Roger to waking up this morning.

I had just poured the milk when James streaked past, his hands over his bits, running into his bedroom. A few minutes later he emerged wearing a pair of shorts and a T-shirt. I pushed his coffee across to him. "At what point does your memory go blank?"

"I remember you ranting in the lift about the Ruskie, saying you were great in bed, I remember we couldn't unlock the door, and we both fell in when the key finally turned. After that, nothing. I doubt if we shagged, the state I was in."

I wriggled, I could feel that something had happened, that slightly bruised feeling that acts as a reminder of a night of passion. "I think we did." I blurted out, "I'm getting a flashback of you saying I was nice to shag, and I can feel the aftermath, you know, down there."

"You on the pill?"

"I had a shot, don't worry."

"Elle, I'm really sorry..."

"It's not your fault. We were both drunk, both responsible. Let's just treat it like one of those things that happens between drunken friends."

"Yeah..." He paused, "wish I could remember it though."

I smacked his arm. "We're meant to forget it ever happened, not try and recall the details. Now, do you want some toast?"

"Please. Is there any orange juice? My mouth feels like it's got fur growing inside it." I passed him the carton, the contents of which he chugged down. "That's better. Now, are you ok? You're not upset about last night are you?" He looked concerned.

"I'm a bit embarrassed," I admitted, "mainly because I don't generally behave like that, and the first time in my life I have a one night stand, it had to be with you."

"I don't normally shag drunken women, and I'm a bit embarrassed too, I'm quite glad you can't remember it, I probably wasn't at my best."

I smirked at him. "Me neither. Listen, let's just forget it. Where have you got to go today to meet Janine?"

"Belvedere. It's in South East London. She's staying with a friend there. I'll get the train at around ten. What've you got planned?"

"I'm gonna nip down and see Oscar about nine. I want to play him that recording, get his advice as to what to do. Ivan's asked him to join the board too, so he needs to know about this." I glanced at the clock, it was only half seven. James rummaged through his kitchen drawer, finally pulling out a box of neurofen. He took two, before offering them to me. I pressed two out of their plastic capsules, and used the last of my coffee to swig them down.

While James made more coffee, I picked up our clothes from the floor, cringing slightly at the sheer embarrassment of finding my knickers outside my bedroom door. I found my handbag on the floor in the hall, and pulled out my phone to check it. There were 22 missed calls, all from Ivan. He'd left a voicemail at one in the morning. I went into my bedroom, and rather tentatively pressed 'play'.

"Elle, I've had a rather disturbing call this evening from Roger, telling me he tried to escort you home from a bar, and you declined, appearing to be drunk. Apparently you were ranting about some drunken rubbish. Elle, I'm not happy about this, and you need to know that I won't put up with public displays of drunk behaviour, nor will I allow you dismiss your security in that way. I don't know why you aren't answering your phone, I can only imagine that you're sleeping off the effects of your appalling lack of judgement. Call me the moment you wake up. We need to have serious words." *Who the fuck does he think he is?*

57

I switched off my phone, and put it on to charge, before heading into the shower. I turned the water up to hot, and immediately began to feel a little better. I stood under the water, thinking about James. We had both reacted the same way, namely embarrassed, but it seemed, each secretly a little bit intrigued. I racked my brain, trying to remember a bit more about the previous night, as I wanted to recall how he felt inside me. The thought of James' cock made my tummy do that delicious squeezing thing.

By the time I'd washed my hair, cleaned my teeth, and put a bit of makeup on, I was starting to feel human again. I put on the little sundress that I'd brought back from France, and slipped on a pair of flipflops. It promised to be a blazing hot day, and I contemplated heading over to Hyde park after seeing Oscar. It was just before nine when I knocked on his door. He opened it dressed in a pair of shorts and a T-shirt. He smiled widely, and invited me in.

It was the first time I'd been inside his apartment. It was a stark contrast to the castle, being ultra modern, and extremely masculine, all decorated in a palette of taupes and greys. It was similar to James' flat, with the addition of a wall between the kitchen and the living room. I sat on the sofa, and looked around, while Oscar disappeared to make the tea. The first thing I noticed was the piano in the corner of the living room. It looked like a baby grand, and was so highly polished, it had an almost mirror like shine. The living room was dominated by a huge TV, which had to be at least 60 inches wide, set against the far wall. Underneath it was an oak unit, which seemed to house an array of gadgetry, including a playstation, which surprised me. On the coffee table was a copy of 'Stuff' magazine, alongside this month's GQ. All in all, it was the bachelor pad of an extremely urbane, and rather stylish man.

Oscar carried in a tray with a teapot, and all the other accoutrements on, and set it down on the coffee table. He then proceeded to pour, and finally handed me my tea in a white cup and saucer. "So you have an issue you need some advice on?"

"Yes. Ivan is planning an umbrella company and superboard to bring all the various companies together under one board, so to speak. Both you and I have been invited to sit on it as non execs." He nodded. "Yesterday morning, Ivan and I met with Paul Lassiter to discuss executive search, primarily to find a finance director, but also to fill the other skills gaps in the executive team. It was all pretty complex, so I recorded it, to help me make notes later. I don't think Ivan saw me press record, but Paul did. I wasn't being secretive, my phone was on the table, although partly hidden by my handbag. Anyway, halfway through, I needed the ladies, and when I came back, Paul couldn't look me in the eye. I figured something had been said while I was in the loo. I'll play you the recording, and see what you think." I pressed play, and fast forwarded to the 20 minute mark.

Oscar listened intently, his face impassive, giving me no clue as to what he was thinking. When it was finished, I switched it off. "Well?"

"I don't really know what to say, it doesn't make sense."

"What do you mean?" I asked, frowning.

"Well, he pursued you hard from day one, was prepared to hand over a multi billion pound company to ensure your safety, and changed his will to leave everything to you. His actions and his words say two different things. I take it you haven't spoken to him about it?"

"No, but his driver was outside the pub last night. I was drunk, very drunk, and said that Ivan should go fuck Penny fucking Harrison, plus a few other choice words, so he may have an inkling by now, plus I'm not returning his calls."

"You can't just avoid him."

"I know, but I couldn't even look at him yesterday afternoon. I just felt sick and humiliated. Then when I was on my way out, Paul Lassiter collared me, and tried to explain it all away. Said Ivan was jealous of you, and was trying to paint a horrible picture of me to put Paul off."

"That's certainly a valid theory I suppose. Have you given any thought as to how you want to deal with this?"

"I sounded Lassiter out about moving back to a city law firm. I'm sure that Ivan will pull his account over this, and I don't want losing the Retinski account on my CV, so it's better that I jump ship before that happens."

"That seems way too drastic. You might miss out on your bonus if you lost Retinski, but I doubt if they'd sack you. Ivan isn't your only client, nor is he your most lucrative, I am. Anyway, I'm sure I can send enough new clients your way to make up for you losing Retinski, I've held back because you seem pretty snowed under at the moment."

"Doesn't it bother you though, what he said about you?"

"No, not really. He's always been envious. That's why I kept the secret of the Faberge eggs from him. It also tells me that he still has no idea why you left me. Confirms that you've been true to your word."

I frowned, "I promised you, it will never be revealed. Whatever the circumstances, my lips are sealed." *Why is he bringing this up again?*

"I think you need to let him know about this recording. We can second guess his motives all we like, but until he's confronted with this, you'll only be guessing. I don't think you'll find peace of mind until you've seen his face when the recording is played to him."

"That's not what I expected you to say."

"Did you expect me to tell you to dump him, and come back to me?"

He doesn't want me either. The thought hit me like a thunderbolt. Dependable, ever present Oscar was rejecting me. Ivan was right, he'd got bored waiting, probably didn't want Ivan's cast off.

"No, I understand that you wouldn't want me back. I'm sorry to have bothered you this morning. I'll leave you to it." I stood up to go.

"Elle, that's not what I meant. Sit down, and don't put words into my mouth."

I sat down. "So what do you mean?"

"I'm trying to think of what's best for you. Clearly this is extremely upsetting for you, and unless you confront the problem, it will eat away at you, and your self esteem. Now, you know my arms would be wide open to welcome you back, but it's important to me that you return because you finally realise that I'm the man who loves you, not because you need to get back at Ivan for being disrespectful."

"I see. So you think I should wait till I see him to put this to him?"

"Definitely, you need to see his face."

"Oscar, can I ask you something, and you tell me the absolute truth?"

"Of course."

"Was he right in what he said? That I'm uptight and boring in bed? I need to know."

"Absolutely not, well, not with me. I think you're the sexiest woman alive. I liked that you were demure enough to keep your boobs covered in that game of dare, but saucy enough to flash your pussy to me in the bedroom. Plus you let me handcuff you to the bed. Hardly laying back and thinking of England is it? That's why you need to tackle this. Already it's made you doubt yourself."

"Yes it has. I guess you're right. I'll see him on Monday morning." I sighed.

"Why not tackle this now? I'm about to drive down to Sussex. I can take you to Ivan's house...and pick you up afterwards. Call him, see if he's there."

I took a deep breath, "alright, but you might have to come and scrape me up before you've even made it up the drive to the castle."

"That's not a problem."

I dialled Ivan's number. He answered on the first ring. "Elle, what the hell are you playing at? I've been out of my mind with worry."

"I'm fine. Are you in Sussex?"

"Yes, do you want me to send Roger to come and get you?"

"No need, Oscar's heading down to Conniscliffe, I can hitch a lift with him. I'll see you in about an hour."

"Great. See you soon." He cut the call. Oscar was getting his keys, and closing the windows.

"Do you need to get anything from your flat?"

"No, I just need my handbag, nothing else." I followed Oscar out of the flat, and into the lift. He pressed the button for the basement garage, and I cooled my back on the mirror walls of the lift. My heart was racing at the thought of confronting Ivan, and of having to listen to his reasons for telling Paul why I was so lacking.

Oscar must have seen how lost in thought I was. He reached over and gently squeezed my shoulder. "I'll be nearby. Don't worry, he won't hurt you. He's a lot of things, but he's not a stupid man."

We drove down in companionable silence, each seemingly lost in our own thoughts. I kept thinking about James, and why he was so horrified about sleeping with me. We were both single, and I wasn't ugly, so it had seemed like a bit of an overreaction on his part, being embarrassed about me seeing his dick. I had actually seen it before he'd rolled over to hide it. It had looked quite normal to me. I resolved to talk to him about it.

"You're very quiet. Are you ok?" Oscar enquired.

"Yeah. Just not looking forward to this," I admitted.

"I bet. Oh, I forgot to tell you, Mr Carey invited me to the legal awards bash next Saturday, on one of the Pearson Hardwick tables. Are you going?"

"Yeah, I got two tickets. At the rate I'm going, I'll be there on my own. Mind you, I could invite my friend Lucy, if she hasn't already got a ticket that is."

"If you don't have an escort, I'll offer to hang off your arm and look pretty." Oscar smiled at me.

"I may well take you up on that. It's a bit of a nuisance being on Saturday night. I'm flying out to Spain early the next morning."

"A holiday will do you the world of good. It's all been pretty stressful for you lately. I'm flying out to Tuscany a week on Friday. I plan to eat and read for a week."

"On your own?" I was surprised. He blushed slightly.

"Yeah. I would have taken you, but I didn't think you'd want to spend a week with me."

"Of course I would. I always enjoy your company. Have you been to Tuscany before?"

"Yes, I have a place there. It's very peaceful. You'd like it."

"I'll pester you for an invite next time."

"It would be my pleasure. It has a great pool, and the food is out of this world. I'd love to take you there, make you relax, drink wine and fatten you up a bit."

"My flatmate told me I'd got a bit thin too."

"I wouldn't say you were too thin, just thinner than you were. There's certainly some room to feed you up a bit."

I smiled at him. "I plan to come back from Spain at least half a stone heavier. James and I both like to eat. It's our mutual love of food that we have in common."

Oscar navigated the country lanes with consummate ease, handling the large Range Rover with confidence and skill on the narrow winding roads, and hairpin bends. I was getting increasingly nervous, the closer we were getting to Derwent.

All too soon, we pulled up outside the gates to Ivan's house. I called Roger to open them for me. As they began to whirr, I pecked Oscar's cheek. "Wish me luck, and I'll probably see you in a little while."

"Just ring me when you need me, and Elle, don't take any of his crap."

Chapter 6

I felt like the condemned man as I trudged up the drive to the house. Ivan was standing in the doorway, waiting, with the dogs at his feet. As soon as they saw me, they came racing over, desperate to say hello, and have some fuss. I petted them, before glancing up at Ivan. He was wearing just shorts, and was barefoot. He smiled tentatively at me. "Hi baby. Sorry about that voicemail I left. Very bad tempered of me to try and spoil your fun." I shrugged, unsure what to say. Ivan frowned slightly at my mute, unsmiling face. "Come on in. Would you like a coffee? Or would you prefer a cold drink?"

"I'll have a cold drink please. Water's fine." I sat down at the kitchen island, while Ivan poured a glass of chilled water, and opened a bottle of coke for himself. I took a long, cool drink. Ivan sat himself down, and looked at me expectantly.

"You look as though something is eating you alive. Would you like to tell me what's bothering you?"

I took a deep breath. "Yesterday, in Smollenskis, when I went to the ladies. I know what you said about me." I watched his face intently.

He frowned, "what am I meant to have said? You shouldn't trust Paul Lassiter you know." I watched Ivan's eyes widen as I pulled out my iPhone, and found the recording. I pressed play. We both listened to the conversation, Ivan's accented voice was unmistakable. He tried to keep his face impassive, but I saw panic in his eyes, especially at the part about Penny Harrison.

"How did you get this?" Was all he had to say for himself. "Did Lassiter give it to you?"

I shook my head. "I was recording all the information during the meeting for my notes. I forgot to switch it off when I went to the loo. The fact that Paul couldn't look me in the eye when I got back alerted me that something had been said. I typed up all the notes from the meeting, and his recommendations, and put them on your desk on Friday afternoon, if you remember. There's no way anyone could have done that from memory."

He steepled his fingers in front of his mouth, and just stared at me for a minute. "I'm sorry Elle, I don't know what to say."

"I see. I only have one question before I go. Are you prepared to answer one question truthfully for me?"

"Of course."

"Am I really that bad in bed? I need to know." To my complete and utter surprise, he began to laugh. I gave him a hard stare.

"Of course not. Hang on, is this why you went out and got drunk last night?" I didn't reply, I just sat there, stone faced, while he made light of my upset. "Elle, don't be silly. I said that to put him off you. I just didn't want to admit to being your devoted puppy, as Lassiter keeps taunting me about you, saying that you left Golding and you'll do the same to me."

"I'm sorry Ivan, but I don't believe you. Firstly, you didn't even admit that we were an item, second, you were totally disrespectful in a way no man would be to a woman he loved, and third, Penny. Bloody. Harrison." I kept my voice low and controlled. "Please answer my question, was I that bad in bed? It's all I really want to know."

"I can't compete with Golding can I? I always knew you'd go back to him, with his top education, society contacts and vast wealth. He's had everything he's ever wanted from the moment he was born. I wanted to take you from him, have something that he wanted, and he wants you desperately. Lassiter wants you too. I was showing off, pretending I didn't care, that you were just one of many, yet to both of them, you are the grand prize."

"You haven't answered my question. I'm not interested in your excuses, just that one question." I held Ivan's gaze.

"The truth is that I'm in love with you, and I'm terrified of losing you. I'm aware that out of the three of us, I'm neither the wealthiest, or the best educated. I'm not as perceptive as Lassiter or as knowledgeable as Oscar. The only thing I had that they were both desperate for was you, so I made out it was no big deal, that you were nothing special, that I had other women too. It was basically a pissing contest, and the most stupid thing I've ever done."

"Answer the question."

He scrubbed his hands over his face. "You know you're not boring in bed. Did you honestly think you were?"

"Yes, I did. Thank you for telling me what I needed to hear. I'll be off now."

"Don't go," he looked panicked, "we need to talk, I need to make it up to you."

"The best thing you can do is make sure this doesn't damage my career."

He frowned. "Why would it do that?"

"Because I've left you. All I ask is that you don't move to another law firm until after I've left Pearson Hardwick. I don't want this tainting my career."

"You don't need to do that. I won't move law firms all the time you're there. Look, this is all my fault, and I don't want you to suffer for it, so don't do anything you'll regret." He looked contrite and rather sad.

"I don't want to stay in Canary Wharf. I'm planning to go back into the city. I'm probably going to have to move, so I may as well have a clean break."

"Move? Why?"

There was no way I was admitting the real reason. "My flatmate is back with his ex, and it's a bit awkward being around them. It's about time I bought my own place rather than living like a student in a flatshare."

"I see, you seem to have made a lot of decisions. What about Oscar? Where does he fit into this?"

"He doesn't. Between the two of you, you've made me the most miserable I've ever been in my entire life. I want out, to get away from all this. Oh, and can you stop tracking my phone please, or I'll change my number."

"Elle, it doesn't have to be like this. Please don't give up on us. I know I make mistakes, but you know how I feel about you. I'll even beg you, please don't make all these changes, give it a little time. Let me prove how much I feel for you, please." If I didn't know better, I'd say he looked like he was about to cry.

"I'd better go. I need to get back to London."

"You only just got here. At least stay for lunch, or a walk in the woods with the girls." He looked anxious. "If you leave me because you don't feel for me, then so be it, but let's at least try and stay friends, and colleagues. We work so incredibly well together, we should at least try and preserve that."

I thought about it. "I don't know if I can do that. At the moment I can hardly bear to look at you. I mean, how would you feel if you heard me telling someone you were crap in bed, had a small dick, and I had to get it off Oscar to keep me satisfied?"

"I'd be devastated, I know I would, but I'd also know that I don't really have a small dick, and I made you come every time we made love. I'd trust what I know deep down."

"What about Penny Harrison?"

"She was the one that Roger delivered home the night you left Oscar. I've not seen her since. That's the truth. She's tried to call me at the office, but Galina filters my calls. She gave up calling my mobile after I didn't answer it when she phoned. I only said I was still seeing her because she's famous, and it would piss Lassiter off." He looked sincere, and contrite.

"You really are a tosser sometimes."

"Yeah, I know."

We walked through the woods in silence, a large, physical gap between us, in stark contrast to previous walks, in which we'd held hands, or Ivan had draped his arm round my shoulders. The girls seemed blissfully unaware, darting through the trees, sniffing everything there was to sniff. I began to wonder why Ivan had asked me to accompany him, given that he appeared to be sulking. It was lovely and cool under the trees, and the scents of the forest began to permeate, relaxing me. I felt my hands unclench, and my shoulders drop.

Ivan broke the silence. "You're starting to relax, I can see it."

"I couldn't have been more uptight if I'd tried. I know I'm an uptight person at the best of times."

"Not really, well maybe in your professional life, but that's how a lawyer should be. Uptight women don't have multiple orgasms, or let anyone stick a butt plug in them." I blushed as he said it. He'd seen, and played with, the most intimate parts of me. Mind you, I'd done the same to him.

"I don't know if you and I can just be colleagues, after everything that's passed between us. I know I'd struggle seeing you with your next girlfriend, and I suspect you'd get arsy about seeing me with another man. A clean break is sometimes better."

"I don't want you changing your life, moving away, just because I behave like a dickhead at times. I should never have said those terrible things, and it was just my ego, and my inferiority complex talking." He paused. "It would rip me apart seeing you with another man, especially Oscar, but I would understand. He's a decent man, and he's been true to you all along, although, in a way, you've been true to him. I still don't know why you left him."

But he's not you, I wanted to scream. "I need some time away from both of you. I care very much for Oscar, love him as a friend, but I'm not in love with him. As for you, yes, I'm in love with you, but I don't really like you very much, especially now."

"Apart from the obvious, why don't you like me?"

I thought for a moment, "because you are controlling, a male chauvinist, because you treat me like a bloke. You generally assume I can be bought off with a shopping trip, and you make sulking an Olympic sport."

"But apart from that?" He smirked, which made me laugh.

"I think it's time to let go of this so called inferiority complex. You're a beautiful billionaire Ivan, women fall at your feet, and men wish they were you. The poverty stricken peasant immigrant is long gone. It's time to stop using it as an excuse."

"I could say the same to you. You behave as though you expect to be dumped at any moment, and you believed I'd have an affair with some dumb actress. None of us see you as the little working class girl that you seem to think you are. When I look at you, I see an extremely intelligent, and highly accomplished woman, with an iron will, all wrapped up in a feminine and sensual body. As an added plus, you don't have a mean bone in you, which is rare in such an ambitious person." He paused, "I do appreciate your qualities you know."

"It didn't sound like it on that recording. You made me sound prissy, boring, and deluded."

"I know. I'm really, truly sorry."

"There's another problem now of course."

"Go on."

"I don't think I could sleep with you again, without a little voice in my head whispering that I was boring, and all the other things."

"That really got to you, didn't it? So despite me admitting I was lying, you still believe I was telling the truth?" I nodded. "I'll have to find a way to change that. I can't bear the thought of never touching you again, of never having this," he waved his hand to indicate the dogs, and the woods, "again." I knew what he meant, our weekends together had a magical quality for both of us. We were best friends, soul mates, and I was going to walk away.

"I need to go." I said. I turned to walk back to the house. Ivan didn't say a word.

I collected my handbag and phone from the kitchen, and walked through to the front door. "Do you need a lift back to London?" I shook my head.

"I'll give Oscar a call when I'm outside. He invited me to lunch at Conniscliffe."

"Is there anything I can do to change your mind, or fix this?"

"No. I don't think there is."

"So be it. Are you still going to meet me Monday morning to see these Americans?"

"If you want me to."

"Yes. I want it very much. Ten, in my office? Is that ok?"

"See you then." I turned and walked down the drive before either of us could say any more. It took every ounce of willpower I possessed not to turn around and fling myself at him, and let him kiss away my misery. Instead, I faced front, and kept walking, until the gates were behind me.

I wandered along the lane outside for about a quarter of a mile, before pulling out my phone and calling Oscar to pick me up.

Ten minutes later, the Range Rover pulled up alongside me, and I hopped in. "How was it?" Oscar asked.

"Basically, as you and Paul predicted. Said he'd lied to show off. I don't really want to talk about it if that's ok."

"Sure. Have you had lunch yet?"

"No, not yet."

"How about a nice lunch, then a long walk around the gardens? They're looking fabulous right now. No hosepipe ban this year."

"Sounds good." I sank into the seat of the car, relieved that I'd faced up to Ivan, and found out the truth of his betrayal. I still regretted leaving behind the red ball gown though.

After a lovely lunch, Oscar and I toured the gardens. The white garden had taken on a softer, more billowing appearance. "This is really at its best in May and June. It's gone over a bit now. The long borders are at their best this time of year though." He led me through the rose arch, along some yew lined walkways, and into a dazzling flower display, shown off by a backdrop of immaculate hedges. "This part is designed for high summer. The flowers all timed to come out together. I'm glad you got the chance to see it at its best."

"It's stunning." Tall spires of flowers punctuated blowsy bright yellow daisies, and the whole effect was a riot of hot, bright colours. Bees buzzed around happily, giving the effect of one of those timeless summer days of childhood. I wanted to lay down on the grass, and just while away the day.

"You look much happier," observed Oscar. "I've been quite worried about you lately."

"I feel....freer, sad, but liberated. Mind you, it would be impossible to be sad for long in such a beautiful place."

"Oh I don't know, I've sat in here and been depressed many times. It usually depends on what you're used to. To me, this place is just home."

"Yeah, I forget that sometimes, it's grander than the castles I visited on school trips, so I sort of treat it like a museum I'm visiting, and really, it's just where you relax and chill."

"When I was a child, I think I explored every inch of this castle. It was a magical place to grow up. I found secret rooms, a priest hole, all sorts of things. If I ever have children, I want that childhood for them, that's why I work so hard to preserve Conniscliffe."

"I can understand that." Marriage and a family with Oscar would represent an easy life. He was kind and gentle, with ingrained good manners, and a proven sense of loyalty and decency. Idly, I wondered if his odd tendencies could be cured with a vibrating butt plug.

"You have a strange look on your face, what's going through your head?" I blushed. *Why does every thought I ever have show on my face?*

"Nothing much." He gave me a searching look.

"So what are your plans for the rest of the weekend?"

"I thought I'd head back to London. I have a stack of work to do by Monday, I need to go to the gym, and sleep off my overindulgence last night."

"You're welcome to stay here you know."

"That's really kind of you, but I have a lot to do at home, and I also need to see James, if he's home tonight that is." Oscar looked quizzical. "His ex has been in touch, wants him back. I think he will. Might mean I have to move out. Threes a crowd and all that. Besides, it's about time I bought a place of my own. Does Goldings do mortgages?"

"You don't need a mortgage, I'll give you the money for an apartment."

"I couldn't possibly accept that, you know that."

"Alright, I'll give you the money, and you can pay me back if you get bonuses. Say 10% of your bonus each year? I won't charge you interest."

"That's incredibly kind of you. How much should I look to spend on a flat?"

"I don't know, up to five mil maybe? If you can get what you want for that. If you need more, just ask."

"I'll add flat hunting onto my list of jobs to do. Ivan's talked me out of leaving Pearson Hardwick, promised me that he won't move to another firm unless I leave."

"That's something, I suppose. You're a bit new into the job to move just yet I would've thought. That in itself might have damaged your career....does that mean you'll look nearby for an apartment?"

"Yes, if I can. I do love living there. It's very convenient for everything, plus it satisfies my 'wanting to live in the city' thing, without having to live somewhere old or rickety."

Oscar glanced up at the castle, "I quite like old and rickety." He laughed at my embarrassment at having insulted his uber grand country pad. "I know what you mean, don't worry. I love my flat. Love that I don't keep having to fix things, and it looks great with modern furnishings. Don't get me wrong, Conniscliffe is where my heart is, but it's quite nice sometimes to not be surrounded by priceless antiques."

I returned to London later that afternoon, arriving home around six, to find James had cooked a meal for Janine, and the two of them making doe eyes at each other. I felt a strange pang of jealousy, and wished that I'd stayed at Conniscliffe. Instead, I took my laptop to my room, and got on with some work. I also rang Lucy, and invited her to the awards bash the following Saturday. She was delighted, as the tickets were pretty much reserved for the partners, and a few high flyers from corporate, so as a family law specialist, she hadn't even had a look-in.

I had just got into writing up a complicated invoice when Ivan rang. "Hi Elle, just thought I'd check that you were ok."

"Yeah, I'm alright. Just doing some work."

"Why are you working on a Saturday night? You sound sad."

"My flatmates girlfriend's here, so I had to get out of the way. Threes a crowd and all that. I can't spend the entire evening in the bath."

"I wish you were here." Ivan spoke softly, not in his phone sex voice, but nearer his 'daddy' voice that he usually reserved for the girls.

"Do you?"

"Of course I do. I miss you terribly. Do you remember our very first Sunday together? I loved it, and that was before we became a couple." I thought back to that day, the easy rapport we had, and the discovery that Ivan was as normal and nice as a Russian billionaire could possibly be, and that he had spaniels.

"Yeah, it was nice, uncomplicated."

"What are you doing tomorrow?"

"Flat hunting. I think I need to move out of here. I'm going to see if I can view some apartments."

"Whereabouts? You're not moving away are you?" He sounded concerned.

"No. If you're not pulling your account, I'm going to stay put. I'm going to look at apartments in this area. I like it here."

"Do you need me to help you out financially?"

"No. But thank you for the offer." I wasn't going to let on that Oscar was lending me the money for a flat.

"The penthouse of the new building next to mine is up for sale. It's called Cinnamon Wharf. It's very secure. Great river views. It's definitely worth a look. It's on with Savills I think."

"I'll give them a call in the morning, although it's a twenty minute walk from work."

"I can always organise a driver for you."

"Ivan, we broke up. I doubt very much that your next girlfriend will take too kindly to you ferrying your ex around for evermore."

"I don't want anyone else. I only want you." He sounded so sad that my heart broke a little. "The girls are upset too. Tania's off her food, and Bella won't speak to me." *I'll give you points for persistence.*

"I'm sure they'll both recover on sausage Sunday."

"It won't be the same without you here. You left all your clothes behind by the way."

"Yes, I know. I thought it would be a bit greedy to ask for them, especially the red dress."

"Well I'm not going to wear it am I? I bought it for you."

"It's not really your colour."

"Very true....have you eaten this evening?"

"No. James cooked for him and Janine, and he hadn't made enough for three. He didn't think I'd be back tonight. I'll have a piece of toast later."

"I wish you'd come down here, I could cook for you, and make you sausage sandwiches in the morning. Mrs Ballard left a fillet of lamb in the fridge for us."

"I need to start flat hunting, plus it's half seven now. By the time I got down to you, it would be nine."

"You can view apartments next week. It's not as though you need to move out tomorrow is it?"

"True, I just feel really awkward here with the two of them." James had been really strange with me when I'd got back from Oscar's. Janine had been pleasant enough, but the pair of them clearly didn't want an audience. They had been tucking into a prawn and pasta concoction when I'd arrived home, and I'd noticed that the fridge had been severely depleted.

"You can always stay with me if you want to. There's plenty of room in my apartment."

"That's kind of you, but that really isn't going to be an option, given the circumstances now is it?"

"We are still friends though. I can still look after you, and help you. I'm just not allowed to make love to you, is that right?"

"I suppose so. Usually when people break up, they stop seeing each other."

"But we'll still be working together, and seeing each other most days, so spending a Sunday together makes no difference. If you stay there, you'll have to spend all day in your room, apart from the hour that you're flat viewing. It won't be much fun. Roger is only at my London place. He could pick you up in five minutes. By the time you get here, the lamb will be ready."

"Separate bedrooms though."

"Whatever you want, your old room is at your disposal. Shall I call Roger, and throw the lamb in the oven?" *Oh fuck it, yes please.*

"Ok. See you in a while."

I gathered up my handbag, keys, laptop and phone, and went into the living room to say goodbye. James and Janine weren't there, and I could hear high pitched yelping noises from James' bedroom. I cringed, and quickly scribbled a note to leave on the island, saying I would be out for the night. I headed down, and waited outside for Roger.

It was a muggy, humid evening, and I was relieved to slide into the air conditioned luxury of the Mercedes. I was also relieved to be away from the flat. Listening to sex noises all evening would have been pretty horrific. At least my mind was made up about moving out. My embarrassment at my drunken shag with James, had been magnified by the fact he was clearly not into me, and very into his girlfriend.

I pulled out my iPhone, and googled 'property for sale in Canary Wharf'. Straightaway, I found the penthouse Ivan had talked about. It was priced at four and a half million, looked a lot like his, and was in a secure, portered block. I emailed the estate agent, left my details to arrange a viewing, and looked at what else was for sale, leaving messages for another six agents. To while away the time during the drive, I wrote a wish list of attributes I wanted in my new apartment. It was relatively short for someone spending up to five million, so I racked my brain to think of things to add to it.

An ensuite bathroom with a good shower, and a bath.

A laundry room, separate from the kitchen.

A parking space, in case I ever learned to drive

A balcony.

A spare bedroom

A study/office (not essential).

I looked at my sad little list. For five million, I didn't seem to be expecting much. I didn't need a built in bar, or home cinema. I preferred going out to the gym, and certainly didn't plan on putting in a sex room as Ivan had.

Chapter 7

Ivan's house smelled fabulous when I walked in. The scent of roasting lamb made my stomach rumble, and the girls were overjoyed to see me again, probably because they suspected that a bit of lamb might find its way into their mouths. He looked delighted to see me, despite my having to be driven over, because I'd been too upset (or pig headed) to stay in the first place. He'd greeted me at the door, the dogs bouncing around with excitement at his feet.

"I'm so glad you came over. Bella was sulking nearly as much as me." I bent down to stroke her ears, only for Tania to shove her out of the way, and stand under my outstretched hand looking expectant. Laughing, I gave her ears a rub, then followed Ivan into the kitchen. He busied himself pouring the wine, and checking the oven, before joining me at the island. "How was Oscar?"

"He was fine. I had a bit of lunch with him, and a walk around the gardens, then went home."

"So what's happening with your flatmate that you want to move out?"

"His ex girlfriend's back on the scene, and I feel like a bit of a spare wheel. They need their privacy if their relationships going to get back on track. Oh, and they ate all my food. Bugger all left in the fridge when I got in, and they were happily tucking into the prawns that I bought. There was barely enough milk left for even a cup of tea in the morning, they'd used it all for lattes."

Ivan winced, "I wouldn't like to see you denied your morning coffee, men have been murdered for less heinous crimes. So is he serious about her?"

"I think so. He proposed to her once, although she refused him, then ran off and married his best mate. He's really weird with me when she's around though, sort of cold, as if he'd rather I wasn't there."

"Are you jealous of her?"

"No." *Yeah, ok, a bit.*

"Even though she's forcing you from your home?"

"I'm not being forced out, it's just made me rethink. It really is time I bought my own place."

"Can I ask, how are you planning to finance it?"

"I have savings. It's not really any of your business. I don't ask you how much money you've got."

"You had access to my bank accounts when I was kidnapped. Didn't you look at them?"

"No. I didn't want to be nosy, well, unless I had to make payments to people on your behalf. You were only gone a night, so the issue never arose. I know you have fifty mil inside Russia, but beyond that I didn't snoop." He smiled at my rather naive reply. Most people would have been raking through his bank accounts at the drop of a hat. It hadn't even occurred to me to snoop. The only thing I was mildly interested in was his study, which he'd asked me not to go into. The weekend he'd been missing, I'd been too paralysed with fear to even think of going for a nose around.

"You only have to ask, if you don't have enough for the flat that you want. I don't mind helping. If not, I'll buy you a nice flat warming gift." He got up to see to dinner. Satisfied it was ready, he pulled it all out of the oven, and began serving.

"Do you want some help?" I asked. He shook his head, before efficiently carving up the lamb, and dividing it between four plates. He added some roast potatoes and veg, cutting up the dog's portions into small pieces, and mixing in a little gravy. He brought all the plates over to the island.

"Theirs needs to cool down a bit. They'll be sick if it's too hot." He placed my plate in front of me, and poured us both more wine. He raised his glass, "to wonderful weekends full of food, wine and good company." We clinked, and drank.

I tucked in to my dinner, groaning as the lamb hit my palate. "This is gorgeous. Where did you learn to cook like this?"

"In Moscow, food was scarce, and what we had was limited and poor quality. One of the things that awed me when I got to the UK was how varied and plentiful the food was, so when I started earning decent money, I set about learning as much as I could about cooking and eating well. I don't have the most sophisticated taste, but I like to prepare food. I find it relaxing, and I hate having to rely on my housekeepers, they always make food too fancy when I'd prefer it plainer."

"Do you like Russian food?"

"Not particularly, although I like caviar and blini. It has to be proper Beluga. I can't bear rye bread though. It reminds me of the old, cheap, black bread. I like mine white, and fresh."

"I don't think I've ever tried caviar. I didn't even eat in a fancy restaurant till I met Oscar. Going out with him, then you, opened my eyes to just how much I don't know about the world. I have a bit of catching up to do."

"You're very young. Most people don't know much at 24."

"True. I feel like I'm just beginning my real education at times. I've been learning about body language. Paul sent me recommendations for some books, which I've been studying. It's really very useful. How to tell when people are lying, that kind of thing."

"That could be dangerous. What were you picking up when I was grovelling earlier?"

"You started off confident, and as I played you the recording, the confidence fell apart, you tried to hide it, but you looked defeated. That's about as far as I've got. They're pretty complicated books."

"Probably a fair assessment of the situation."

"Changing the subject, what've you been up to this afternoon?"

"Sulked, took some phone calls, sulked a bit more, read some risk analysis, did a little paperwork, then did some serious sulking, until I called you."

"I see, so are you representing Russia or England in the Olympic sulking championships in Rio?" He laughed his rich, deep laugh.

"You have a lovely way with words. I've missed you this week. I don't think anyone can make fun of me like you can."

"That's because women are too busy drooling, and men are too scared of you."

"True, you know you're the first person in at least ten years to call me a tosser."

"A richly deserved moniker, certainly in this case." I paused. "So does that mean that you never behave like a tosser to anyone else? Or that nobody else dares to tell you when you're being one?"

He looked thoughtful, "I think it's a bit of one, and a bit of the other. I tend to keep people at arm's length, so nothing is ever that personal. I'm closer to you than I've ever been with any woman."

"Even Dascha? You were with her a long time, surely you knew each other well?"

"Not really. I worked seven days a week, extremely long hours, so I didn't actually have to spend much time with her. She had her shopping, her lovers and her hobbies, so as long as she had access to my money, she didn't bother me."

"Did you just say she had lovers?"

"Yeah." He pulled a face. "She was into the BDSM scene, which I'm not, and I wouldn't let her tie me up or inflict pain, which she enjoyed. We were sexually incompatible, so she took lovers for all that stuff. It suited me."

"No wonder you think I'm boring in bed." I was reeling from his revelation. It was a world away from my own sexual experiences, and not a world I had the remotest interest in.

"No, quite the opposite. She just wanted to tie men up and whip them. That's not sex. I hated it, let her try it once, and said never again. I just couldn't see where the enjoyment was. I know you and I were a little kinky and adventurous, but it was always sex, you know, with an orgasm at the end of it."

"I thought BDSM was a sex thing, shows how much I know..."

"Dascha used to say that giving pain *was* sex to her. I told you before, she was a psycho." I shuddered, not wanting to visualise Ivan being whipped, he was way too alpha and too sensual a lover for all that. "At some point, I need to go over to Windsor and sort out their house. I dread to think what we'll find there. Would you mind coming with me? I don't really fancy going on my own."

"Sure, whenever you like. I don't mind at all." I finished eating, and pushed my plate away. Ivan checked that the girl's helpings had cooled enough, and set the plates down on the floor for them. They practically inhaled the roast lamb dinner, which made us both laugh. "Tania's got her appetite back then?"

"Looks like it. They've both been little ratbags all afternoon since you left. Bella's been driving me nuts, barking every five minutes to go out, then barking to come back in. When I said no to her after the fifth time, she slunk off and wouldn't speak to me."

I shared out the leftovers on my plate between the two of them, and cleared our dinner things away into the dishwasher, before we went into the lounge, and flopped onto the sofas. Ivan put the telly on, but the combination of my late night the night before, and three glasses of wine, made my eyelids start drooping. I was vaguely aware of Ivan carrying me upstairs, but didn't fully wake up.

I woke up the next morning still wearing my T-shirt and shorts, in the spare room, with Ivan fast asleep beside me. I tried to slip out of bed without disturbing him, but the moment my foot touched the floor, he opened his eyes. "Morning. I'm sorry, I meant to go back to my own bed before you woke up. I must have fallen asleep."

"I'll go and make us some drinks. What were you doing in here anyway?"

"I just wanted a cuddle before I went to bed, so I lay down beside you, and must have nodded off. I'm sorry, are you upset with me?" I shook my head, amused that this supremely confident, alpha male could admit to needing a snuggle.

I made our drinks, and took them back upstairs, purposely sitting on the sofa in the room, rather than perch on the side of the bed while Ivan was in it. "So what's the plan for the day?"

"Well, it looks a bit cloudy, so I think breakfast, a walk, and after that, we could go over to Windsor and check out Vlad's house, if you want, that is."

"I don't mind coming along for a good nose. Have you got the keys?"

"Yes, the police had them, sent everything over to Lucy, who sent them to me. I've not been there for a few years, so I'm quite eager to see it again. Dascha moved back there last year when we split, so it's only the one house to deal with."

"Can I use your gym this morning? I need a run and a workout. I didn't do one yesterday."

"Sure. I can be making breakfast while you're doing that. It'll be ready by the time you're finished." We drank our coffees, and I headed downstairs to the gym. I didn't even bother to change, knowing I'd be showering afterwards. I plugged my headphones into my iPhone, and ran for a full, fast paced, twenty minutes, before working my way methodically around the weights machines.

After finishing, I pulled out my earbuds, and could hear the radio blasting out in the kitchen. I could also hear Russian accented singing. Curious, I padded down the corridor, to see Ivan holding up bits of sausage, singing to the dogs, and the three of them dancing around.

"I know you want it, I know you want it, I know you want it, but you're a good girrrl." He sang, holding the sausage just out of their reach. He didn't see me, as he howled along to 'blurred lines'. I stood and watched, amused, as the dogs bounced up on their hind legs, as if they were dancing to his singing. As the song came to an end, he noticed me standing there. "Breakfast's ready. How long have you been there?"

"Most of the song." I smirked, as he blushed slightly.

"It's their favourite record at the moment."

"I could tell, the way they were dancing to it...." I bent down to pet Bella, "and have you got a crush on Robin Thicke, naughty girl?" She did that doggy smile thing, and hung her tongue out, which made us both laugh.

After breakfast, I showered and dressed, before we took the dogs out. This time, I observed Ivan closely, and saw what he meant about tension lifting in the woods. His shoulders dropped, and his hands relaxed. I wondered just how stressed he actually got, working as much as he did, with the responsibilities that he shouldered. "What stresses you out the most?" I asked.

"Other people," he replied immediately, "I'm not good at being around people a lot. I have to put up with it at work, but I'm quite solitary. It's why I'm not overly friendly with my security." I had noticed that he didn't seem to talk to them much, considering they trailed around with him most of the time. "I learnt the hard way to take a full day off every week, turn my phone off, and concentrate on the two girls." He paused, "my body began to object to lack of sleep, stress, and constant pressure. I suffered insomnia, palpitations, and passed out in my office once. I made changes after that."

"You have to look after yourself first. That's what my mum used to say, not that she was a great advert for it. You seem quite laid back now though, well, for someone who runs as many companies as you do."

"I internalise the stress, at least that's what I think I do. I hate anyone seeing me as weak, as it leaves an opening to exploit, like Dascha did."

"Loving someone isn't being weak, it's being a normal human being."

"True, it goes back to my bravado with Paul, admitting I was madly in love seemed like admitting I was weak." He looked down at the floor as he spoke, as if he didn't want to see my reaction.

"Do you think Oscar's weak then? He admitted being in love when we were together."

"Yeah, a bit. I thought it was amusing at the time how he trailed around after you, and behaved as though you were some sort of goddess. Thought he was being adolescent, until I spent that first Sunday with you. Then I understood."

"I think the pair of you are emotionally stunted to be honest. You with your 'I'm a poor immigrant' spiel, and Oscar with his 'I have to put up with being a bank chairman' crap. Both of you need to count your blessings a bit more."

Ivan laughed, "trust you to say it like it is. Yes, I'm probably a bit undeveloped in the relationship area. I never really had to try to get a woman before, they usually flung themselves at me, and were devastated when I got bored with them."

"Maybe they should have called you out for being a tosser more often."

"Possibly." He smiled his movie star smile.

We made our way back to the house, and once the girls were delivered into the care of their team, we set off for Windsor. It didn't take long from Sussex, and within an hour, we were pulling up outside a pair of enormous iron gates. "I hope Nico changed the codes," muttered Ivan, as our driver tapped away at the keypad.

The gates opened, and we continued down a long driveway, towards a large, faux Georgian house. "Wow. This place is enormous!" I exclaimed. It was way bigger than Ivan's Sussex home, which was huge by most people's standards.

"I'm hoping all my codes for the internal security work, otherwise we'll have alarms going off, and god knows what else." He pulled out a set of keys, and opened the front door. As soon as we stepped inside, a beeping noise began, and Ivan tapped some numbers into an alarm pad near the door. We both breathed a sigh of relief when the beeping stopped.

"What happened to all his household staff, and security detail?" I was curious.

"I let them go immediately. I didn't want anyone in here. Nico came over to secure everything external, set up our own security system, and make sure it was safe."

"So you knew your codes would work then?"

"Oh yes, the external ones, not the internal ones. Sorry, I was having a dumb moment."

We explored the downstairs. It was opulent in a rather overdone sort of way, with lots of gilding, and ornate furnishings. "Very typical oligarch taste," Ivan said, wrinkling his nose a little. The kitchen was vast, and beautifully fitted. It also contained every gadget a cook could ever want.

"What are you going to do with all this stuff? And the house?" I asked.

"Sell the house I suppose, I don't want it for anything. I know it's bigger than Sussex, and worth a lot more, but Windsor is more built up, and less private, although the security here is very good, and it has got woodland. I'm not sure what to do with the contents. They're way too good to just throw out, but are not my taste."

"Donate to charity maybe? Or rent the whole thing out?"

"Could do. It does seem a shame to just sell it, and I don't need the money." *How the other half live.*

We went upstairs to check out the bedrooms. The master bedroom was strangely traditional, a bit like the bedrooms at Conniscliffe, with heavy drapes, and old paintings hung round the walls. "I'd put a bet on that these are black market paintings. If they were kosher, he'd have hung them downstairs, and shown off about them."

I looked closely at the signatures, trying to decipher who they were by. I made out Degas, and one by Van Gogh. "I'd suggest these be returned to their rightful owners if they really are stolen. This is the ideal opportunity."

"True. I'll speak to Oscar, see if he knows anything about them." He pulled out his phone, switched it on, and snapped some photos. "Dascha's apartment is the other side of the house, so shall we check out the rest of these rooms first?" He nosed around the walk in wardrobe, before checking behind each of the paintings. I looked quizzically at him. "Looking for the safe," he said.

"Study, I would have thought." I replied.

We worked our way through the rooms, until we came across Vlad's study. Ivan searched through cupboards, and behind pictures, until he found the safe hidden behind an abstract painting. He tried all the keys on the ring, finally managing to open it with the second to last one. I peered in, over Ivan's shoulder. The safe appeared to be full of cash, stacks of it, in fifty pound notes, banded in £1000 packs. Ivan pulled it out of the safe, and piled it onto the desk. I counted it up. There were 600 packs, so £600000. "My god, why did he have so much cash here?"

"That would have been his day to day petty cash. It's not much considering what he was worth. Six hundred grand wouldn't last him long with Dascha around. There must be another, larger safe somewhere." Ivan carried on ferreting around in the safe, slipping a couple of flash drives in his pocket, and reading some papers. "There's a letter here for Dascha, in the event of his death.

The main safe is in his bedroom, and he gives the code. Come, let's look." He piled the cash back in the safe and locked it, replacing the picture across it. We went back to the bedroom, and pushed the bed across, revealing a trapdoor.

Ivan lifted it up, to reveal a safe door, set into the floor. He tapped in the code, and we heard a click. He heaved the heavy door open, and we both leaned forward, although I had a peculiar sense that we were intruding into something private.

The safe was stuffed with cash. We had no way of knowing how much was in there, without emptying it out, as we couldn't see how deep the box was. Ivan began pulling it out, heaping it on the floor beside him, while I counted it. It took us ages, as the box went down about a metre, and was at least a metre wide. It ended up at just under eight million, plus some diamonds, and a pack of deeds, which Ivan would need to look at closely, as they were written in Russian.

"I've never seen so much money. It's unreal." I exclaimed, thinking that had Ivan not returned, it would have all been mine, a vaguely unsettling thought.

"The problem with lots of cash is how to spend it. Money laundering laws are pretty strict nowadays. Cash like that is usually murky. There's only so many clothes you can buy, and meals you can eat. When you start trying to pay for cars and houses with it, it attracts attention." He piled it back into the safe, apart from a large stack. "You can have some fun with this, treat yourself."

"I couldn't accept this, you know that."

"I don't want it for anything. Use it for your holiday then." He moved it aside while we pushed the bed back into position. "Now, the bit I'm dreading, Dascha's apartment." He picked up the folder of deeds, and the stack of money, and placed it all on a table at the top of the stairs, before leading me down the corridor to the left hand side of the house.

Her room was ultra modern, with a sleek, white, padded bed, and acres of white carpet. Although very stylish, it was a cold, rather impersonal room, made by a designer, with no hint as to the person who had once inhabited it. "How come she moved in with her dad, rather than getting her own place?" I asked.

"She hated being alone, so couldn't have lived by herself. When I kicked her out, it was the natural place to go. She was a really strange woman."

"How old was she?"

"30." I looked around the room, there were two doors leading off it. Ivan opened one, and poked his head round. "Bathroom," he announced. I opened the other, and walked through into a vast wardrobe room, larger than most people's bedrooms.

"Oh.My.God. Look at the stuff in here." There were rails of clothes, an entire wall devoted to shelves of shoes, and a storage unit displaying handbags of every shape, size and colour. "I guess you weren't joking when you said she liked to spend." I picked up a Chanel handbag, and turned it over in my hands. It looked pristine, as though it had never been used. I opened it to find a lipstick, and a wad of cash.

"What do you want to do with all this?" Ivan asked. I looked at him quizzically.

"That's not my decision to make. This all belongs to you."

"Ok, I'll phrase that differently, would you like to have any of this? It's no use to me, but it seems criminal to just throw it all away. You're welcome to it, that's if you want it. Some people are squeamish about having things that belonged to someone else." I moved to the shoe racks. She was size six, same as me. I looked at the Jimmy Choos, and Laboutins covetously. *I'm not too proud to have all this.*

I moved to the clothes rails, all were size eight, the same as me. She had been slightly taller, but a decent tailor could sort that. "Would you think I was skanky if I asked to keep all this?"

"Not at all. It would be criminal to waste it. She may have been a nasty cow, but she had very good taste in clothes. Most of this probably hasn't even been worn. I'll arrange for Nico to get it shipped to your place." He pulled open some drawers, pulling a face at her underwear drawer. There was no way I was asking to keep that.

A couple of the drawers contained jewellery. Ivan picked up a handbag, and threw all the pieces into it, before zipping it up, and handing it to me. "You may as well take that home. I bought her most of that, so I'd rather you had it."

"Isn't it a bit weird, seeing me wearing all her stuff?" Ivan shrugged.

"Not really, it's just clothes and objects. I barely took any notice of her at the best of times, so I wouldn't have a clue if you were wearing something of hers or not."

We moved on, and went to the next room down the corridor. It turned out to be fitted out for her bizarre sexual tastes, with paddles, canes and whips on a rack along one wall, a padded bench, and various restraining devices fitted to the walls and the ceiling. "Gross," announced Ivan. "This can all be slung out straightaway."

It took us most of the afternoon to explore the house and grounds. Nico had set up a security team, based in a small, separate building, to watch the property round the clock. There were banks of CCTV monitors, and sensors around the perimeter of the land. It must have cost a fortune. Ivan sent a guard out into Windsor to pick us up a Starbucks, as there was no fresh milk, and we sat and drank our coffees in the park-like garden, while Nico organised some men and a van to load up all the contents of the dressing room.

"Did you come here often when Vlad was alive?" I asked.

"Fairly often. I got along ok with him, and he encouraged me a lot in my business. Gave me the seed money to start up, and introduced me to a lot of contacts. He thought Dascha and I would marry, so he wanted me to be successful so that I could take care of her. At least that's what he told me at the time," he said, rather mysteriously.

"How come nothing happened to you when you dumped her?"

"His only saving grace was that he was an animal lover. Bella and Tania were the puppies of two of his spaniels, both gone now sadly, but he loved both pups, and was appalled when Dascha went for Bella. Said he didn't blame me for leaving her. He loved his daughter, but he wasn't blind to her. Hence why I was able to escape unharmed." *Why do you look like you're lying?*

I rang James to see if he'd be home to let the van people deliver all the clothes and stuff. He sounded a bit strange, but told me he wasn't going out, and it would be fine to send them straight to the flat. Ivan picked up his files, handed me the stack of cash, locked up, and we headed back to Sussex.

Chapter 8

"Stay here tonight as well? We don't have to be at our meeting till ten tomorrow, plenty of time for you to get ready in the morning."

"I have a load of paperwork to do. I was planning to go home this evening, plus of course, I have a room full of clothes to sort out."

He put his knife and fork down, and pouted slightly. "I like Sunday nights with you. Don't worry, I won't jump you. I'll even sleep in my own bed."

"I really need to get back, and get myself organised for tomorrow. I have a busy week ahead."

"What about next weekend?"

"I'm out Saturday night, and I'm going away Sunday morning remember?"

He pouted some more, "Out where?"

"The law society awards. My friend Lucy's coming with me. It's a work thing. I could do without it, what with going away the next day, but work want me to attend. It's good for networking."

"Hmm, probably be a bunch of lawyers all chatting you up."

"That'd be nice. I've not been chatted up for ages."

"I hope you're joking."

"Yeah, I'm joking. I'm off men."

"I've been nice all weekend. Even you have to admit that."

"Yeah, you've been lovely. If this carries on, you might redeem yourself one day. I haven't forgotten your bad behaviour you know."

"You're a hard woman."

I arrived home about half six, dropped off by Nico, who insisted on seeing me into the lift. Given that I had a bag of jewellery, and a bag of cash, it probably wasn't a bad idea. I let myself in and called out a cheery 'hi, I'm home.'

James was in the kitchen, wiping down the surfaces. "Hiya. Did you know that the contents of Imelda Marcos' shoe rack, and the whole of Harrods ladies wear department arrived earlier?"

"Yeah. It's a bit of a long story."

"Shall I make us a coffee, and you can tell me?"

"Sure." I hopped up onto a stool, and watched as he made lattes. "Where's Janine?"

"Gone home. So come on, who bought you all that stuff?" I told him about the house at Windsor, and the dressing room. I pulled the jewellery out, and we looked at the various pieces. "Is this all real?" He asked, turning a sapphire pendant over in his hands.

"Apparently. I gather she used to spend Ivan's money like water. She had a rich daddy as well, so he probably spoilt her too." He whistled through his teeth.

"What's in the other bag?"

"We found a load of cash. Ivan gave me some for our holiday. I've not even counted it yet."

"About our holiday...." James trailed off.

"This is where you tell me you want to take Janine instead of me, isn't it?"

"She's a bit suspicious of you, and after what happened the other night, I don't really blame her. I thought that maybe she could come with us, get to know you. She might be better about you living here."

"I've decided to buy a place. It's about time I had my own home, so Janine doesn't have to worry, I'll be out of the way soon enough. Listen, I'm sure I can go to Tuscany with Oscar, so please don't feel bad, just take Janine." I was upset about missing out on our holiday, but tried to hide it. James looked really sheepish about the whole thing, and given how weird he was about drunken-shag-gate, I wasn't entirely sure spending two weeks together was a good idea. I certainly didn't want to play gooseberry with the pair of them.

"Are you sure? I don't mind you coming too."

"I'll give it a miss, thanks. Now, if you don't mind, I'll crack on with sorting out these clothes. I need to do some laundry too." I could feel the tears welling up, and didn't want James to see them.

"Do you want something to eat? I filled the fridge back up."

"I ate at Ivan's thanks." I took my coffee, and my bags, and headed to my bedroom. It looked like a warehouse, with boxes everywhere. I set my coffee down, and let the tears spill out. It was a mixture of disappointment at not going on a holiday I'd been looking forward to, and the sense of having lost James as a friend, that had upset me so much. There was a knock at the door. "Not now James," I said. He ignored me, and came in, plonking himself down next to me on the bed.

"I knew you were upset."

"It's nothing, don't worry." I sniffed loudly, and began to look in one of the boxes, avoiding his eyes.

"It's not 'nothing' if you're crying. Come on, tell me." He pulled me by the hand to sit down.

"I'm just disappointed, that's all. I turned down offers of holidays with both Ivan and Oscar, and had an argument with Ivan about going with you, and all for nothing. I get ditched when something better comes along." James looked a bit horrified.

"Oh Elle, I'm so sorry. I just assumed that with all these men chasing around after you, that you wouldn't be bothered, and would've rather gone with Ivan. If I'd known how upset you'd be, I wouldn't have asked Janine to come."

I sniffed in a very unladylike way, "it's not just that, ever since you got back, you've been weird with me, as if you don't want me around, I made the decision to move out yesterday. I'm viewing a flat tomorrow. If needs be, I can stay at Ivan's until it all goes through."

"You don't need to do that, Elle, I'm really sorry if I made you feel uncomfortable. I'm embarrassed about our drunken night, and I feel guilty for cheating on Janine."

"We don't know for sure that we cheated on anyone."

James looked down at the floor. "Yeah, we did....I didn't tell you the whole truth."

"I suggest you enlighten me now then."

"Alright, but promise me you won't be angry?"

"I promise."

"We came up in the lift, and you were ranting about the Ruskie, saying you were nice to shag. I challenged you to prove it, and you dragged me into the flat by my T-shirt, stripped off, and I fancied you too much to stop. I shagged you just the once, and then you passed out, and I feel like a total shit for taking advantage of you when you were drunk. The next morning, I was horrified at what I'd done."

"Why were you so embarrassed at me seeing you nude?" It was a question that had been bugging me. James blushed.

"I don't know. Fear of not measuring up to the big dicked alpha males that you normally go out with I suppose. They don't have to get you pissed first do they? I did, because I knew that sober you wouldn't have ever considered it."

I felt total sympathy for him. He looked so ashamed and contrite. "James, I never had any inkling that you had the remotest interest in me at all. I just thought you considered me a friend, or a sort of kid sister. I would've handled things differently if I'd known."

James gave me a searching look. "How would you have handled things then?"

"I would have jumped you that morning when we woke up, rather than being so stupidly embarrassed about it. I was curious about you too." *That's it, the cat's out of the bag.*

James didn't reply, just stared at me for a few moments, before leaning in, and giving me the softest kiss. We both let the kiss linger, a small, chaste connection, before he pressed a little more firmly, his tongue meeting mine, shyly at first, before becoming bolder. His arms wrapped around me, pulling me close. I relaxed into his embrace, and wrapped my arms around his waist, feeling him physically for the first time. It felt.....wrong.

He must have felt the same, as he pulled away. "I wanted to do that for the longest time, but..." He trailed off.

"It didn't feel right, did it?" I said softly. He shook his head.

"I'm so sorry Elle, I thought it would be all fireworks and celestial choruses, but..."

"Same for me. Want to know what I think?" He nodded, "I think you're in love with Janine, and I'm in love with the Ruskie Ratbag. We're both good looking people, so there was always going to be an attraction, but now we've acknowledged and explored it, we can admit that it's either not the right time, or that the chemistry isn't there, and let it go."

"I think you're spot on with your assessment. Can we get back to being best friends?" He looked relieved.

"Yeah. Although I don't think it's all that fair that you asked your girlfriend on our holiday. I would never have done that to you."

"Sorry about that. She was giving me so much grief about it. Why don't you ask Ivan to come? Then the four of us can go."

"Doubt if he'd be able to at such short notice. I will ask though."

"What are you gonna do with all these clothes and things? I doubt if they'll all fit in your closet. The shoes definitely won't."

"I might keep a lot of them packed up until after I move. I need to work my way through them, see what needs altering or cleaning, and sort them all out. There's a lot there, so it'll take a while. I'm gonna go through all the handbags first. There was a wad of cash in the first one I picked up."

"I'll give you a hand if you like." He pulled open the first box of handbags, and between us, we went through all of them, throwing the contents onto the bed. Each one seemed to hold makeup, perfume, and a wad of cash. When we were done, James sorted the cash into piles of a thousand pounds per heap. There was twenty five grand in total. I counted the pile of cash Ivan had given me, and in total, I had just over two hundred thousand pounds. James whistled through his teeth, "generous bugger isn't he?"

"The handbags alone must be worth more than that," I said, stroking a Hermes bag. "All of these are designer, average price about five grand. There's at least 100 here. I began to go through all the cosmetics, sorting it into keep and throw piles, while James made more coffee.

"Rather than throw all that, you should take it into work, and see if the secretaries want it."

"Good idea." I piled it all into a carrier bag, and set it down next to my gym bag, ready for the morning. I put a washload of laundry on, and tidied the boxes as best I could, before shoving the cash in my knicker drawer. I kept the jewellery hidden in the handbag, stuffed in the closet amongst all the others.

I decided to give Ivan a call about the holiday. I didn't expect his phone to be switched on, but it was.

"Hi babe, what's up?" he said as he answered on the first ring.

"James has invited Janine on holiday. Would there be any chance you'd be able to join us too?" He went a bit quiet.

"You go next Sunday don't you?"

"Yeah, I know it's short notice."

"I could fly over for the weekend, but not the whole two weeks. I pencilled in two weeks in France in August, I have to organise these things in advance." *You didn't invite me to join you?*

"Ok, not to worry, it was just an idea. See you tomorrow."

"Night."

I went into the living room. James was sprawled out over the couch. "Ivan can't take the time off, so I'm gonna let you and Janine go on your own. I don't fancy playing gooseberry."

"Oh Elle, I feel so bad about this whole thing. We wouldn't make you feel uncomfortable, I promise."

"Can we leave the subject now please? I've said no." James turned back to the telly in a bit of a huff. I went to my room, and got on with some work, ready to hit the ground running the next day.

The next morning, I was at my desk by half seven, checking my schedule, and sorting out the work I'd got ready the night before. By ten, I'd got tons done, and was strolling into the boardroom at Retinski. I sat back, and watched Ivan outline his plans to the American end of the Conde Nast board. They all behaved identically to the UK directors, sitting a little straighter, eyes gleaming with greed at what could lay before them.

They all seemed very polished, and astute to the point of slyness. Vaguely, I mused that we'd all have to watch our backs with such sharp characters around. I really didn't like the finance guy, nor the PR director, who gave me the creeps. I sat and made some notes as Ivan asked questions about the American operations, which were larger than the UK ones, but not as profitable. It looked to me as though they had let their costs run away, but their revenues had been somewhat static for the last few years. By joining everything into the umbrella company, we could cut costs significantly, and get a better grip of the outgoings. That only left the issue of growing the revenue. I made a note to explore the possibility of involving Joan Lester in giving them some assistance.

Ivan took them all out to lunch, while I went back to my office to work on setting up the umbrella company. He had decided on an English sounding name, Beltan Industries plc. I worked my way through the paperwork required to create the conglomerate, listing the various companies as subsidiaries. I called Lewis to see if he was free to check over what I'd done, as it had been pretty complex, and I wanted his nod that it was all completed correctly.

"You're on the list of directors as a non exec. I thought you weren't going to do it?"

"That was Retinski. This is the umbrella that controls all of it. Not stuffed full of Russians, so I'm happier with this one."

"Good politicking Elle, not only a seat on the board of a vast conglomerate, but the job of setting it up too. Resigning from Retinski was a great move. I'm learning a lot from you."

"It wasn't like that Lewis. This was more about controlling a huge collection of vastly different companies, and finding a board that would keep everyone happy. It's not all about me you know." I was a bit annoyed. Ivan wasn't doing this just for me, and Lewis' insinuation that I was manipulating Ivan was wrong and a bit snide.

"Whatever the motivation, it's a hell of a feather in your cap."

"And Pearson Hardwick's. You have direct access to one of the biggest conglomerates in the world now. Quite a coup for the firm."

"Quite. You will be the golden girl when Ms Pearson hears about this." *He's jealous.*

Lewis went back to his office, and I sat and contemplated his behaviour. I figured it was only to be expected that my older, wiser colleagues would be a bit put out that I'd only just started my career, and had waltzed into a non exec role that Lewis would have sacrificed his left testicle for, with the pay check that eclipsed anything I could earn as an ordinary corporate lawyer.

Laura came in holding the file she'd typed up for me in one hand, and a cup of tea in the other. "All that makeup's gone from the staff room. They were like a pack of vultures, fighting over it. Where did you get it from?"

"Dascha's house. Think she had a bit of a shopping illness. I'll see if there's anything else there next time I go." I felt a bit greedy keeping all the bags and clothes for myself, and resolved to bring in anything I didn't want.

Ivan emailed me just before I headed home, asking me to meet him and Paul in Smollenskis at eight the next morning. He said he might join the Americans for dinner that evening, so wouldn't be around. He did invite me, but I still had work to do that evening, and I had a flat to view.

Roger drove me over to Cinnamon Wharf, and the estate agent was waiting outside as we pulled up. It was a similar type of block to the one I lived in, with the addition of a 24 hour concierge in reception. I looked around at the marble and glass entrance hall, with its sculptures and tasteful decor. "How much do the cheapest flats here sell for?" I asked the agent.

"Three hundred and fifty thousand. Did you want to look at one?" He asked, probably thinking I couldn't afford the penthouse.

"No thanks. There's no social housing here is there?"

He shook his head, "no, all privately owned. 90 percent are sold, mostly owner occupiers. Only three have been bought by companies, probably for their executives, rather than general rental. You won't get a neighbour on housing benefit, if that's what you're asking." He pressed the button for the lift. "The penthouse has two parking spaces in the underground garage. Service charge is ten thousand a year. There's a management company in place, with residents as directors." The lift pinged as we reached the twelfth floor. There was only one front door. *This flat must be vast.* He unlocked it, and stepped aside to let me in.

The apartment took my breath away. It was flooded with light from a wall of floor to ceiling windows overlooking a sunken terrace, and the river. It was huge, open plan, with a gleaming and glossy white kitchen area at one end, and plenty of space for sofas, and a dining table in the main reception. It had cream tiled floor, which the agent explained was limestone, with underfloor heating throughout. He showed me around the kitchen area, with its built in appliances, enormous cooker, and double size fridge. It had two doors leading off, one of which was the separate laundry room I'd put on my wish list. The other was a walk in pantry, fitted with shelves and a wine fridge. *Lovely.*

The apartment had four bedrooms, as well as a separate study. The master bedroom had river views from more floor to ceiling windows, a gorgeous ensuite, with a very fancy shower as well as a jacuzzi bath. The dressing room was quite large, and nicely fitted. I figured it would be fine for my work clothes, and I could use one of the other bedrooms for the rest.

The second bedroom also had a walk in closet and ensuite, which would be great for guests. The other two rooms were plainer, and looked out onto the street. Perfect for my handbag and shoe collections. I checked out the study, which was beautifully fitted out in pale oak.

"The piece de resistance for this penthouse is the terrace," said the agent, pushing open the wall of windows. They concertina'd open, exposing the entire reception room to the terrace. I stepped outside. The terrace was slightly lowered, so as not to interfere with the views of the river, and had Perspex rails. It wrapped around three sides of the apartment, and was the same limestone as inside. I wandered along to the end. I could see straight onto Ivan's terrace, which meant he could see onto mine. *Not so great.*

It was tremendous bad fortune that Ivan stepped outside as I was standing there, and even worse when he was followed out by a dark haired woman. Her body language was flirtatious, and coquettish. I waited to see if anyone else joined them. I wanted to be wrong, but it felt like a kick in the guts after our weekend. I took out my phone, and called him. I watched as he pulled his phone out of his pocket.

"Hi, how did it go this afternoon?" He asked, as I observed him pouring two glasses of wine.

"Yeah. Done as far as I can. Are you out with the yanks?"

"Yeah, just in the car now, heading over to the west end. Are you at home?"

"No. I'm viewing a flat, next to yours, and wondered who that woman is, ya lying bastard." I watched as he stood up, and looked straight at me. I clicked off my phone, and headed inside.

"Any other similar apartments, but in a different location on your books?" I asked the agent.

"Yes. I have another two places you can view." I followed him out, informed Roger that I wouldn't be needing him, and went off to view the other two apartments.

The second one was perfect, near work, and as large and well appointed as the first. It was slightly more money, at 4.75 million, but really did tick all my boxes. I headed home, and went up to see Oscar.

He answered the door wearing just shorts. "Hey Elle, how did the flat viewing go?" He waved me in, and went off to fetch another glass to pour me some wine.

"Great. Found the perfect apartment, just down the road from here."

"Thought you were looking at Cinnamon Wharf?"

"Yeah I did, but the balcony looked straight onto Ivan's balcony, where he was entertaining a lady friend, while telling me he was out on a business dinner." Oscar winced.

"That explains why he called me, to ask if I'd seen you. Did you switch your phone off?"

"Yeah. Didn't want to listen to his excuses. He was meant to be trying to win me back, not getting caught lying and entertaining another woman. Anyway. Two things, first, I'd like to put an offer in on an apartment. It's 4.75 mil. Is that ok?"

"Yes, of course. Offer four and a half though first, they should go for it as you're a cash buyer. I'll transfer the money into your account this week, as soon as you give me the details. Now what was the other thing?"

"Can I join you in Tuscany? Only James has invited his girlfriend on our holiday, and I don't want to be a gooseberry with the two of them. That leaves me with two weeks booked off with nowhere to go, and no one to go with."

He smiled widely, "I'd be delighted. I can see if I can arrange a flight for Monday if you'd prefer. It doesn't matter when I go."

"That would be fantastic. Thank you so much." I flung my arms round him, hugging him tight. It felt ridiculously good to be pressed up against him again. He hugged me back, resting his chin on my shoulder.

I pulled away, and picked up my glass, we toasted our holiday, and I took a long sip, feeling the tension begin to leave my shoulders. Oscar promised to call me with our flight details the following day, and take my account details. I hugged him goodnight, and went home.

James and Janine were out, so I made a coffee, and checked my emails, immediately seeing the one from Ivan.

To: Elle Reynolds
From: Ivan Porenski
Date: July 8th 2013
Subject: sorry, yet again

Dearest Elle.

Yet again another email to say sorry. I shouldn't have said I was in the car when I wasn't. There's nothing going on with Natalya (the woman you saw), I just didn't want to have to explain who she was, or my business with her. I did in fact head over to meet the yanks shortly afterwards, which they can verify. I know this doesn't look good, but I beg you to trust me. I have no romantic or sexual entanglement with her, never have, and have no intention of it. She is just doing a job for me, and needed a last minute meeting yesterday.

Your devoted puppy
Ivan

I read it a couple of times before replying.

To: Ivan Porenski
From: Elle Reynolds
Date: July 8th 2013
Subject: yet again you're a tosser

Ivan

Exactly how many chances did you expect? Don't worry, I won't be buying that apartment, as I don't fancy being watched on the terrace with my new boyfriend.

As for 'Natalya' (if that's even her real name), do as you wish. You are a single man after all.

See you tomorrow at eight, as arranged.

Regards
Elle

I pressed 'send' with a flourish. I knew Ivan would go batshit crazy about my holiday with Oscar, but as he hadn't invited me to join him in August, I figured he couldn't really say anything. I closed my laptop, and had a look in the fridge, before making myself a slice of toast and a cup of tea.

Chapter 9

I met Paul and Ivan in Smollenskis the following morning, as arranged. Ivan seemed anxious, and rather nervy around me, and Paul was observing us both very closely. I handed Ivan the files containing everything that needed signing to set up the new umbrella company. I explained that there were enough directors already in place to go ahead, and begin trading under the new entity. I was pleased to hear that Ivan had decided to go with Gail Hayward as the finance director, rather than her American counterpart, who I really hadn't liked.

Paul listened as Ivan listed the skills that the board still needed, and agreed to search for one mining exec, and a non exec with an engineering background. By nine, we'd discussed everything we needed to, so I took my leave, and went back to my office. Ivan had looked as if he'd wanted to say something, but kept quiet, just saying that he'd see me later.

The day started off fairly quiet. Lots of colleagues were away, and activity on the mergers and acquisitions front had ground to a bit of a halt. I checked that all my time sheets and invoices were up to date, and read through a couple of cases regarding umbrella companies for conglomerates. Oscar called me at half eleven to say he'd booked a flight for Monday morning at eleven, and would pick me up from my flat at nine. It turned out we were going by private jet, so didn't have to schlep over to Gatwick. I gave him my account details, and called the estate agent to place an offer on the apartment, explaining that I was a cash buyer, and looking for a fast completion.

While I was waiting for the agent to call me back, I checked our internal staff lists to see if we had a specialist residential conveyancer. I could have done it myself at a push, but I wasn't an expert in that field, and someone who did that type of work regularly would be faster and more likely to spot issues. I discovered that one of Lucy's colleagues handled residential sales, and gave her a call.

"Claire Plant speaking."

"Hi, it's Elle Reynolds, I'm a friend of Lucy Elliot's, based over at Canary Wharf. I'm buying an apartment, and wondered if you could handle the purchase for me?"

"Hello Elle, yes of course I can. I take it you have a property in mind?"

"Yes, just waiting to hear if my offer's accepted. It's a leasehold though, 999 years, in a new block."

"Pretty straightforward. How quick do you need? Have you got anything to sell? And how are you financing the purchase?"

"As quick as poss please, nothing to sell, and I'm paying cash."

"Blimey, you corporates do get paid well. Lucy told me she's going to the law awards with you Saturday night, she's beyond excited. I had no hope of a ticket being in lowly residential conveyancing."

"Aw, I'm sure it will just be lots of smiling and clapping crusty old men. I must give Lucy a call regarding times and stuff. So how quickly can you get this purchase pushed through?"

"Depends totally on the other side, with leasehold it also comes down to how good the paperwork is for the management company, and if there are any ongoing issues. If everything is totally in order, about three weeks."

"That would be fantastic. I'm going on holiday next Monday, so can you try and organise anything I need to sign before that? I can deal with everything else by phone and email while I'm away." She confirmed her email address, and we said goodbye. No sooner had I put the phone down, it rang again, this time the estate agent.

My offer of 4.5 million had been accepted, subject to a 28 day exchange. I gave him Claire's details, confirmed all mine, and took the full address of the property, which I emailed to Claire as we spoke. Laura arrived with a cup of tea, just as I was punching the air in delight.

"You seem happy?" She enquired.

"Had my offer accepted on an apartment. This calls for a celebration I think. Are you free for lunch?" We ended up in the bistro, enjoying a lovely lunch, and toasting my new apartment with prosecco.

"Have you thought about how you'll do it up?" Laura asked.

I shook my head, "I only saw it last night. There's so many things I'll need to get. I live in rented at the moment, so I don't own a stick of furniture. There's a lot built in, but I need sofas, table and chairs, a bed, everything."

"That's so exciting, being able to buy everything from scratch. You'll be able to have it just as you want. Are you going modern, or traditional?"

"Modern. I want sectional sofas, the kitchen is open plan, and is glossy white, so I think pale, soft shades of cream, grey and taupe will work best. It's so exciting, I've never bought furniture before." My home in Welling had been furnished with mainly hand me downs from neighbours, and even a junk shop find was a big purchase. I thought of the two hundred thousand in my knicker drawer, and shivered with excitement.

Back in my office, I scanned through furniture websites, drooling over the myriad designs of settees available, when my phone rang. It was Oscar, and he sounded serious. "Elle, we have a problem. Someone from Barclays has told the press that they were manipulating the LIBOR rates, said they were pressured into it by their superiors. All hell's breaking loose. This could have massive implications for the banking system. Can you speak to Carey, and find out what the position is regarding actions that the Bank of England can take please?"

"Will do. I'll call you back in a bit." I trotted along the corridor to Mr Carey's office, and told him the problem. His eyes widened.

"This could have enormous consequences for the banks which are caught. They could be fined vast sums, or forced to pay compensation for the difference between what the rate was, and what it should have been. Depends how big a deal the press make of this really. He switched on the news. Straightaway, we saw reporters outside Barclays head office, hounding the CEO as he left the building. It was being portrayed that the banks had colluded to rip off the British people even more than they had over the bailout.

"Goldings didn't take a bailout during the crash did they?" I said.

"No. They had enough cash reserves to weather the storm, plus they didn't merge with any competitors which may have brought problems, like the Lloyds/HBOS debacle. I hope that publishing their figures every day exonerates them and deflects this problem quickly." Mr Carey called Oscar, and spoke to him, explaining the risks, and advising him what to do. I listened, impressed by what a wily old fox Mr Carey was.

They drafted a press release, stressing that Goldings operated under strict policies of integrity, honesty, and prudence. They released their calculation of the rate every day on their website, alongside the official LIBOR rate, and were confident that all their procedures would stand up to the closest scrutiny. As a bank, they were in good shape, hadn't needed a taxpayer funded bailout, and operated the highest standards of corporate governance, overseen by independent lawyers.

After the call, I went back to my office. I checked the Reuters, and saw immediately that the CEOs of Barclays, Natwest, and Lloyds were under pressure. Goldings hadn't been mentioned.

There were reporters outside the tower as I left that evening, and even some outside our flats. I made sure they couldn't see my code and gain access to the building, and hoped the other residents did the same. James had the telly on when I got home. He made a coffee as I watched various bank CEOs get hounded outside their premises. "This is a huge story, the press appear to be baying for blood," said James.

"I just hope it doesn't affect Oscar. It shouldn't, but who knows how these things are going to play out." I quickly called Oscar to let him know there were reporters outside. He groaned.

"This seems to be the press' latest plaything. They're like a dog with a bone. I released that press statement, and they don't seem to be baying for my blood at the moment. The other banks are having a much rougher ride than we are, mainly because of the anger over their bailouts."

"I'm home this evening if you need me. I'd suggest you don't give a comment if you're accosted."

"Poor Oscar, looks like he's going to have a rough few days," said James, nodding at the TV after I'd finished my call. The BBC commentator was calling for the banks to compensate their customers, sack their senior management, and basically nationalise the lot of them. James dished up some casserole, and I watched as Oscar was pounced on as he left the tower.

"What's it feel like to be the only honest banker in Britain?" Yelled a reporter.

"Are you disappointed in the behaviour of the other banks?" Shouted another.

"Will you be taking legal action against the other banks for rate fixing?"

I could see the astonishment on Oscar's face. They were not the questions he was expecting. "Gentlemen, I can't possibly comment until all the facts are known, and I trust the Bank of England to take any action that's appropriate. It's not my place to comment on other companies. I can only assure you that there has been no price fixing or manipulation at Goldings. Our integrity and honesty in our dealings are extremely important to both us, and our clients."

He strode away, presumably heading home. Ten minutes later he called me. "Was that on the news?"

"Yep. It came across very well. You looked and sounded sincere."

"I wasn't expecting all that 'most honest banker' stuff. Where did that come from?"

"Maybe the other banks tried to conceal, or refused to acknowledge the press anger. By being upfront, you may have diffused, or deflected it. I wouldn't relax yet though, a lot can happen over the next few days. On a happier note, my offer of 4.5 mil was accepted today."

"Well, that's a bit of good news isn't it? I put 5 mil in your account this afternoon, so you're good to go. I'm going to lay low, and keep quiet if I can over the next few days. Let all this blow over."

"Very wise. It really doesn't sound as though they're gunning for you at this stage, so let's just hope it stays that way." I finished the call, and turned to James. "Where's Janine?"

"Out with a friend, she'll be back later. What was you on about when you said your offer of 4.5 mil was accepted?"

"I put an offer in on an apartment today, and it was accepted. It's about five minutes from here, on St Saviours dock. It's lovely."

"I'm pleased for you." *You don't look it.*

With no work to do that evening, I decided to start working my way through all the clothes, trying them on, and separating them into piles for cleaning, alterations or taking into work. I started on the nearest box, pulling everything out onto my bed, and checking everything for stains and loose hems as I went. Most of the garments were still in dry cleaning covers, and looked pristine. There were some beautiful items, and I grudgingly admitted that the cow had good taste. The trousers seemed to fit me perfectly, and I deduced that, although she'd been taller, proportionally she must have had short legs. My alteration pile seemed to only contain long dresses, which were only about two inches too long. I was a bit ashamed that there were only two items in the 'take into work' pile, mainly because they were a bit big for me. I resolved to be a bit less greedy with the next box.

I heard a knock at the front door, and assumed it was Janine returning, so let James get it. I was standing in my room in my bra and knickers when Ivan walked in. Instinctively I tried to cover myself. "Don't bother, I've seen it all before," he snapped. I pulled on my robe.

"Hello Ivan, to what do I owe this pleasure?"

"Your phone. You're not answering. Yet again." I rummaged round in my bag, frowning.

"I hasn't rung this evening.." I pulled it out, and saw that it was on silent, and that I had ten missed calls from Ivan. "It was on silent," I muttered, "what did you want?"

"I wanted to discuss Natalya."

I sat down on the bed, "ok, go ahead."

"It wasn't how it looked. She's a private investigator. I commissioned her to do a job for me in Russia. She needed to see me urgently with some news."

"I see."

"I asked her to look into the circumstances of my parent's deaths, and a rumour that I heard as a child."

"And that made her all flirty with you?"

"She was just reacting the same as all women do, except you that is. She came to take a sample of my DNA, and tell me her findings so far."

"Which was?"

"Vlad's henchmen killed my parents Elle, I always wondered why the bastards didn't kill me as well, they could have done. Apparently they were under strict orders to ensure nothing happened to me."

I frowned, "why did Vlad do that, if he really was behind the murder of your parents?"

"That question has bugged me, well, at the time I didn't know Vlad was behind it, but I always wondered why I was spared. The man who took them away said dad was not my father."

"Right..."

"It looks like Vlad was my father, which means Dascha was my half sister, and he wanted us to marry."

"That's sick. Imagine if you'd had kids?"

Ivan shuddered, "I feel sick knowing I had a relationship with my own half sister, that's bad enough, but having a psychopath like Vlad as a father is horrific. I just hope it's not hereditary."

"No wonder he helped you so much, setting up."

"Yeah, he covered that by telling me it was for Dascha. A hospital in Moscow gave Natalya a sample of his DNA from a biopsy they did for him. In a few days, I'll know the truth." He scrubbed his hands over his face. "I was friendly with the man who killed my mother."

"Why were they killed?"

"Vlad basically stole the factory where my father worked. I didn't know until recently who 'the businessman' was. My parents were activists in the protest movement, as all the workers were thrown into even more poverty than under the communist regime.

We could barely afford to eat, and it was getting worse. Vlad's men stamped out all dissent quickly and mercilessly. I gave the workers a pay rise, and better working conditions when I was in Moscow the other week, and discovered that the factory was part of Vlad's estate. They were so grateful, it was pitiful."

"Why didn't you tell me all this before?" I asked softly.

He stared out of the window for a while. "You don't like me seeing where you're from, I'm the same. I'm from peasant stock, from the grottiest slums of Moscow. Those people are still there, dying young from the conditions they work in, and the poverty they endure. It so easily could have been me, and if my parents hadn't been murdered, it probably would've been."

"You don't know that, all this could have happened regardless."

He shook his head. "No, I know I would have stayed. I was a bit of a mummy's boy. I watched them dragged out of our tenement, and saw my father executed in the street in front of everyone." Tears were streaming down his face as he relived the horror. He swiped them away. "I prayed so hard that they'd let my mum go, but they took her and some other woman to the gates of the factory, and killed them there. I heard the shots, and I knew it was her. They left her body there as a warning to the other workers not to get above their position, or cause trouble. I didn't know what to do. I had no other family, or money for a burial. I couldn't even arrange a grave. All the other neighbours were too scared to help me, so I had to dig two paupers graves on some scrubland to bury them. Then I ran away."

"So he killed the woman he had a relationship with?"

Ivan nodded. "I don't know if my father ever knew there was a chance I wasn't his. Bear in mind, I was born long before Vlad became successful. I don't know if it was an affair, rape, or anything."

"Baby I'm sorry, this must be so hard for you." I hugged him, holding him tight. "Regardless of who your father is, you're still the same person, that won't change. Neither us are the product of our parents."

"There's only one bright spot. If Vlad was my father, proven by DNA, I'll get my 13% inheritance tax back."

"True, but you still won't have any living family. I wish I had siblings or cousins. I wouldn't feel so alone."

"I don't care about having any family. I've been on my own since I was fifteen. I hate to think you feel alone. You have me."

"Do I? I bought a flat today. You don't know where, what it's like, anything. You don't know my favourite colour, the music I like, the books I read. I don't 'have' you Ivan. I have the tiny bit of you that you choose to share with me. Is it any wonder we fall out so much when you're so secretive?"

"I wish I was a good boyfriend, and knew how to make you feel loved and cherished. It's like there's a secret that I'm not privy to, you know, how to make a woman happy."

"You are pretty rubbish at it," I teased, "unbelievably stingy with the flowers too." I paused, "I need to tell you, I'm not going away with James and Janine now. I'm going to Tuscany with Oscar. He invited me, and I need a break. I did ask you to come on holiday first though," I added hastily. I cringed, expecting an eruption.

"And I said no, that I booked August, and didn't invite you..." Ivan trailed off. I nodded. "I meant to ask you, but you were so intent on not sleeping with me, I just..." I looked at him expectantly. "Ok, I'm a tosser."

I made us both coffee, and Ivan sat on my bed while I carried on sorting through the clothes. I told him about my new flat, and my ideas for the furniture. He offered to hire an interior designer to help me, which I accepted gracefully. He yes or no'd each outfit I tried on, showing a surprisingly good sense of style. The pile to be taken into work grew quite a bit. "Which dress are you wearing on Saturday night? He asked.

"The tickets said it was white tie, so I thought I'd wear the strapless champagne one that you bought me. I've been waiting for an event to wear it to."

"I'm going to make it my mission to take you out more. Show you off to the world. You're too young and lovely to stay home as much as we do."

"Smooth, Ivan. You're turning into a bit of a charmer."

"It's a shame I'm not taking you Saturday. Your friend's going isn't she?"

"Yes, you've met Lucy. I need to speak to her about timings. We have to be in the city by seven at the latest."

"I'll lend you the Bentley, and Roger. The two of you can arrive in style, and be seen safely home afterwards."

"Thanks."

He pulled me onto his lap, and wrapped his arms around me. "When can I make love to you? I've been so patient, and I can see your nipples through your bra. It's been driving me crazy all evening." He nuzzled my neck, pressing little kisses over my shoulder. I could feel him hardening underneath me, which seemed to ignite my slumbering libido. "Can I at least take your bra off, and feel your tits?" he murmured against my shoulder. He reached round, and unclipped my bra, before pulling it off, and letting it drop to the floor. "I've missed your breasts. You have the best nipples I've ever seen." He was using his 'phone sex' voice. I melted into a hormonal mush.

He captured a nipple in his lips, and sucked hard, causing me to arch into him, while he rolled and pinched the other with his fingers. "Please tell me when I can make love to you. I can barely control myself," he murmured against my breast. I stroked his erection through his shorts, causing him to groan. "Please let me make love to you. I'll beg if you want." He sounded needy and desperate. He lifted his face to mine, and kissed me, pressing his tongue into my mouth, in a show of barely restrained animal passion.

"Yes, make love to me now." No sooner were the words out of my mouth, than Ivan had my knickers yanked down, his shorts kicked off, and I was laying on my back on the bed. He crawled up my body, kissing and licking my heated skin.

"I need to fuck you hard first. I won't last long, I'm too turned on." He pressed inside me, stretching and filling me with his thick, solid erection. He fucked me at a hard, primal pace, completely dominating my body. I could barely move as he pinned me to the bed, taking me as he wanted. Just the sheer sexual power of the man, and his desperation for me, turned me on beyond belief. As he pounded me, I felt the familiar quickening of an impending orgasm. He kissed me as I called out, swallowing my cries of passion. As I pulsed around him, he stilled, and let go, resting his forehead against mine. "I've missed you so much baby, please don't let's fall out again."

I stretched like a cat underneath him, boneless and languid after my orgasm. "Don't fall asleep, please, I'm looking forward to round two," Ivan said, looking a little alarmed.

"I'm not going to sleep, not when I've got your big dick to play with," I purred. He rolled off, and lay on his back. I licked and sucked his nipples, each in turn, and stroked the silky skin of his torso. I loved how sensitive his nipples were. He practically arched off the bed in pleasure as I rolled them between my fingers. I kissed my way down to the tip of his cock, which was back to a full strength erection, and leaking pre-cum. Settling myself between his legs, I massaged his anus as I licked his balls, and pressed tiny kisses up his inner thighs. He sighed loudly, giving in to the sensual pleasure I was inflicting on him. *Boring in bed? I don't think so..*

I slowly licked my way up the shaft of his cock, avoiding the sensitive tip, until I had nudged my finger into his anus. He gasped as I massaged his prostrate at the same time as I sucked his cock, swirling my tongue repeatedly over the crest. "Oh god, oh god, don't stop, oh god that feels good," he garbled as I teased and played with him. "Oh no, no, I'm gonna come, stop, stop." I ignored him, and continued my sensual torture until he spurted hotly into my mouth.

"You proved your point, sexy girl. Your turn now, and I'm not gonna show you any mercy." He flipped me onto my back, and lifted my hips, pulling my knees up to my tummy, and pinning my legs open with his arms, so that I was totally open and exposed to him. He began with long, lush licks, before sucking my swollen clit. I groaned with the pleasure, feeling wanton and horny, as he lapped and sucked at the most intimate parts of me.

He changed position to slide two fingers into me, and began pumping them in and out. He pressed down on my tummy, just above my pubis, which felt astonishing. He kept his fingers pumping and rubbing my g spot as he slapped my clit several times, then pressed down again.

"Let go baby," he commanded, as my legs stiffened. I came with a muffled cry, and to my total horror, saw liquid squirt out of me.

"Oh my god! I'm so sorry, I don't know what happened." I was mortified. He grinned, looking very pleased with himself.

"I gave you what's called a 'squirting orgasm'," he said, "it's supposed to be the most intense a woman can have."

"It looks like I wet the bed," I muttered, still embarrassed. He scooped me into his arms, and gave me a deep, lush, kiss.

"No, it looks like you had a giant orgasm. I'll sleep on the damp patch, I don't mind. Now, I think my cock's recovered since your earlier fun. Can we have a slow one?" *Jesus, is the man insatiable?* "You, on top, so I can see you, and touch those beautiful breasts." He rolled me onto him. I straddled him, and sank down onto his cock, holding still for a moment to get used to the sensation. He watched my face intently as he stroked his hands over my waist and ribs, in a sensual gesture.

I began to move slowly, closing my eyes, as he kneaded and fondled my breasts. I tilted my head back to push them into his hands, revelling in the sheer sensuality of our connection. "Open your eyes, let me see you....please." He murmured. I bent over him, and gazed into his eyes, light blue into sapphire, seeing his face relaxed with pleasure. "You are so beautiful, so sexy," he whispered, "I could never get enough of you." He cupped my face, and drew me to him for a kiss.

We made it last, moving slowly, just enjoying each other's bodies, with neither of us chasing an orgasm. When I eventually came, it rolled through me in waves, massaging his cock deep inside me, causing him to find his own release. Afterwards, I lay in his arms, neither of us speaking for a while. Eventually I broke the silence, "Would you like a drink?"

"Can I have something cold? Water or juice, something like that please." I threw on a robe, washed my hands, and padded out to the kitchen. James and Janine were cuddled up on the sofa.

"Hi Elle, not seen you all evening." Janine said.

"My boyfriend's here," I said by way of explanation, "is there any juice left?" She nodded, and I went over to the fridge and poured out two glasses. I grabbed some breadsticks and soft cheese, and carried it all back to the bedroom. James raised his eyebrow as I walked past.

"Brought us some sustenance."I announced as I returned. Ivan sat up and took the glasses of juice off me, placing them on the bedside table. I dumped the rest on the bed beside him.

"Great, I'm starving. Sex always makes me hungry," he said, pulling out a breadstick, and scooping up some cheese, taking a bite, before offering it to me. We ended up feeding each other, with Ivan groaning as I licked Philadelphia off his fingers. "Careful, I'll end up hard again. You'll break my cock if you don't let it rest."

"I wouldn't want to do that," I smirked as I bent down to give it a little kiss. It twitched, despite being soft. "I agree, no more tonight, anyway, I'm a little sore, and I want to change the sheet before we sleep. It's full of crumbs as well as whatever it was that came out of me."

Ivan helped me change the sheet, before throwing the duvet back over, and sliding in, his arms outstretched. I snuggled into him, breathing his gorgeous scent, and feeling his heart beat steadily as he wrapped himself around me. "I will be the man you fall in love with, I'm determined," he whispered.

"You already are," I replied, my eyes closed as sleep beckoned.

Chapter 10

I wafted the fresh coffee under his nose, hoping that the aroma would wake him up. When that failed, I poked him. "Come on sleeping beauty, time to wake up." He opened one eye, and turned his head to look at the clock.

"It's half five. Why're you getting me up so early?"

"I need to be at the gym by six." I was already wearing my gym kit, and had my bag ready with my work clothes and heels. I sipped my coffee as he struggled up onto his elbows, his face all creased from the pillow, and his messy, dark, curls resembling a birds nest. He took a long slurp of coffee, before swinging his legs out of bed, and padding over to my bathroom. A few minutes later he came out. "Can I borrow your toothbrush?" I nodded, hoping he wouldn't take too long. "Don't worry, I'll just brush my teeth, and I'll be out of your way," he called out as he went back into the bathroom. I made the bed, and gathered up my keys, handbag, and the bag full of clothes to take to work, and waited.

"I can get them brought up to your office, save you lugging them," he said, seeing me laden down like a pack pony.

"Would you? That would be great," I replied, handing him the bag. We went down in the lift, to find Nico waiting outside.

I had a relatively quiet day, the most exciting part being an extended lunch to pay a visit to a beauty salon to get my waxing and mani/pedi done for both Saturday night, and my holiday. I gave the Brazilian wax another go, and was relieved to find it wasn't so painful second time around. After work, I headed over to Guiseppe's salon for a trim and blowdry.

I'd just walked out, feeling fabulous, when I bumped into Paul. "Hello again. How's everything?" he asked, smiling widely.

"Good thanks. How's the search going for our new execs?"

"Identified a few already, and made contact. It hopefully won't take too long. You look like you just had your hair done."

"Yep. Do you like it? I'm going to an awards do on Saturday, so I wanted it freshly cut in case I wear it down."

"I'm sure you'll be the belle of the ball."

"I doubt it. I'm going with a friend, and she's the archetypal long legged blonde with impeccable breeding. I scrub up quite well, but I'm not in her league." I knew Lucy would look amazing, plus she was hoping to meet a nice barrister or corporate, so would no doubt make an effort.

"I don't think you need to worry. By the way, how are things with you and Ivan now? The other morning you both seemed terribly awkward with each other."

"Yeah, we're ok now thanks. I decided to stay at Pearson Hardwick, so sorry to have wasted your time, if you looked for a move for me."

"Not a problem. Just let me know when I need to look, although my guess is, that when the time comes, they'll be looking for you, not the other way round. There is something I did want to ask you though," he said, looking a little anxious.

"Go on."

"I have a ball coming up on the third of August, and need someone to accompany me. Would you be free that evening?"

"I'm not sure... Can I check my schedule tomorrow and let you know?"

"Certainly. It's the investment managers annual fundraiser. Great networking opportunities for both of us." *Oh you know how to dangle a carrot Paul.*

"Ok, I'll email you tomorrow. I'd better go." We said our goodbyes, and I headed home. James had made a lasagne, which he popped into the oven as I walked in. "What you been up to today?" I asked.

"Pottering about, banked my paycheque from Apple, played on my playstation, that's about it. What about you?"

I told him about my day. When I got to the bit about Paul asking me to the fundraiser, he frowned. "Is that wise? I know he's a friend of Ivan's, but it seems he's trying to edge his way in. I'd be careful there if I was you. Make sure you discuss it with Ivan first."

"He is a client, so I need to tread a little carefully. Where's Janine?"

"Job interview at Retinski, they're looking for a receptionist." *At six in the evening?*

"I thought they only employed Russian speakers."

"She speaks a bit of Russian. She did languages at uni, fluent in French and Italian, conversational in Russian and Polish." James looked extremely proud of her as he spoke, "she's no slouch you know."

"I never thought she was."

"So can you put in a word for her? I'd really like her to get a job locally, as she's going to be living here."

"So she's moving in?"

"Yeah."

"Hopefully I'll be moved out in about three weeks. Better that you have your privacy.

"Elle, I'm not pushing you out. I wouldn't do that to you. Stay here as long as you need to." I didn't reply, just taking my bag and phone, and heading into my bedroom to continue sorting clothes. Half hour later, I heard Janine return, sounding excited as she chattered to James. Five minutes later, Ivan called.

"Hi baby, what're you up to this evening?"

"Nothing much. What about you?"

"I'm waiting on a phone call, but that's all. Shall we eat out?"

"Great. You want to choose, or shall I call Quintessentially?"

"Give them a call. I'll pick you up in ten." I changed into a dress, and retouched my makeup, after a quick conversation with the concierge service.

As I headed out, James yelled "dinners nearly ready."

"Eating out tonight thanks." He looked annoyed, but didn't reply. Janine was perched on a stool, sipping a glass of wine, and looking pleased with herself. "Have a nice evening," I called out, before closing the front door.

Ivan was outside in the Bentley. "So where are we going?"

"Hakkasan tonight, over in Mayfair. Does that suit?"

"Great. I love Chinese."

Our meal was gorgeous, really top quality Chinese, with impeccable service. Ivan seemed relaxed and happy, even after taking the phone call he was expecting, jabbering in Russian to someone. I always found it hard to tell whether he was angry or not, when I listened to him speak in his mother tongue. He told me about his day, asked about mine, and said he liked my hair.

"Was Ranenkiov working late this evening?" I asked.

Ivan frowned, "no, why?"

"My flatmate's girlfriend had an interview at yours this evening for a receptionists job. It just seemed a bit late. She didn't get back till half six."

"Not at my place. We're not looking for a receptionist, as far as I know, anyway, that kind of thing is done during the business day. I doubt if Ranenkiov would interview candidates though. The office manager would do it, and she went home at half five."

I frowned, "How odd. I don't trust her one bit to be honest. She seems...sly. I don't know, maybe because she ran off with James' best friend, I just expect her to be sneaky."

"Gut instincts are usually right. Make sure you keep your jewellery in your safe if she's around."

"I don't have a safe."

"Use mine then. I'll pick it up when I drop you home. You can always ask Oscar for a deposit box at his bank, and transfer it all there."

"Good idea. I'll sort it tomorrow. I need to get some Euros anyway, ready for France."

"About France...you and Oscar, you won't sleep with him will you?"

"No, of course not. He's just a dear friend nowadays. I'm just looking forward to lazing around, and catching up on some reading. As I said before, if I wanted to sleep with someone else, I'd break it off with you first. Oh, that reminds me. I bumped into Paul today. He's asked me to accompany him to some do, said it was a networking opportunity."

"I see." He looked cross. "What did you say?"

"I said I'd get back to him tomorrow, when I've checked my schedule. It's a shame you have something arranged that evening already, isn't it?"

He caught on, "I'm sure he'll be terribly disappointed. When is it?"

"August the third."

"I'm sure we'll be away somewhere that weekend."

I sniggered, "Poor Paul, he'll have to find out the hard way that you don't 'share nicely'."

"I don't share full stop, and I'm not totally comfortable about you being so close to Oscar, but I do know it was my own fault." He reached over to grasp my hand, bringing it to his lips for a soft kiss. "I know you can be trusted. I'd never doubt you."

We made our way home a little before ten, after a great evening. I loved being out with Ivan, he was fun, well mannered, and I loved watching other women go weak at the knees for him. We arrived back at the flat, and kissed all the way up in the lift.

I walked in to find James looking distraught. He was sitting at the island, with his head in his hands. "What on earth is wrong?" I asked, instantly concerned.

"I don't know. I think she's left me again. She was fine, and asked me to go to the shop for her. When I came back, she wasn't here. No note, nothing. She's not answering her phone either. I don't understand what's happened, we didn't have a row or anything."

I glanced at Ivan quickly, instantly sharing the same thought. I turned tail, and ran to my room. The door to my dressing room was open. My knicker drawer was hanging open, the money missing. Thankfully, I'd left the jewellery in the handbag that Ivan had stuffed it in, which was still intact. I flew back to the kitchen. "Did you tell her about that money? It's all gone."

"What about the jewellery?" Asked Ivan, looking remarkably calm.

"Still there, thankfully. That fucking bitch helped herself to the cash, and ran for it." I yelled. James looked like he was going to cry.

"Elle, I'm gonna call the police. I'm so, so very sorry. I'll replace it."

"Don't call the police. The money was murky. They're going to want to know why you had it, and where it's from. Let me make some calls." Ivan seemed very unruffled about the whole thing. He pulled out his phone, and called someone, speaking rapidly in Russian. He asked James for Janine's phone number, and relayed it to the person on the other end, followed by a photograph from James' mobile. Eventually he clicked off his phone. "Now, have you checked to see if anything else has been taken?" I had my cards and phone with me, so apart from the jewellery and laptop, which was on the island, I had nothing else of any value. James checked his study and bedroom.

"Nothing of mine. I'm so sorry Elle, I should've kept my mouth shut. I would never in a million years have thought she could do something like this."

"She left you for your best mate James, she's clearly a sneaky bitch, oh, and she wasn't at Retinski for an interview this evening. I don't know where she was, probably planning this with her next lover," I added, rather spitefully.

"Elle, come on, it's only a little cash. The poor man's lost his woman over it." Ivan said, with rather too much compassion for my liking. He walked around the island, and filled the kettle up. I sat and watched, as Ivan made three cups of tea, placing one in front of James, who looked like he was in shock.

"I don't understand why she didn't come to me, if she needed some money," he said, "I would've helped her. I already invited her to move in here, so she could get a job, and get back on her feet."

"Why did she leave her husband?" Ivan asked.

"I don't know, she wouldn't tell me, just said it had all gone wrong between them, and she'd realised she'd made a terrible mistake, you know, leaving me for him."

"Hmm. Well, we can probably get the money back. What happens from there is up to you." Ivan replied.

"What do you mean?" I asked, "and who did you call?"

"My security company. They'll find her, and if she still has the money, they'll retrieve it. It's what happens after that, whether you want her prosecuted, punished, or just to leave you alone. I suspect that James will want some answers, to get his own closure on this."

"I want to ask her a million questions," said James. "I want to know if this was a moment of madness, or whether she came back with the intention of robbing me. She knows I'm ok for money. Mind you, her husband wasn't skint."

"Most people who steal have an addiction or problem. Was she secretive in other ways?" I asked.

"Yeah, I suppose so. I was never allowed to touch her phone, and she always took her handbag everywhere, even into the bathroom. That's not really normal is it?" We all glanced at my bag laying open on the island with my phone poking out.

"No, not really," I said.

"So when they find her, you want to speak to her?" Ivan interjected.

"Yeah, if they find her. Who exactly is looking for her?"

"A private security company. They can find a needle in a haystack. They'll track her phone, scan CCTV, that type of thing. They're normally pretty quick, unless she had the nous to throw her phone away."

We all sipped our tea, and waited, James with his head in his hands. "You know, that was the first time in my entire life that I actually had any money." I said.

"I thought you had money to buy this flat?" Ivan asked, frowning.

"I meant money that wasn't earmarked, just for frittering," I said, quickly covering myself for my flippant comment.

"How much was there?" He asked.

"Two hundred thousand, plus or minus a few quid. I hope they get it back tonight. I need to get some Euros tomorrow."

"I'll get them for you, don't worry about that." James said.

We all jumped when Ivan's phone rang. He looked at the number, and answered in Russian. I tried to gauge what was happening from his facial expressions, but as usual, he looked impassive, as if he was discussing the weather. After a couple of minutes, he handed the phone to James. "Ask away." James took the phone into his bedroom. "They found her, and her male accomplice in London City airport, trying to buy a flight to Rome. Unfortunately for her, flights are infrequent, and she would have had to wait until the morning."

"What a bitch. I knew there was something shady about her. Poor James, he really did love her. I hope for his sake that he never sees her again."

"I would be devastated. When I think, you had full access to everything, and you didn't even look, let alone take as much as a fiver..." He trailed off.

"I'm not a thief, and I know that if I needed anything, I could ask. If anything, I feel a little embarrassed about all the gifts and things that have been showered on me. I love nice things as much as the next girl, but it does make me feel a bit greedy. Plus of course, this has happened, and I can't help thinking that if temptation hadn't been put in her way..."

"She would have stolen from James. She had an accomplice Elle, she meant to steal. Now, in some ways it's better it was you than James, because I can take care of it. James had to work hard for his money, we just found yours. It also gives you an insight as to why I have so much security. I can't bear to be stolen from."

"I've never really been a target before, well, mainly because I've never had anything worth nicking." Ivan smiled at me indulgently.

"I'm so pleased that at long last I've been able to fix something for you. It's been rather too much the other way round. I like looking after you."

"Bloody caveman," I teased. "I'm going to buy you a nice present when I'm away."

"So are you going on holiday with James now, or Oscar?"

"Dunno, I just wish I was going with you. It'd be more exciting than just reading and eating." I winked at him, which made him smile. "Maybe I could do the first week with Oscar, then meet James in Spain for the second week."

"Just let me know, and I'll lend you my jet. I'm not going anywhere." He leaned forward, and softly kissed me. We were interrupted by the buzzer from the main door. I answered the video entry, and saw a military looking man.

"Delivery for Mr Porenski," he said. Ivan was immediately by my side.

"Code word?"

"Goddess" Ivan buzzed him in. A few minutes later, he took delivery of a carrier bag containing the cash.

"You'd better check how much is there," he said, handing it to me. I counted it all, and there was about £700 short, which I presumed, she'd spent on flights. I stuffed it all back in the bag, and was clearing up our cups when James returned looking ashen. He handed the phone back to Ivan.

"The fella wants to speak to you." Ivan spoke to whoever was on the other end in Russian, before ending the call, and shoving the phone in his pocket.

"So?" I looked at James expectantly.

"Oh god, where to start. Well, first off, she came to me thinking I'd be a good target. She left Oz because she was in trouble with the police. She wouldn't say exactly why, but I got the impression it was theft from her employer. Apparently her and Tryst split up ages ago, because she'd met some Italian bloke. They needed money fast, because she's pregnant, and knew she wouldn't be able to deceive me for long before it showed. I didn't even bank my cheque till today, so it wouldn't clear till next week. Apart from that, I didn't have enough cash for her to be bothered. When she knew about yours, I told her last night by the way, she changed plans. She met this Antonio earlier to tell him they'd be leaving tonight, and the rest you know."

"Oh James, how disappointing for you," I said. My heart went out to him.

"That's a bit of an understatement," he replied, "that woman has ripped me apart twice now, and I let her. I just feel like a total idiot."

"We all behave like idiots when we're in love, forgiving when we shouldn't," I said, shooting Ivan a pointed look. He had the grace to look a bit sheepish. "What's going to happen to her?" I asked him.

Ivan shifted on the stool. "She'll be on the next plane to Rome. They have their tickets. I gather my security scared the life out of the pair of them, and told her I'd taken a contract out, so she can never return to London again."

"Have you?" I asked.

He shook his head, "of course not, I don't do things like that, but she won't know any different. I gather she tried to blame it all on the boyfriend."

"She told me she was jealous of Elle, said it wasn't fair that Elle got everything so easily, had it all fall in her lap. That was how she tried to justify her actions." James interjected.

"Easily? Is that what the bitch thought?" I felt my fury rising. "Up until I moved here, I've had to work my arse off for everything. You saw what I walked into this flat with, I had fuck all to my name. My own mother died penniless so I could go to Cambridge. I came from total poverty, but I never stooped low enough to nick anything. Bitch."

"Do you know how sexy you are when you're angry?" Ivan said, trying to diffuse my anger. "She knew nothing. Don't let her twisted opinions affect you. She was just a lazy and envious person, and anyway, it's all been sorted. You can get your Euros as planned."

"What do you want to do about this holiday?" James asked.

"Let me talk to Oscar, maybe I'll do a week with you and a week with him. He changed his dates to accommodate me, so I can't just drop him. I'll speak to him. In the meantime, it's nearly one in the morning, and I'm almost dead on my feet. I have to be up in a few hours, so I'm going to get a bit of sleep." I took my bags and wandered over to my bedroom, with Ivan following. Within seconds we'd stripped off, and snuggled up under the covers. He felt solid and warm, his strong arms wrapped around me, making me feel safe.

"Are you too tired?" He whispered.

"Hmm? Yeah, sorry."

"Don't worry. I'll pencil in a session tomorrow. Go to sleep." He didn't have to tell me twice.

I still woke up at five, *the curse of the early bird,* I thought. Ivan was out for the count, so I padded out to the kitchen to fix myself a strong coffee. Even James wasn't awake. I opened my laptop, and flicked through my emails, spotting one from Claire Plant, sent the day before. Reading it, she informed me that contracts had been issued by the vendor of the flat, which I could sign before I went away, along with a few other land registry, and lease documents. If I could place the money in their client account before I went, she could aim to exchange and complete while I was away, as the documentation on the apartment appeared to be in good order. I emailed back that I would check my schedule, and email her a time as soon as I got into work. I made a mental note to put my chequebook in my handbag. A frisson of excitement ran down my spine. I'd never had my own home before, it had always seemed like an impossible dream. I couldn't wait for the moment of walking into that apartment, and knowing it was mine.

"What are you smiling about?" James said, interrupting my musings.

"Got an email asking me to sign contracts for my new flat today. I'm excited. It'll be the first time living somewhere not rented."

"Really? Not even your childhood home?"

"Council."

"Well, I never would have guessed. I knew you didn't come from a rich family, but... Anyway, another coffee?"

"Yeah, go on, I'm not gonna go to the gym this morning. I doubt if I'll be able to peel sleeping beauty off my bed in time."

"He's a decent man. Very calm in a crisis. He was surprisingly kind too."

"You should see him with his spaniels, mind you, we were wrong about Osc, he was lovely with Ivan's dogs. They adore him too, he spent ages playing with them."

James raised an eyebrow, "I would never have expected that, would've thought he was more likely to have them between two slices of bread." We both giggled. "Now, what do you want to do about this holiday? I know this is my fault for messing you about, so if you can't come, I will understand."

"I thought I'd spend a week with each of you. Ivan offered me his jet, so I can fly over. Is that a good compromise?"

"Great. We both need some R and R, you especially. It's been a stressful time for you. New job, moving house, new boyfriend, plus your mum. Four life events in one year is enough to drain anyone."

"This week alone has been rather too exciting for my liking, although I'm pleased that Ivan and I seem to be back on track."

"The two of you look right together. He's a decent man, not what I expected an oligarch to be. I think he's definitely in love with you, he has this sort of softness when he looks at you."

"Yeah, he's a good man, despite being a Ruskie Ratbag at times. Now, what about you? Please don't tell me I'm gonna see the return of the heartbreak beard and scraggy hair?"

He shook his head, "I'm gonna find myself a nice brunette, I've had it with blondes. In some ways this episode laid a lot to rest. I blamed myself for her leaving me for Trystan, thought I was in some way lacking. She obviously has a world of issues of her own, I mean, she was sleeping with me for god's sake, and she was pregnant with another man's child. How must he have felt?" James looked disgusted.

"At least you got a few shags out of it."

He smirked, "yeah, it's like riding a bike, you never forget."

We chatted for a while about the events of the previous night, until I glanced at the clock, it was nearly half six. I made all three of us more coffee, and took mine and Ivan's into my bedroom. He was still out cold, so I prodded him. "Coffees here." He opened his eyes, and looked at the clock.

"Not quite as ungodly an hour as normal. Did you get a lay in?"

"No, I've been chatting to James. Thought I'd give the gym a miss, and let you sleep in a bit. We did have quite a late night."

"Well, you're gonna have another one tonight, hopefully in my pleasure room."

My belly squeezed, "mmm, can't wait. I like your swing contraption."

"If you're not careful, I'll visit your office at lunchtime. Mines a bit too open for any fun. I happen to know that yours is lockable and soundproofed."

"Now I know why you insisted on it. Are you coming for a shower?" He slurped down his coffee, before following me into the bathroom. I set it to tropical flow from the large overhead fitting, and let the deluge flow over me. Ivan shampooed my hair, and lathered me all over with body wash. I did the same to him, ogling his naked body rather shamelessly.

"If you're not careful, I'll end up taking you up against the wall," he said, as I washed him, taking particular care to wash his dick extremely thoroughly. "You really are asking for trouble," he purred, before grasping my face for a deep, lush kiss. His hand slipped down between my legs, where he stroked my clit, making me as horny as hell. I groaned as he slipped a finger inside, then two, pumping me slowly, while pressing his thumb against my clitoris. I grasped his cock, which was rock hard, and swirled my thumb over the tip. I felt myself pressed against the cool, tiled wall of the shower. Ivan lifted me up, and I wrapped my legs around his waist, as he guided his cock into me.

He hammered into me hard, pounding me relentlessly, as the water flowed over us. I reached between us to rub my clit, desperate for an orgasm to relieve the tension building up inside.

"Come on, come for me baby, I need you to come all over my cock." He whispered in his phone sex voice. I rubbed a little faster, until I came gloriously hard, my insides contracting viciously, blocking out everything but the feeling of his cock, ploughing in and out. I felt him swell, and let go, his cock throbbing as he spurted into me. He kissed me again, a deep, grateful kiss, as we both got our breath back. "You, my darling, are exquisite, and I'll never get enough of you."

"Hmm, so are you. That was the nicest shower I've had in a long time," I purred. I re-washed myself quickly, and hopped out to dry myself. My legs were a little wobbly, so I went and sat at my dressing table to quickly dry my hair.

I stuffed some cash, and the cheque book in my handbag, and asked Ivan to put the rest in his safe, with the jewellery, as he was going home before he went into the office. After a cheery goodbye to James, we left to drop me at work.

Chapter 11

I bounced into work, excited to be off for a fortnight, and knowing that I wouldn't have a terribly busy day. My time sheets, and other paperwork was all up to date, and none of my projects would require too much attention. I checked my schedule, and made an appointment to see Claire at ten, and arranged to pop up and see Lucy afterwards. I planned to nip out at lunchtime to get my Euros, and stock up on sun lotion. Laura organised a taxi, and I made my way over to head office.

I signed all the forms that Claire had prepared, checked the details of the management company for the apartment block, and wrote an eye watering cheque to cover all the costs to completion. Claire had seemed very thorough and knowledgeable as she explained the lease, and it's various clauses. I was relieved that there wasn't a 'no animals' clause, in case the girls came for a visit, and I was pleased to find out that there would be no problem exchanging and completing on the same day.

I looked around Claire's office as she fussed around with the file. It was one of the older ones in the building, with mahogany panelling, and a large, old fashioned desk, much like I'd expected when I'd dreamed of becoming a lawyer during my degree. It had that lovely, slightly musty smell of old papers, and even older books. She saw me looking around. "Bet this is a bit different to your place. Lucy told me its spectacular."

"Yeah, it's a great building. This office is gorgeous though, I was just thinking how it was what I expected mine to be when I qualified. I love the old panelling and stuff. My office is lovely, but it's a bit bare."

"With a view to die for, I expect. There has to be some perks to be had for the crazy hours you lot have to do over in corporate. Personally, I couldn't do it. I have to leave at five on the dot to pick my little one up from his childminder."

"I think in the four months I've been there, I've had one early finish. Most of the time I try and get away before seven, but I'm at my desk by half seven in the morning, and often have to entertain clients, so don't get home till after nine at night. It's not all posh offices and long lunches, I do loads of drudgey contract work too."

I popped up to see Lucy once I'd finished with Claire. We discussed outfits, and arranged that she should be at my place at six, so that we could be picked up by Roger at quarter past. She quizzed me about how I'd be wearing my hair, and said that she'd be wearing hers up, as her dress wasn't strapless. It turned out that she was on annual leave as well for the next two weeks, but had nothing really planned.

I got a taxi back to Canary Wharf, in time for lunch. My first stop was the bank, where I bought £5000 worth of Euros, grimacing at the exchange rate, then into Boots to buy sunscreen, insect spray, and toiletries. At one o'clock I trotted back to my office, ready to wrap up all my work.

"Glad you're back, I know you're in holiday mode, but would you sit in on a negotiation please?" Lewis had poked his head round my door.

"Sure." I grabbed a notebook and pen, and followed Lewis down the corridor to one of the meeting rooms. There were three men seated, our client was introduced to me as Graham Baxter, the owner of a music publishing company. The other party was the creator of a website that had shamelessly ripped off the copyrights that Graham legitimately owned. We had sued on Graham's behalf, and it was due to go to hearing on Monday. Today's negotiation was to see if an out of court settlement could be reached. I quickly text Laura to say that if I called, she was to leave the line open, and be silent. I had learnt a few tricks from Ivan.

Lewis had calculated the level of damages he expected the judge to award, based on Graham's last year's accounts, and doubled it to get a starting point. I saw the opposing side take a sharp breath when Lewis gave the figure. "Please bear in mind, gentlemen, that the judge will also be awarding costs, which, as of this moment, are.." He looked at the file, "ten thousand, four hundred pounds. Now, I'm sure I don't need to tell you that pulling the top team from Pearson Hardwick into court is an expensive business, so please be aware that costs are likely to quadruple if you lose on Monday."

The opposition went pale. "I need to speak to my lawyer alone please." I pressed 'call' on my phone, and tucked it under the cushion of my chair, before following the two men out of the room.

"We must remain totally silent. Is that understood?" Both nodded. We crept into my office, and listened on Laura's speakerphone to the opposition berating his lawyer, and begging him to let him settle today. He told the lawyer that the evidence was so damning that he wouldn't have a hope in hell's chance of winning in court. He also admitted that he'd made around eighty grand out of the scam before it had been uncovered, which was the settlement figure Lewis had opened with.

After ten minutes, we went back in. I surreptitiously retrieved my phone, and ended the call. Lewis played hardball, refusing to back down to the level he would have done previously, and finally settling on 70k, to include all costs, plus the website permanently removed. Graham breathed a sigh of relief as the two opponents slunk out of the room, after signing to say that they accepted the out of court settlement. "Now I just have to get the money out of him. That won't be easy."

"This is a legally binding document. We can apply to the high court if he doesn't pay. Their bailiffs will sort it." Lewis said, shaking his hand.

When Graham had gone, he turned to me, "where did you learn that little trick? Not strictly ethical of course."

"Porenski, who else?" I smiled. "That was fantastic negotiating Lewis. Great result."

"I know a trick or two as well. Now, any news on Goldings?"

"Not as far as I know. Let me check the news." We went into my office, and I clicked on Reuters. "Barclay's CEO has resigned, looks like Lloyds is under pressure too. Nothing about Goldings. I'll give Oscar a call to make sure." I picked up the phone, and was put straight through. "Hi Oscar, anymore fallout from the LIBOR scandal?"

"Only the fact that we're snowed under with new account openings, including most of the prestige corporate ones. Think we're being seen as a safe haven. I'll be glad to get away, it's like a madhouse here."

"You know about the CEO of Barclays going?"

"Yes, spoke to him a couple of hours ago. Serves him right to be honest, they really were ridiculously greedy, and the strategy was never going to work. They are going to have to do a rights issue before this is all over, mark my words. I'll point the next CEO in your direction, maybe you can keep them on the straight and narrow."

"I'm glad to hear that you're ok. By the way, do you want a lift tomorrow night? I've got the Bentley and a driver taking Lucy and I, you're welcome to join us. We're being picked up from mine at 6.15."

"That would be super, thank you. A pretty lady on both arms. Can't think of anything nicer. Listen, I'd better go. I'll come up to your flat at six tomorrow." We said our goodbyes, and I ended the call.

"At least you can go on holiday knowing alls right with your clients," said Lewis.

"Yep, speaking of which, it's nearly five. Have you got anymore tasks for me?"

"No, go have your holiday. Have a great time." Lewis smiled, and waved as he walked out of my office. I gathered up my shopping from earlier, and quickly called Roger. He answered after the first ring.

"Hi Roger, I don't suppose you're free to drop me home? Only I've got a ton of stuff to carry, and I still need to pick up my dry cleaning."

"I'm presently waiting downstairs for you." *This is so cool.* I went straight down and dumped all my shopping with him, before zipping into the mall to pick up my cleaning and the dresses I'd had altered. Within twenty minutes, I was home, with all my gear on the sofa, where I'd asked Roger to leave it.

"You're home nice and early. Thought you might end up working late to clear everything before they let you go." James said, as he pushed a coffee towards me.

"Nope, I spent all week being incredibly organised, so unless there's a disaster, I'm off for a whole fortnight." I did a little happy dance, which made James snort. I put my cleaning away, and did some laundry, wanting to keep on top of everything. I got James to help me pull my suitcase down from the top shelf of my closet, ready for packing.

"Bit early if you're not going till Monday, isn't it?" James remarked.

"I don't care, I just want the excitement of it. I haven't packed for a holiday since forever, so I'm gonna make the most of it."

"I bet you have a list."

"Of course, they don't call me Mrs Uptight- And- Organised for nothing you know." James grinned at my obvious enthusiasm, and hooked his arm around my neck, pulling me to him so that he could plant a wet kiss on the side of my forehead. Smiling, he went off to pour out a glass of wine each.

"Are you eating here tonight?" He called out.

"No, I'm seeing Ivan tonight, so I'll probably eat with him." James returned carrying two glasses, and handed one to me. "Heard anymore from Janine?"

He shook his head, "No, and I don't expect to. It's time for me to move on, and find someone nice. There's got to be a woman out there somewhere."

"You won't have much trouble, the girls'l be tripping over their tongues when you strut down to that pool in your shorts."

"Doubt it, but thanks for the compliment." He looked embarrassed. "Have you loaded up your kindle?"

"Yup, loads of trashy chicklit, and a few murder mysteries as well. Gotta keep myself busy by the pool." I was interrupted by Ivan calling. "Hi babe, how was your day?" I chirped.

"Long and boring. All that's kept me going was the thought of tonight. I bought new batteries, and everything.." I caught on to what he was talking about. With James sitting opposite, I couldn't exactly say too much.

"Excellent news, are we eating at yours?"

"Yeah, my housekeeper made a roast. You need to keep your energy levels up for what I've got planned. Shall I send Roger over? Are you ready now?"

"Yep, give me five minutes for a quick shower, and I'll be sorted. See you in a bit."

Ivan pulled me into a strong embrace as soon as I stepped out of the lift, pushing my hair back gently, he kissed me deeply, his tongue stroking mine, as the dogs danced around our feet, desperate to say hello too. I bent down to pet them, rubbing their soft little heads as they happily wagged their tails. "I wasn't sure if we'd be going to Sussex tonight," I said.

"I'm going down tomorrow. I wanted the swing at my disposal," he smirked, "plus of course, I'm gonna have two very boring weeks, so I'll make the most of you while I can." He poured some wine, and pushed a glass over to me.

"I'm sure we'll talk on the phone, text and email. I'm not going to Outer Mongolia you know. You could always hop on your jet and come and join us, then we won't have to go two weeks without any sex."

"Hmm, quite a tempting offer. I might surprise you." He pulled two plates of food from the warming drawer of his oven. "The girls have already had theirs, so don't listen to any lies about not being fed today." He placed a roast chicken dinner in front of me, poured some more wine, and sat down to eat his. Both dogs immediately positioned themselves at our feet, looking hopeful.

"Spaniel eyes are so difficult to resist," I mused.

"That's what they depend on. I wonder if it would work for me too," he said, widening his eyes, to give me a puppy dog look. The effect was rather spoilt by his sapphire irises glittering in the early evening sun.

I smiled, "Not really, they need to be chocolate button coloured to fully elicit the sympathy vote. Yours are too blue and sparkly. Besides, you're going to eat your fill, then have as much sex as you can handle. Exactly what else could you possibly want?"

"That sounds great. I just wish I was the one taking you away, seeing you so excited to be off for two weeks. I wish it was me that could laze around reading beside you, although to be honest, I'm just thrilled that we're lovers again. I love it when you answer the phone all happy and call me 'babe'."

"Mm, I like it too. I wish it was just us two going away as well, but there'll be other holidays. I might see about taking a long weekend when you're in France, that's if you want me there," I added.

"I want you there for the whole two weeks. I love spending lazy time with you. I'm hoping little miss here won't try and swim to Africa this time." He looked pointedly at Bella, who wagged her tail in response.

I slipped the two dogs the remainder of my chicken, and took our plates to the dishwasher. Ivan scooted around the island to capture me in his arms. I could feel his hot breath on my neck, as he whispered something in Russian. "What did you just say?" I asked.

"Nothing much, just something I'm practising. Now, more wine? Or straight to the pleasure room?"

"How about a quick drink on the terrace? Let our dinner go down before we start bouncing about." He took my hand, led me outside, and pulled me onto his lap. It was a beautiful, warm evening, and the river shimmered below us. I sipped my wine, before placing the glass on the table, and running my hands over his strong shoulders, and into his silky, dark hair. He pulled me into a kiss, pressing his tongue into my mouth in a gentle, but possessive movement. He pulled away to put his glass down, then wrapped his arms around me, his hands roaming over my back as if they were searching for a bit of bare skin to stroke.

"Come, I don't want to wait any longer. I want to see you naked, and feel your desire. I want to see you desperate for my cock." He was using his phone sex voice. I turned to mush. He led me into the apartment, and along the corridor to the pleasure room, carefully closing the door behind him. He threw off his shorts and vest, and lay on the bed. "Strip for me, please." He picked up a remote, pressed a button, and the room was filled with the strains of Savage Garden. *Insatiable? Good choice.*

I stripped slowly, turning it into a show for him. I let him have glimpse of a nipple before covering it again, and coyly flashing my freshly waxed pussy, turning as I pulled my knickers down. Ivan lay on the bed, lazily stroking his cock, and watching me intently.

"Bend over, I want to see your pussy from behind." He purred the command, but it had an authoritative edge. I complied immediately, opening my legs slightly to give him a better view.

"You look so beautiful," he said softly, "tonight, will you let me restrain you? Make me feel as though I own you, body and soul?" *He wants to own the world.*

"Ok, but if I don't like it, you promise me you'll stop?"

"Of course. I never want you to feel uncomfortable. Tonight is for your pleasure as much as mine." He slid off the bed, and walked over to the cabinet to retrieve a pair of leather cuffs. "Stand up please." I did as he asked, and watched in the mirror as he cuffed my arms behind my back. When I was secure, he kissed his way down my shoulder, pausing only to cup my breasts in his hands, holding them with the gentlest touch. I could feel his breath on my back, as he kissed his way across to the other shoulder. I shivered with anticipation, feeling myself get hot and slick.

He stood behind me, watching in the mirror as one hand caressed its way down my body to slide rhythmically over my clit. I could feel his erection digging into my buttock as he looked mesmerised, watching himself pleasuring me.

"Can you see how much your pussy likes this? How wet it's getting for me?" I could see his fingers glistening with evidence of my arousal. "I think it wants my cock."

"Oh god, yes please." I was shamelessly horny for him.

"Not yet baby, I want to feel your desire. I *need* to know you desire me, and only me."

"It's only you," I whispered, fascinated by the sight of him watching himself. He pressed his fingers to my lips.

"Taste how much I turn you on." I sucked on his fingers, tasting the musky sweetness of my own juices, before he withdrew them, and sucked on them himself. He turned me round, and kissed me again, before dropping to his knees, and burying his nose in the apex of my thighs. He inhaled deeply, "you smell so good." He guided my legs a little further open, and slid his middle finger into me, curling it towards him, to tickle my spot. With his other hand, he parted my lips, to gently suck on my clitoris, which was twitching and throbbing wildly.

134

He must have felt the familiar quivering of my impending orgasm, because he stopped abruptly, withdrawing his finger, and leaving my clit engorged and bereft. *So this is your game?* "Don't you need a hard fuck first? You know, to get you ready?" I asked.

"No. I had a wank before you arrived. You're not getting fucked that easily baby." He purred. He bent me over the bed and caressed my bottom, lingering on my anus for a while. I could see his erection straining, and wondered how long he was going to hold out, before he gave me a good fucking.

He padded over to the cabinet, and pulled out some toys. I felt something cool and smooth slide into me. "Try and hold that in place." He murmured. It kept feeling as though it was slipping out, no matter how much I clenched my inner muscles around it. Ivan kept sliding it back in, but it was too smooth to provide any friction. "You're too wet and turned on to hold it, aren't you?"

"Yes, I need your cock."

He chuckled, "all in good time baby." With that, he rolled me onto my side, the dildo slipping out onto the bed. He slid it back into me, before pressing a vibrator onto my clit. I arched into the welcome sensation, desperate to reach an orgasm to relieve the tremendous pressure building inside me.

He took it away. *Bastard.* I cried out in frustration, as my orgasm melted away. I tried to rub my legs together to get some relief, but Ivan had other ideas. "You want my cock?"

"Yes please." He helped me off the bed, but instead of undoing me, and putting me in the swing, he guided me down onto my knees, and pressed his cock to my lips. *Two can play at this game lover boy.* I closed my mouth resolutely, pressing my lips together firmly.

"Like that is it? That won't get you fucked baby." He bent his legs, and grasped my tits, squashing them together around his cock, which he rubbed rhythmically back and forth. "Do you like me fucking your tits?" He demanded, as his index fingers flicked my nipples in time with his thrusts. I felt the sensation travel right down to my groin. I groaned. "If you suck my cock, I'll put you on the swing and fuck you."

I opened my mouth, straining to lick the tip of his dick as it bobbed up and down between my tits. "Such a good girl. You want to suck it?" I nodded my assent, and he abandoned my breasts to press the tip of his cock into my mouth. I sucked greedily, swirling my tongue over the wide crest, tasting his pre-cum. His movements grew a little more urgent. I could tell he was being careful not to choke me, but as his breathing grew more ragged, he pushed a little too far, and I gagged. "Baby I'm sorry, I got carried away," he said, looking mortified.

"I'm fine. Give me back your cock." He smiled, and gently teased my lips with the tip. I captured it in my mouth, and sucked hard, which caused him to gasp.

"Ok, I give in, turn round, and let me uncuff you. I need to fuck you." He undid the cuffs, and gently rubbed my shoulders, before helping me into the swing. I lay there, anticipating the tremendous orgasm to come, my clit pulsing and twitching. He stared at it for a few moments. "You have the prettiest pussy. I need to taste it a little more."

He raised the swing, and buried his face in me, licking and lapping at my juices. I was almost mindless with the need to come. "Please baby, I'm gonna come, and I want your cock." I felt the swing lower.

"Your wish is my command," he said, slamming into me. I gasped at the size of it, stretching me inside. He fucked me at a fast pace, the crest of his dick rubbing repeatedly over my g spot. He was really taking no prisoners. He pressed the vibrator onto my clit, and I fell into my orgasm.

I screamed as I came, the earlier denial priming me to climax so hard that I saw stars. He carried on at a relentless pace until I felt my next orgasm brewing. It rolled through me, making my body convulse in spasms of pure pleasure. "That's it baby, just go with it," he murmured, not missing a beat. He was swinging me onto his cock harder and harder, pressing the vibrator onto my clit. He turned up the speed of it, and I cried out, unsure if I could take any more ecstasy. "One more baby, let it go. I know you can," he breathed, slamming his body into mine.

It felt as though I'd fallen off a cliff, my body seemed to shatter, as another orgasm ripped through me. My insides contracted viciously, and I think I blacked out for a moment. I felt Ivan swell, and still, as he pumped me full of semen, his body shuddering, and slicked with sweat. We stayed still and silent for a few minutes, with him pressed deep inside me. Eventually, he softened, and his cock slipped out. "That was amazing," I murmured.

"Yeah, it's always special with you." He stood upright, and wiped the sweat off his face, before helping me out of the swing, catching me before I slumped onto the floor like a sack of potatoes, because my legs were too wobbly to carry me. He laid me tenderly on the bed, and snuggled in beside me, kissing me softly. "You are exquisite, beautiful girl. Have you any idea how much I love you?"

"Mmm, I love you too baby. I am totally wrung out."

"Are you hungry? Thirsty?"

"Thirsty, something cold, and yeah, I could eat if you are." Ivan pulled on a robe, and took another one from the back of the door, helping me into it, as though I was a child. He took my hand, and led me down to the kitchen. I perched on a bar stool while he poured two large glasses of apple juice. I watched as he drained his, and poured another one.

He smiled at me rather shyly, then turned to ferret around in his large fridge, pulling out a strange looking tin, some crème fraiche, and a pack of little pancakes. "Caviar and blinis, only the best Beluga for you of course." I watched, fascinated as he opened them all up, and showed me how to spread a little of the crème fraiche on the blini, and pile a little caviar on top. He held it out for me to take a bite.

It felt like little pearls of salty fishiness were bursting on my tongue. "You like?" He asked. I nodded my head, and took another bite. He finished the rest of that one, and started preparing another, ignoring the girls at his feet begging for a morsel.

"Does this remind you of home?" I asked.

"No, I never had it until I'd been in London a few years. The only things that remind me of home are anything pickled, rye bread, and salted meat. I avoid all three like the plague." He took a big pile of caviar. "I was born to enjoy only the good things in life I think."

"Just a good time boy," I teased.

"That's me. I make no apology for it." He leaned forward and softly kissed me.

We snuggled down with the dogs to sleep, I was so exhausted, I fell into a deep, dreamless slumber, not even waking until nearly seven the next morning.

I glanced at the clock, delighted that I'd managed a lay in. I pulled on the robe, and wandered along to the pleasure room to retrieve my clothes from the night before, pulling them on, then heading to the kitchen to make a drink.

I sat on the terrace with my coffee, watching the boats go by on the river. I fantasised about doing this same thing every Saturday morning once I'd got my new apartment. I was busy daydreaming when the dogs came skidding out, closely followed by Ivan.

"Morning baby, you looked like you were a million miles away." He said, kissing me.

"Yeah, I was just dreaming about my new flat. It's got a terrace like this too, overlooks St Saviours dock though, as well as the river."

"We should use some of that cash on the furnishings. It's a good way of getting rid of it. I booked an interior designer for the Saturday morning. Hopefully it will be yours by then. She can help you decide how to choose your new furniture."

"That'd be great."

"Are we still going to the crematorium that day?" He asked.

"Yeah, won't take long though. I just have to pick a spot, and scatter her ashes."

"We could go straight to Sussex from there. Have some quiet time. You might be a little emotional."

"Yeah, that's a good idea. Maybe go over to Windsor, and see if there's any more stuff for the girls at work. They loved all the cast offs."

"Sure. We can pick up some more cash too. I want to get a safe fitted for you, for your jewellery and cash."

"I forgot to ask Oscar about deposit boxes, plus my boss was sitting in front of me when I spoke to him, so I figured it was better to keep quiet, and leave the stuff here for the time being. I need a little cash for tonight though, for drinks mainly." *Why do I feel embarrassed asking?*

"You need to look through the jewellery too, see if there's a nice diamond set to go with your dress."

We spent the morning chatting, drinking coffee, and playing with the dogs. It was lovely, lazy, and easy going. We felt so comfortable together that time seemed to pass unreasonably quickly. At mid day, I had to head home to get myself ready for my hair appointment, telling Ivan I'd call him in the morning to send a car for me to join him in Sussex.

Chapter 12

Back home, James was doing his ironing ready for packing. I said hi, and disappeared for a long shower, which involved lots of exfoliation and an application of self tan.

"Can you tan my back please?" I asked James, handing him the tube. "Don't forget to wash your hands after though, or they'll go orange." I stood with my back to him, and slipped my robe down to give him access to my shoulders and back. "No peeking," I said sternly.

He rubbed the tan rather gingerly across my skin, making sure it was properly covered. "There you go, all done." He handed me the tube, and went straight to the kitchen sink to scrub at his hands.

Back in my room, I threw on a track suit, and took a photo of my dress for Guiseppe. With my hair still wet, I skipped along to the salon. Guiseppe and Andre greeted me like an old friend, and sat me down with a cup of coffee to discuss my 'look' for the evening. I showed them the picture of the dress that I'd snapped on my phone, and Guiseppe declared that my hair should be put up, to show off my neck and shoulders to best advantage, and use a clip that I'd found in the jewellery pile.

He proceeded to roll up my hair, and put me under a dryer. Andre cleansed and primed my face while I was drying. He did my makeup while I still had the rollers in, using shades of gold and bronze that would complement my dress. Guiseppe declared my makeup 'perfecto' and proceeded to work on my hair, piling it onto my head in an intricate knot. He finished it with the diamante clip, (at least I thought it was diamante , although I wasn't sure, knowing Dascha), which glittered beautifully under the salon lights. "A masterpiece" I declared, staring at myself in the mirror. I kissed them both goodbye, paid my bill, and left.

Back home, James stared at me when I walked in. "Blimey, you scrub up alright don't you?"

"Thanks. They're magicians in that salon." I looked at the clock, and saw that it was five. "I'd best get dressed, Lucy will be here soon." I went through to my room, and put on my dress, shoes and jewellery. I heard the buzzer go for the entry system, and James letting someone up.

I opened the door to Lucy, air kissing her hello. "You look totally gorgeous," I exclaimed. She was wearing a baby blue Grecian style gown, which showed off her lithe, golden limbs to their best advantage. Her feet were encased in impossibly high heeled sandals, encrusted with blue stones, and her blonde hair was in a soft side bun. I felt a bit of a midget standing next to her, despite my three inch heeled Jimmy Choos.

"You look incredible," she replied, "James! Long time no see. Looking as handsome as ever."

"You don't look like kid sis anymore. You look lovely Luce, you keeping well?"

"All good thanks. Doesn't Elle look amazing?"

"Yeah, she looks lovely." James replied.

"She looks better than 'lovely'. You look like Keira Knightley's prettier sister," she said to me, "doesn't she James?"

"Yeah. I'm sure you'll both be the belles of the ball. Now, would you like a glass of wine while you wait for your car?" He went off to fetch the drinks.

"So, do we know who else is going tonight?" Lucy asked.

"Not sure. We're being escorted by Oscar Golding. He's one of my clients, and a friend."

"And an ex," James called out from the kitchen.

"Yeah, well, that was a while ago now. These days he's just a good friend," I said. James returned with our drinks, and I sipped mine gratefully.

Lucy looked thoughtful, "Oscar Golding, as in Lord Golding?"

"Yep."

She looked delighted. "He's beyond gorgeous, plus of course he's rich and well connected. I'm sure you know that already though."

"Oh yes. He's been very kind to me. He's a nice guy. Looking forward to escorting the two of us tonight."

"He's definitely an ex? You won't get cross if I flirt will you?" Lucy was serious.

"Absolutely not. I even told his mother that I should introduce the two of you. I've got a feeling that you might be just his type. Really don't worry about me, I'm with Ivan now."

"How come you're not bringing him tonight?"

"We had a row, and I dumped him. We're back together now, and getting along really well. I invited you before he'd managed to get round me. Oscar was invited by one of the partners. He's an important client."

"I'll be on my very best behaviour, and try not to jump him." We both giggled, then both jumped when there was a knock at the door. I opened it, still smiling. My smile vanished, and my jaw dropped at the first sight of Oscar in full, pristine white tie. Most men look handsome in black tie, Oscar especially, but in white tie, he really was something else. Lucy was taken aback too, although she was doing a better job of covering it than I was.

"Elle, you look beautiful, really stunning, and introduce me to your gorgeous friend." He kissed me quickly on the cheek, and turned his attention to Lucy, who was flashing her megawatt smile.

"This is Lucy, a colleague of mine at Pearson Hardwick." I watched as he kissed the back of her hand, looking a bit enchanted. "Lucy, this is Oscar, our escort this evening."

"Delighted to meet you," said Lucy, beaming.

"How come I haven't met you before? I'm at your offices quite often," asked Oscar.

"I'm based at our head office in the city. I specialise in family law, not corporate like Elle. I rarely get call to visit our Canary Wharf offices," Lucy explained.

While they were chatting, I checked my bag, to make sure I had everything I needed, and saw a text from Roger to say that he was downstairs. "Our car's here. Shall we make our way down?" I said goodbye to James, and the three of us went down in the lift, and got into the car. Oscar sat between Lucy and I, and I'm sure I caught him looking at her shoes. The pair of them chatted easily during the drive over to Inner Temple.

There was quite a line of cars pulling up at the entrance to the banqueting hall, and quite a few people milling around. When it was our turn, two liveried gentlemen opened the car doors, and we stepped out. Oscar stood in the middle of us, and grasped my elbow, as well as Lucy's to escort us both in.

The reception hall was packed, throngs of mainly men were standing in groups chatting and laughing. Oscar flagged down a passing waiter, and handed glasses of champagne to Lucy and I, before taking one for himself. I spotted the Pearson Hardwick group, and we made our way over to say hello. Ms Pearson looked extremely elegant in a dove grey designer gown, her hair blow dried into flicky waves around her face. "Elle, you look lovely dear. That dress is divine. Lucy, how nice to see you here." She turned to Oscar, "Lord Golding, I'm so glad you could come. Hopefully not too difficult a week for you, with all these problems going on?"

"Thank you for inviting me, I must say, all you ladies look extremely elegant this evening," Ms Pearson actually blushed, "and I have to say that thanks to both Elle and Mr Carey, I've had a very good week. We've had the highest number of account openings in our history, including a lot of prestigious corporate ones. So far, I'm having a good scandal."

I spotted Peter and Matt from my office, and excused myself to go and say hello. They looked less at ease in their ensembles than Oscar, who looked like he'd been born wearing his. They both complimented me on my dress, and asked who Lucy was. When I explained that she was one of our colleagues from head office, I swear I saw Peter dribble.

"Clever enough to be a lawyer, and looks like a model? Jeez. She is one hot lady. Looks like Golding thinks so too," said Matt. I glanced over to see Oscar gazing at her, a look of total enchantment on his face. I felt a tiny pang, as I realised that I'd lost my fallback position, but the truth had been that I didn't want to sleep with him again. It was right to let him go.

He sat between Lucy and I at dinner, barely noticing that I was there. I chatted to Lewis, who was seated on my other side. I heard Oscar ask Lucy if she was going away this year.

"I'm trying to, well, I was meant to be going with my ex, but we cancelled it when we split. I kept the time off booked, and I thought I'd visit my parents in their villa in Southern Tuscany, only I've not been able to get a flight out. I'll keep trying all next week, but so far they've all been fully booked, even from places like Manchester and Glasgow."

I dug Oscar in the ribs, and whispered, "can't she come on ours?"

He whispered back, "we're sharing with the Smythe-Robertsons, there isn't room. I already promised them a lift. They couldn't get flights either."

"Well, I could go to Spain with James, and take Ivan's jet down to you next weekend. Give you a clear run with Lucy if you like. Go on, invite her."

"Are you sure?" he asked

"What are you two whispering about?" Lucy asked. I nodded at Oscar, and smiled at him.

"I'm flying out there on Monday," said Oscar, "you're very welcome to join me on my jet."

"That would be fantastic," Lucy exclaimed, "what a stroke of luck."

"Well, I've got a family with five children hitching a lift too, so you might not think it quite so lucky. One of them's a baby, so there may be some screaming, and it's a relatively small jet." He turned to me, "I wish I hadn't offered the Smythe-Robertsons a lift really, but I felt a bit mean."

"Henry and Penelope?" Lucy said. Oscar nodded.

"You know them?"

"Oh yes, we often meet up in Tuscany. Our villa is only about a mile from theirs. We've christmassed with them before too, in their Cotswold house."

I tuned out as they chatted happily about the people they knew, and turned my thought towards Spain. As soon as the awards were over, I excused myself and went to the ladies to phone James. He answered straightaway. "Is everything alright?"

"Yeah, everything's great, because I'm coming to Spain with you in the morning."

"Yay! How come?"

"Fixed Osc and Lucy up, she needs a flight out to Tuscany, so I'm letting her have my place, and I'll take Ivan's jet over next weekend. Whatever you do, don't let me sleep in. What time we gotta leave?"

"Cabs coming at half six, we have to be at Gatwick by eight. Flights at ten. I'll make sure I've got your ticket ready. You have a 22 kilo luggage allowance."

"I'll pack when I get home. James, I'm so excited. Listen, I'd better go, I need to call Ivan and let him know that there's a change of plan."

"Ok, I'll see you later on. Have fun."

I quickly called Ivan. "Hey babe, we have a change of plan, Oscar is taking Lucy on Monday, so I'm going to Spain in the morning instead. Am I still ok to borrow your jet next weekend to fly from Spain to Italy?"

He went quiet...."have you been matchmaking?"

"Yeah, a bit. But they've really hit it off, and it gives Oscar a bit of a clear run with Lucy without me getting in the way."

"I'm delighted, I sort of thought you were keeping Oscar on ice..." He trailed off.

"Don't be silly. Oscars a great friend, but that's all. He's like a smitten kitten with Lucy. She seems very taken with him too. It's very cute."

"Cute is not a word I'd ever use to describe Oscar. Listen, have a great time in Spain, and I'll sort out my Jet for next Saturday. Is that ok?"

"More than ok. I hope you can come out too. I'm gonna miss you so much next week. Just don't forget that I love you."

"I love you too baby. Ya sobirayus zhenit'sya na tebe."

"What does that mean?" I was curious, as it sounded like the phrase he'd whispered the night before.

"Doesn't matter. I'll tell you soon. Go and have fun."

We said our goodbyes, and I went back into the ballroom. I spotted Oscar and Lucy deep in conversation at the table, their body language indicating that they were indeed, very into each other. I decided to leave them alone, and joined Lewis and Ms Pearson, near the bar. "Might be you getting an award next year Elle," she said, "you could easily go up for the 'rising star' category."

"Yes, but look at the head hunters crowding around this year's winner," pointed out Lewis, nodding towards the young man who'd been awarded that honour.

"At least Pearson Hardwick won the 'best litigator' prize, and best 'investor in people' award. That's quite something. You must be very proud." I said to Ms Pearson.

She beamed, "I have a feeling that corporate is where the prizes will be won next year. I think we may have a few more banks on board by then. Now, if we can get the Conde Nast account too, well, that would be a huge coup."

"I'm working on it. I accepted the position of company secretary on the board of the umbrella company that I set up to combine Conde Nast, Retinski, and various other companies. With Retinski already a client, I doubt if the other companies would have much choice. Odey and Corbett are gonna lose another one."

Ms Pearson raised her glass in a toast. "To the sharpest corporate lawyers in London." We clinked, and drank.

I mingled and networked a little, mainly chatting to my colleagues, although a chinless wonder made a feeble attempt at chatting me up. Oscar and Lucy were deep in conversation, so I left them to it. In truth, I was itching to get home and pack.

It seemed to take forever to get to midnight, despite it being such an important and glamorous 'do'. I was relieved when Oscar and Lucy approached to ask if I was ready to leave. "We're planning to go over to Whisky Mist for a drink. Would you like to come?" Lucy asked.

"I need my bed," I lied, thinking they were both a bit overdressed for a bar. Roger was waiting outside, and we all got into the Bentley. We dropped the two of them off outside the bar, and I watched them walk in holding hands, before Roger pulled away to drive me back to the docklands.

As soon as I got in, I made a coffee, stripped off, and began my packing. With an uber-full wardrobe, it was relatively easy to get carried away, and pack too much. I worked my way methodically through my list, making sure I packed carefully to avoid creasing. It was nearly four in the morning by the time I'd finished. I didn't dare risk going to sleep in case I didn't wake up, so instead, I sorted my handbag, checking that I had money, debit card, passport, and phone numbers for lost and stolen services. I took my hair down, hid the clip and jewellery, and hung my dress back in the closet.

By the time I'd showered, washed and dried my hair, put some makeup on, and got dressed, James was up. "Hey little Elle, didn't you go to bed?" He asked, eyeing my suitcase by the door.

"No, I'll have to sleep on the plane. I didn't get in till nearly one, so by the time I'd packed, it was time to get ready. I busied myself making James a coffee. He drank it quickly, and shuffled off to have a shower and get dressed.

The cab arrived bang on half six, and after James had checked he had the tickets and his passport, we set off for Gatwick. We got there in good time, as the traffic was light, and checked in straightaway. "Shall we go through security and find somewhere for a bit of breakfast?" James suggested.

"Good idea. I'd like to visit duty free too, and the sunglasses shop if we've got time." We passed through security without issue, and wandered around the vast shopping area inside the terminal. As we were quite early, we had loads of time, so found a table in Cafe Rouge, and scoffed a full English each. It felt like we were already on holiday.

We looked around duty free, where I bought a bottle of perfume, some aftershave for Ivan, and a new mascara, then bought some magazines in Smiths, some bottled water, and a bag of sweets for the flight. I was delighted to find a Sunglasses Hut, and we each bought ourselves a new pair of shades. By the time our flight was called, I was exhausted.

I think I fell asleep the moment we sat down on the plane. I vaguely recall James doing up my seatbelt. It felt like my eyes had only been closed for a moment before he was shaking my shoulder to wake me up and tell me we'd landed. I hadn't even been aware that we'd taken off.

I took a long swig of water, and wiped my fingers under my eyes, as we taxied to the terminal. "That was the shortest flight I've ever taken," I said.

James grinned, "Apart from the fact that you drooled on my shoulder, it was the quietest I've ever seen you. I think the stewardesses thought you'd been drugged."

I looked at the damp patch on his T-shirt, "sorry about that." He just looked amused. With a bit of sleep under my belt, I felt a lot better. We whizzed through the terminal, got our cases, and found a taxi to take us to our hotel.

We pulled up outside a rather grand looking place, larger than a huge villa, but smaller than the high rise tower block hotels which peppered the Spanish coast. It looked extremely swanky and exclusive. The taxi driver pulled our cases out of the boot, and placed them at the entrance. James paid and tipped him, and we went inside to check in.

"Mr Harrison and Ms Reynolds? Yes, your suite's ready for you. May I have your passports please?" We handed over our passports. "These will be returned tomorrow. Your bags will be collected in a moment. Would you like to take a seat, and enjoy a glass of sangria, with our compliments?" We sat down on the sofas in the cool, elegant lobby, and a waiter appeared with two glasses of sangria, filled with pieces of fruit. I sipped mine slowly, savouring the fruity, citrusy flavours. About ten minutes later, a porter appeared to take us to our suite.

We walked past an enormous pool, with people laying flat out around it on loungers, looking like lizards sunning themselves. A few people were swimming, and a group were clustered around the swim up bar at one end. It was beautifully peaceful. "Where are all the kids?" I asked.

"It's an adult only hotel. I didn't think you'd want to be surrounded by squealing children," said James.

"Oh well done, I didn't know they did that." I beamed. I loved it there already. We followed the porter into a small block, and up a flight of stairs. He drew a key card out of his pocket, and opened a door, gesturing for us to go in. After passing through a tiny lobby, we stepped into a living room area, all done in creams and beiges, with doors opening out onto a balcony. I stepped outside, and gazed at the perfect sea view. It had a little bistro table and chairs too, for watching the sunset.

Back inside, James tipped the porter, and handed me my key card. We checked out the bedrooms, and I took the pool view one, and let James have the larger sea view room, as he'd be staying longer. "Do you want to unpack now, or throw a bikini on and go explore?" James asked. "I don't mind either way."

"Can I fling a bikini on and have a look round?" I was eager to see the beach. James lugged my case into the room, and left to find a pair of shorts. I rummaged through, and found a bikini, a sarong, and a pair of flip flops. I quickly changed, and went back into the living area.

"Anything you need to put in the safe?" James asked, as he put his wallet, watch and our tickets in. I grabbed my handbag, and threw it in, taking just enough money for some food and drinks, which I poked into my bikini top. "Don't forget that's in there if you jump into the pool."

We strolled round the grounds, checking out the restaurant and bars, one of which was right on the beach. We stopped at a barbecue area, and sat and had a grilled steak each, with an icy cold beer to wash it down. "We need to get some lotion on if we're going back out. This sun's fierce," I said, noticing James' nose had gone a bit pink during our walk.

We discovered that we could charge everything to the room, which was handy, and set off back to the room for beach towels and sun lotion. I was pleased to discover that the gym was just a short walk away. We sunbathed and swam for a couple of hours, then went up and unpacked, showered, and went down for dinner.

I just couldn't stay awake long enough to go out drinking, so James watched a bit of telly in the room, and I crashed in my bed, after texting Ivan to tell him all was fine.

Next morning I was back to normal, and up early. I made some coffee, while James trotted down to the pool to bag our sun loungers. I packed my beach bag, and we headed down to breakfast. "So, what would you like to do today?" I asked.

"Flop around by the pool, drink some beers, eat, maybe a bit of reading, hit a bar tonight? How does that grab you?"

"Sounds like a plan. I might try out the gym, and add a game of volleyball to that itinerary, and I'd really like to make a start on some of the trashy chicklit books I downloaded." We lingered over breakfast, drinking coffees, and checking out the other guests. A small, slim brunette caught James' eye.

"She looks interesting. Killer body too," he whispered. I looked over, and saw the woman he was talking about. She had long, dark hair, big boobs, a tiny waist, and a pretty and animated, smiling face.

"If I was a lesbian, she'd probably be my type too. As I'm not a lesbian, I'll let you have first dibs," I teased, "have you seen if she's here with a boyfriend?"

"I don't think so. She walked in with that tall girl over there."

"Might be gay."

"Nah. Doesn't look like either ones a lesbo. Neither of them are manly." We both watched as she chose her breakfast, and went to sit outside.

"So she's your type then?" I asked.

"Not really, but I think I'm cured of the fascination with blondes. I want someone totally different from Janine in every way." A touch of sadness clouded his handsome face.

"So what other girlfriends have you had? I've only ever heard about her?"

"Oh, I was a bit of a tart before I met her. Different girl every week, you know. I never really met anyone I wanted to settle with, although there were some nice girls. I liked a lot of variety. I couldn't even tell you what it was about her that was so different, but I fell in love, and the rest is history."

"Maybe a bit of tarting around will do you good. Get you back into the swing of things," I said. James just smiled. "Anyway, shall we go and get some lotion on? I need to start work on my tan." We wandered back to the pool, and James showed me which sunbeds he'd picked. I unpacked the beach bag, and carefully coated myself in cream. "Can you do my back please?" I asked, handing the bottle to James. He squirted a blob on my back, and quickly rubbed it in. "You need to go under the straps please, otherwise I'll burn," I pointed out. He lifted the straps rather gingerly, and swiped some cream around.

150

I did his back, taking care to coat him really well. He wasn't as muscular as Ivan, but considering he didn't work out, he was in quite good shape. I handed him a lipstick shaped tube. "Factor 60, for your nose." He rubbed a bit on, and satisfied we were both coated in sunscreen, I settled onto the sun lounger, and switched on my kindle. I was engrossed in my story when I heard James ask for a fresh orange, and ask me what I wanted. "I'll have the same please." Five minutes later, a glass of icy cold, freshly squeezed orange was placed in front of me by the waiter. James signed the chit, and tipped him a couple of euros. I sipped my drink and said, "this is the life eh?"

We spent the day swimming, reading, eating and people watching. That afternoon, the sports organiser set up a pool volleyball net, and asked for volunteers. I immediately said yes, and got in, as did the dark haired girl from breakfast. As luck would have it, we were on the same team. I'd played a bit at uni, mainly to break up the monotony of my relentless swimming, so I was fairly ok at it. She was also pretty good, plus we had a couple of German men on our team who were fairly competitive too. We trounced the other side, who were all British men, and hopelessly unfit, having swum down from the bar for the game. They were probably a bit pissed too.

When we were declared the victors, we all high fived each other. "That sounds like a London accent," said dark haired girl.

"It is indeed. I live in London. You sound like a Londoner too."

"Certainly am. I live in Rotherhithe. Which part are you from?"

"Canary Wharf, just the other side of the river from you. Want a drink?" We swam down to the bar at the end, and perched on the submerged seats. Over cold beers, I discovered that her name was Lynzi, she was holidaying with her friend, Becca, and was a junior doctor at Guys hospital. They'd arrived Saturday, and were there for two weeks.

"I think your boyfriend's asleep," she said, looking over at James, who was indeed asleep.

"Oh, he's not my boyfriend, he's my flatmate. I left my boyfriend at home. We booked this holiday before I met Ivan," I explained.

"Really? So is he single?" she asked. *You're interested.*

"Who James? Yeah. Split up with someone before we came away. He's a bit upset about it," I confided, "says he'll never go out with a blonde again. I didn't like her much from the start though, James is a nice guy, and she was a bit of a cow. Plus she used to eat all my food."

"I'd be livid if someone did that to me. I used to hate it when I was a student, in shared digs, and people would say 'it's only a bit of milk' as if you're being petty at them using the last bit and leaving nothing for the morning."

"I'll introduce you when he wakes up, if you like."

"Ok, but you're sure you're not together?"

"Totally sure. My boyfriend wouldn't have been happy about me coming away with him if he wasn't sure we really are just friends. James behaves as if I'm his kid sister most of the time. Ivan, my fella, thinks it's quite funny how James feeds me up, and ensures we have a full fridge. He worked away recently, and I got a bit thin and poorly looking."

"So let me get this straight, he's single, ridiculously good looking, and a good cook?" She looked incredulous, "I think this might turn out to be a very good holiday."

"I'll introduce you." We clinked beer bottles and drank. Becca, her friend, came and joined us, and we chatted for a while about the places we liked in London, music and clothes. We were interrupted by James swimming over to say hello. "Woken up then?" I teased.

"Yeah. I was having a lovely sleep. Sorry I didn't help in the volleyball match, but I was feeling too lazy to jump around." He smiled at Lynzi as I introduced them. I chatted to Becca for a while, and when I discovered that she was a gym bunny too, I suggested a workout. James and Lynzi both groaned.

"It's alright, I won't make you come with us, but can you bring the beach bag up with you when you're finished?" Becca and I went off to check out the gym.

After my workout, I walked by the pool, but James was nowhere to be seen. I went up to the room, and heard him singing in the shower. I swigged at a bottle of water, and sat out on the balcony until he'd finished. He came out with a towel wrapped round his waist. "Good workout?"

"Yeah, not bad. You and Lynzi seemed to hit it off ok."

"She's really nice. They're going to join us for dinner tonight, if that's ok with you?"

"Great. You look perkier. You've caught the sun too."

"Wanna see my white bit?" He undid the towel a little, and showed me the stark white line where his shorts had been. "I'm surprised you don't go topless. At least half the women here do."

"That'd go down well with the Ruskie Ratbag when I get home wouldn't it? He'll be making sure I've got white bits. I think he'd be a bit caveman about other men seeing my tits." James nodded in agreement. I went off to jump in the shower and get ready.

Chapter 13

The rest of the week followed a similar pattern of sunbathing, eating, reading and hanging out with Lynzi and Becca. We checked out the local clubs, ate in some great restaurants and played in the pool like a bunch of teenagers. I watched as James and Lynzi grew closer, and more relaxed with each other. I didn't mind at all, as Becca was a blast, and shared my love of fitness. By Friday afternoon, I was tanned, relaxed, and hoping that Ivan would try and come over the next day with his plane.

"It's such a shame you're going tomorrow," said Becca, "those two barely look at anyone but each other," she added, nodding at James and Lynzi. We were all sitting at the swim up bar in the pool.

"I know, but I promised my friends that I'd visit, and I really hope my boyfriend makes it over tomorrow. I've missed him terribly."

"Why would he come if you're going to fly out to Tuscany?" She asked, confused.

James butted in, "it's his plane she's borrowing for the flight. He's got his own jet."

"Trouble is, he hates flying, so avoids it where he can. He did text to ask for the address of the hotel to send a car, so I think that means he's not coming." I was a little concerned that I'd not heard much from Ivan all week. He'd replied to my texts, but not volunteered any of his own.

"Wow, he must be loaded," said Becca.

"Hmm, yeah, a bit," I admitted, "but I guess I'm more used to it now, so I don't really think about it. He's just the man I'm in love with, rather than 'an oligarch'." I did little air quotes with my fingers.

"I'm very glad to hear it," said a deep, Russian voice, as a pair of arms wrapped around me from behind. "I missed you baby, and I just couldn't stay away a minute longer." I spun round and flung my arms around his neck.

"I missed you so much," I whispered in his ear, "I'm having a super time, but it's even better now you're here." We grinned at each other. I turned to the others, and introduced Ivan. I noticed that Becca looked a little overcome, the usual 'Ivan' effect. James looked pleased to see him, and ordered another round of beers for us all. I glanced up to see Nico and another guard standing nearby, in the shade, dressed in suits, and felt a little sorry for them. "Do they need a drink or anything?" We swam away from the bar.

"No baby, they'll be fine. I think Nico has everyone on six hour shifts, so they don't have to stand in the heat for too long. I spoke to Oscar yesterday, and we're flying out to him on Sunday morning. Is that ok?"

"Great. I've got a feeling that James will be just fine here on his own." We both looked over to see James and Lynzi sharing a secret smile.

"You, my darling, have been matchmaking again, haven't you?" He kissed the tip of my nose.

"Not really. They both fancied each other from the start. I just got talking to Lynzi and introduced them. I feel a bit sorry for Becca though, she's gonna be a bit lonely next week I think."

"Maybe she'll meet someone too. I've got some good news for you. I don't have to fly back to London until Monday evening, so we have the whole weekend together."

"That's brilliant news!" I exclaimed, throwing my arms around his neck again.

"Careful baby, I've not seen you all week, and your tits are rubbing up against me. You know what that does." I looked down, and could see the tent in his shorts. I stepped away from him so he could get it under control. We pootled about in the pool for a while, then re-joined the others at the bar for cold beers.

We all ate in the attached restaurant that night. It was sort of posh tapas, which worked well for a group of five. Ivan and James got on well, and I think James was secretly pleased to have a bit of male company for a change. Becca was eyeing up a German man who had arrived a few days before. I watched as they kept looking at each other flirtily. "I think she'll be just fine next week," Ivan whispered in my ear.

We enjoyed a relaxed meal, laughing at Lynzi's doctor jokes, and Becca's funny stories about hospital life. Ivan sat with his arm round my shoulder, stroking my arm. "Are you staying in my room tonight, or did you book a room?" I asked.

"I'm staying in yours. They only had one room available, which my guards are using. Are you ready for bed then?"

"We're gonna head off up to bed. See you all in the morning," I said to the others. I got up, and left, Ivan following behind. "Was that a bit obvious?" I asked him.

He smirked, "I'm sure they know what we'll be up to, but yeah, very obvious." He pulled me into a deep kiss underneath an archway of sweetly scented flowers. "Oh Elle, what have you done to me?" he gasped as he pulled away, "I've been useless all week, counting the hours till I could see you again." I gripped his hand, and practically dragged him up to the room.

The great thing about hot countries, is that you don't need to wear a lot of clothes. Within thirty seconds I was naked, and on the bed. Less than thirty seconds later, so was Ivan.

"Hard fuck first?" I gasped, knowing it would mean a longer, slower session afterwards.

"Standing up. Let me fuck you up against the wall." He quickly felt to see if I was ready. Satisfied that I was already wet and horny, he lifted me slightly, and held me as I wrapped my legs around him. He guided his cock into me, and began to pound me hard and fast. I stroked the silky skin of his shoulders, and reached down to caress one of his nipples, rolling the sensitive little nub in my fingers. I felt his movements speed slightly, I glanced down, and saw his cock sliding in and out. The sheer *horniness* of it pushed me into an orgasm. I dug my nails into his shoulder as I pulsed around him, unable to move or close my legs. I felt him jerk inside me as he came, and watched his face soften as he found his relief.

My legs were a bit wobbly when he put me down, so I immediately lay on the bed, pulling him down with me in a tangle of limbs. He immediately went for my breasts, sucking, licking and fondling them. "I've missed these so much. You have such beautiful breasts," he murmured. I stroked his beautiful skin, feeling his muscular arms and chest, running my fingers through his silky curls. He shifted lower, gently parting my lips to suck on my clit. I arched off the bed, lost in the sensual pleasure that he was inflicting.

I tugged at him to climb on top of me. He crawled up my body, licking and kissing as he went. I almost came the moment he entered me, and I tried desperately to control it. He pulled himself up on his knees, and carried on fucking me, while gazing at my body. He licked his thumb, and pressed it onto my clit, rubbing tiny circles as he pumped. I came with a scream, and tried to close my legs to control my clitoris, which was throbbing wildly. He pinned my legs open and carried on pounding me, swivelling his hips to make my orgasm go on and on.

He must have felt my orgasm begin to subside, as I felt him still and let go. I lowered a leg so that he could roll down beside me. "I missed you," he said.

"Missed you more," I replied, snuggling into his arms, and breathing in his wonderful scent. He smelt like home.

The next morning, I left Ivan sleeping, and went into the living area to make a coffee. James appeared as I was boiling the kettle, having done his sun lounger bagging duties. "Did you bag five?" I asked.

"Of course." I lined up three cups, and spooned coffee into each one. "Erm, can you do another one with two sugars in please?" James asked, looking rather pleased with himself.

"Get you, Casanova," I teased as I organised another cup.

"Like you weren't doing the exact same thing?" He retorted. We both smirked at each other. I took Ivan's coffee in to him, and put it on the table beside him. He was sleeping like a baby, so I left him to it, and sat out on the balcony to drink mine. James came out to join me.

"Did you wear yours out too?" I asked.

"Yeah, she's out sparko. I take it Ivan's still asleep?"

"Like a baby."

"What do you think of Lynzi?" James asked, rather suddenly.

"I really like her. I think she's clever, hardworking, and open. I had a bad vibe from Janine from the start. I don't get that from Lynzi. More importantly, what do you think of her?"

"I think she's great. You know I fancied her from the moment I saw her, but as I've got to know her, I think she's even more attractive. I really like her sense of humour too."

"Yeah, she's good fun. A nice person too. I bet you carry on seeing her at home."

"I hope so," he admitted. We were interrupted by Ivan, sipping his coffee.

"Morning. Everyone sleep well?" James and I both chorused 'yes'. "I did too, after James finished murdering his girl in there," Ivan teased, "talk about loud.." Both men smirked.

"Do you want us to get out of the way, so that she doesn't have to do a walk of shame?" I asked, "we can meet you at breakfast if you like."

"Do you mind?" James asked. I shook my head, amused.

I gathered up my beach bag, towels, etc, and Ivan and I went down to breakfast, finding a large table for all of us. "This must all be quite a novelty to you, holidaying with other people?" I said.

"I like it though. It's very....social, but it's nice. You seem very relaxed and happy." He cocked his head to one side, as he watched my face.

"I've really enjoyed it. It's a lovely hotel, no kids, and I like meeting new people. It feels less... rarefied. I know that if we stayed in a hotel, it would be the presidential suite with a private pool and a posse of guards preventing anyone from speaking to us. I'd love it, because I'd be there with you, but this has been great too. I love seeing you be normal."

He smiled at me. "I can't really help who I am. I like seeing you like this though. Maybe we should have a hotel holiday every year as well as my villa." I beamed at him. Just the fact that he was talking about the future, made me feel secure.

"Have you been reading those 'be a good boyfriend' books?"

"If I had, I would have remembered to order flowers for your room."

"James gets terrible hayfever, so I'm glad you didn't," I replied, smiling a soppy smile at him. We were joined by James and Lynzi, both bearing plates of toast and scrambled eggs. Becca arrived five minutes later, looking extremely happy. It turned out that she'd got talking to the German after James and Lynzi had left, and was meeting him for dinner that night.

After breakfast, we all decided on a game of beach volleyball, with Lynzi and I versus the other three. Becca went off to fetch a ball from the sports organiser, and we made our way down to the beach.

"Do those poor guards trail everywhere?" Lynzi asked.

"Yep. He gets edgy without them. Probably don't need them here, but he was kidnapped several weeks ago in Russia. It was terrifying."

Realisation dawned on Lynzi's face, "I thought he looked a bit familiar, is he Ivan Porenski?" I nodded. "No wonder he's got his own plane. Sorry, I didn't put two and two together."

"Out of context. You wouldn't expect to see him somewhere like this. It's a novelty for me too, and him. He normally holidays in a villa, surrounded by staff and security."

"Isn't this all a bit, well, ordinary for him?" she asked, clearly curious.

"No, I don't think so. He's enjoying it, and although he's wealthy, he's quite ordinary too. We don't eat caviar for breakfast or anything like that." We took our places on the volleyball court. "Ready for us to whip your arses?" I called out.

"No chance baby, we have Becca, the secret weapon, on our side," Ivan called back, as I launched the ball into the air, and straight past his head. It landed at Becca's feet. "Hey, I wasn't ready," he grumbled.

"A poor excuse," yelled Lynzi, catching the ball from Becca. She served a stonker, which James scrabbled to reach, just managing to keep it in the air. Ivan managed to get it over the net, and I slammed it back, jumping to get to it high, and wallop it to the ground.

"Nico! Can you play volleyball?" Ivan yelled, "we need reinforcements." Nico nodded, and looked around to make sure nobody was watching as he took off his jacket, gun holster and tie, handing them to the other guard, before removing his shoes and socks, and rolling up his trousers.

With Nico on their team, it was much more evenly matched, and they beat us 29/30. We all went off to the pool while Nico called for another guard so he could go off for a shower, and change. "That was fun," said Ivan, "you really are good at sports. There has to be something I can beat you at."

"I'm rubbish at tiddlywinks, maybe we should try that." He looked at me quizzically, clearly having no idea what I was talking about. "Doesn't matter," I said, jumping into the pool. The rest of the day passed all too quickly in a blur of laughter, food, and alcohol. I woke up Sunday morning with a bit of a hangover, having had a late night with the group of Germans that Becca's new beau was part of.

I looked over to see Ivan splayed out like a starfish, clearly out cold, and went to make myself a restorative cup of coffee. James was already out on the balcony, swigging coffee. I made him a fresh one, and sat down beside him. "Is Lynzi here?" I asked.

"Yeah, fast asleep. We were both a bit hammered last night. Those Germans like a drink don't they?" I nodded in agreement. "What time are you flying out?"

"About ten. Thankfully it's not a long flight. I might not get my fingers broken this time."

"Is he that bad?"

"Yep. Sweats, shakes, and can't stand up. I feel sorry for him, it must be hell."

"Wow, who'd have thought it?" He swigged his coffee.

"You gonna be alright here on your own?" I asked.

James smiled, "I think I'm going to be just fine. I know at the moment it could be classed as a holiday romance, but I do actually think it'll be more than that. She only lives a ten minute drive away, through the tunnel, so I'm going to carry on seeing her, if she wants to that is."

We drank our coffee in companionable silence, and watched the Mediterranean Sea for a while. "I need to go pack, I think we're leaving straight after breakfast." I made more coffee, and went into the room. Ivan stirred slightly as I put his cup down on the bedside table. Quietly, I pulled open my case, and put my laundry at the bottom, covered by a layer of shoes, and methodically re-packed my clean clothes on top. I left out just my clothes for that day, and the toiletries I needed. Afterwards, I packed Ivan's weekend bag, leaving out a pair of shorts and a T-shirt, as well as his shaving gear, and toothbrush. Eventually, his eyes opened.

"Morning sleeping beauty," I said, as he struggled onto his elbows to sip his lukewarm coffee. He pulled a face at it.

"Morning baby. God, my heads banging," he glanced at my case, "have you packed the headache tablets already?" I nodded to a packet of neurofen that I'd left out, just in case, and went to fetch him a bottle of water, and boil the kettle for a fresh coffee. He sat up in bed, and drank, looking pretty rough, although 'rough' for Ivan was the sort of look that graced magazines. I thought he looked sexy as hell with a bit of stubble, and his hair mussed up.

"Shall we shower after breakfast? I asked, "I'm a bit hungry after all that vodka last night. I need some food inside me." The German lot had insisted on a vodka based drinking game, as soon as they'd learnt that Ivan was Russian. It had all been a great laugh at the time...

"Yes, ok. Maybe food will make me feel a little better." He swung his legs out of bed and threw on the clothes I'd left out. We went downstairs, and ate.

I felt a lot better after a full English, and copious amounts of orange juice and coffee. By the time I'd showered, I was almost back to normal. Ivan seemed to perk up too once he had some food inside him.

The porter collected our bags, and after hugging James and the others goodbye, we went to the front desk to check out. While Ivan sorted his bill, I paid for all the food and drink that James and I had charged to the room, as a nice little surprise for him.

The flight to Tuscany was thankfully quite short, although Ivan, as usual, was rooted to the seat, sweating and shaking. He didn't even bother to try and hide it from me this time. He held my hand in an iron grip, as I read my kindle one handed.

Oscar had sent a pair of cars to meet us when we landed, and I sat looking at the landscape as we drove down to his villa, inhibited by having Nico in with us due to space restrictions in the car full of guards behind. Eventually, we came to a pair of gates, which were open, and travelled along a dusty road through what looked like a vast estate.

I took a sharp intake of breath at my first view of the 'villa', which looked more like a mini castle. "Wow, I thought it would be nice, but it's really quite something, isn't it?" Ivan said. Oscar and Lucy were waiting by the front door.

"I'm so pleased you could come. Ivan, nice to see you. I trust you had a good flight?" Oscar said, as we got out of the car. "Come on through, I'll show you to your room, then a drink on the terrace before lunch."

"Lucy! Lovely to see you." I looked quizzically at her.

"Tell you later," she whispered, looking a little embarrassed.

"This villa is spectacular Oscar. How long have you had it?" Ivan asked as we followed Oscar through the hall, and up the rather grand staircase.

"My Father bought it about forty years ago, as a bit of a wreck, and restored it as a bit of a project, probably to give him a break from patching up Conniscliffe. He did enjoy organising builders. The estate is managed for us though, I don't really have to deal with it much these days."

Our room was delightful, with an enormous bed, crisp white linen sheets, and a view over rolling hills, set into fields. As usual, Oscar had had a luxury bathroom fitted, which was as big as most people's living rooms.

The terrace outside was lovely, made of ancient looking stone, and arranged around a rather lovely pool. It had a covered area, as well as an open area, with sun loungers, and a couple of parasols. We sat at the large table in the covered part, and drank cold, white, Italian wine, brought out by a butler clad in pale linen, rather than the usual butler attire that Jones at Conniscliffe wore.

"So have you heard any news about what's happening back home?" I asked.

"Well, the CEO of Natwest resigned, quite rightly I might add. The CEO of Lloyds is still clinging on by his fingertips. Goldings is having a bit of a bonanza from the whole scandal, although, as the banks bankers, it isn't without repercussions completely. It all comes down to what action the Bank of England takes. If they imposed punitive fines, the consequences could ripple outwards, but I'm lobbying the chairman to make sure that doesn't happen."

"So does that mean I'll be looking after a couple more banks when I get home?" I asked.

"Yep, 'fraid so. You'll probably need to oversee a couple of rights issues too. They're going to need to generate vast amounts of cash fairly quickly."

"Baby, between Oscar and I, you'll make partner sooner than you think," Ivan interjected.

"Nobody under the age of 40 has ever made partner before. I still have a long way to go."

"There's a first time for everything," Lucy chirped. "Ms Pearson does seem rather fond of you, and to pull in that many prestige clients couldn't go unnoticed."

"Plus you're going to get Conde Nast too, don't forget that," added Ivan.

"Best I flop about and relax then. Seems like I'm gonna be hitting the ground running next week."

"I have something to tell you," said Ivan, "I spoke to Ms Pearson in the week, and arranged another week off for you in August. To come to the South of France, to make up for being a rubbish boyfriend."

"That's brilliant news," I beamed. "You really seem to be able to get round her."

"He probably flashes his film star smile at her," laughed Oscar, "she's a sucker for a pretty face."

"She's a sucker for a big wallet, and the prospect of Conde Nast," replied Ivan, smiling at me, his eyes shining with...love?

We had a glorious lunch on the terrace, Oscar was right about the food, it was the freshest, most flavourful Italian food I'd ever tasted. Afterwards, Lucy and I flopped onto the sun loungers, while Oscar went off to show Ivan round the estate. I watched as they walked away, deep in conversation. I took off my shorts and vest, and lay flat on the comfortable steamer chair. Lucy did the same. She looked incredible in a bikini.

"Right, come on, spill," I said to Lucy. She sat up on the side of her lounger, and leaned forward.

"I haven't even been to visit my parents yet. We only got dressed this morning for the first time since we got here. Elle, we're in love, and it's fantastic."

I looked at her, and noticed that she didn't actually look any more tanned than she did on Saturday night at the ball. "We went to Whisky Mist, and talked until it closed. He came back to mine, and had a coffee, didn't leave till four in the morning. Met me for brunch next day, and we haven't been apart since. Elle, he's everything I ever dreamed of and more."

"I'm so pleased for the two of you. I did tell his mother that I'd introduce you. I thought you'd get on well." Despite my little pang at losing my fallback position, I was pleased for them both. Oscar had looked happy and relaxed, if a touch tired, and Lucy was positively glowing as she spoke about him.

"It's all moved quite fast, but we've both hinted at the word 'love'," she added, "he's just so...what can I say? Gentlemanly, sexy, clever, kind..."

"Rich, powerful.."I said, we both giggled.

"Yeah, that as well. We are definitely compatible in the bedroom." *Really Luce? Blimey.* "You and Ivan look happy together. He's incredibly good looking isn't he? I bet you have to fight other women off, not many men are that.." she struggled for the word, "pretty. I bet he's a sex god too."

"Oh yes. Definitely a sex god. It's going really well. I'm happy. I think he's happy with me, and we're extremely compatible. I feel comfortable with him."

"Elle, can I ask, why did you and Oscar split?"

"Just wasn't the right chemistry," I lied smoothly, "he's better with you."

"Yeah, that's what he told me too. His mother liked you though?"

"Eventually. Can I give you a tip? Type up her church newsletter, and set it out nicely in word. Check the spelling of anything the dozy vicar writes, and she'll think you're wonderful. She's actually lovely, and a real blast. I really enjoy her company now."

"Good advice, I'll do that," she smiled.

The butler interrupted us with glasses of cold, freshly squeezed orange juice, and icy cold flannels to refresh us. We chatted about Spain, and the hotel I'd stayed in, until the men returned. I watched as Oscar leaned over to give Lucy a soft kiss, his hand resting gently on her shoulder, as if he needed to be touching her at all times. They looked impossibly good together. I also saw Ivan watching. *What if he goes for Lucy now to rip her away from Oscar? It's what he did with me.*

"Are you ok baby? Not too hot?" he asked.

"No, I'm fine thanks, although that pool looks rather inviting."

We had a super afternoon and evening. Oscar and Ivan were both on good form, and I watched their interactions with rapt fascination. They were both powerful, alpha males, but seemed at ease together, and not as competitive as I would have expected. We talked about Ivan's villa in France, which he described as 'modest', until I laughed, and told Lucy it was enormous, bloody gorgeous, and had a view to die for.

That night, we lay in bed talking about Oscar and Lucy. "Are you surprised?" Ivan asked.

"No, funny enough, I thought they'd get on well. She's very much his type, and she's a little aristocratic too. I never met her ex, so I had no idea whether or not Oscar would be her ideal man, but they seem to have hit it off."

"He's very loved up. I can tell. Does that bother you?"

I looked up at him, "Not at all. I'm delighted for him, I'm more worried about you."

He frowned, "in what way?"

I took a deep breath, "because of the things you said to Paul. You only wanted me in order to piss Oscar off. I'm worried that now he doesn't want me anymore, neither will you." *There, I've said it.*

Ivan drew me into his arms, "Were you honestly worried? Baby, none of that was true, I've told you many times. How I feel about you has nothing to do with how Oscar felt about you, he was just a rival, nothing more, nothing less. Did you think I'd chase after Lucy now?"

"It crossed my mind," I admitted.

"She's a nice girl, but she's not you. She doesn't have your amazing mind, nor your pretty face. She doesn't have your iron backbone, and she most certainly wouldn't understand my hangups about my background. You have absolutely nothing to worry about. My heart belongs solely to you. I worry more about other men stealing you away because I'm a rubbish boyfriend."

"Don't keep saying that. You're not always a rubbish boyfriend, sometimes you're wonderful."

"I try. I'm learning. I was pleased you didn't go topless in Spain. I was worried," he said, changing the subject.

"For your eyes only. I figured you wouldn't like it, so I kept them covered Mr Caveman." He cupped my left breast with his hand, holding it gently.

"See, that's why I love you. You understand me perfectly. Other women wouldn't have given it a second thought. Ya lublu tebia ee hotchu zhenitsia na tebe."

I prodded him in the ribs, "Don't talk Russian. What does that mean?"

"I'll tell you soon," he said, before kissing me softly. We made love slowly that night, mindful that we were in someone else's house.

Chapter 14

The next morning I woke early as usual, and went downstairs in search of coffee. I found the kitchen, complete with a tiny Italian woman making breakfast pastries. She waved me off to sit on the terrace, promising to make me a latte, (in pidgin English). I sat outside, looking at the beautiful view, and five minutes later she appeared with both a latte, and a tea tray with teapot, accoutrements, and a milk jug set in a bowl of crushed ice. I drank the latte first, then poured out a tea. After about half an hour, Oscar wandered out.

"Morning, sleep well?" he enquired.

"Very well thank you. It's a very comfortable bed." The tiny woman reappeared with another tray, and took the first one away. I poured myself another tea, while Oscar sipped his latte.

"It's working out well with you and Lucy by the sounds of it?" I asked.

He beamed. "She's lovely. I didn't think I'd meet anyone who would measure up to you, but she does, and I'm genuinely happy."

"I'm glad for you. You deserve to be loved, and be happy. Do you think she might be 'the one'?" I watched as he pinked up slightly.

"It's early days, but yes, I think she is. She's bright and clever, but not fiercely intellectual, beautiful, but not overdone, and she loves my dirty talk."

"Sounds like a match made in heaven," I said, smiling at him. "The two of you look great together, and she doesn't seem at all intimidated by your wealth."

"Her family is well off, so yes, she's comfortable around money. It's not been an issue." He paused. "You and Ivan seem very relaxed with each other. He seems to smile when you're around. I think the two of you fit together very well, although it pains me to say it." He grinned to show me he was teasing.

"Yeah, we're good. He's trying hard."

Breakfast was quite a lavish affair, with lovely pastries, rich cheeses, and fresh bread served alongside the usual bacon and eggs. "I said I'd feed you up a bit," said Oscar, as I reached for another pastry.

"She doesn't eat enough. I keep telling her she gets too thin," agreed Ivan. I patted my rather round tummy, and sat back in the chair, smiling, as Ivan squeezed my hand.

"I know what I meant to ask you," said Oscar, "what happened to Mrs Smith from Derwent Engineering? Has it gone to court yet?"

"Yes, she pleaded guilty. She only got six months though, because of her age. The hearing was last week."

"I didn't know. How come I wasn't asked to testify?" I asked.

Ivan shrugged, "She pleaded guilty, so there was no trial. It was only a sentencing hearing. I didn't have to go either."

"Mother was asking, there were lots of rumours flying round the village, so I promised her I'd ask you."

"Anything else happen last week?" I asked, looking at Ivan.

"Not really. Lassiter came up with some potential execs who I'm meeting this week, and Andrei found someone to rent the Windsor house. A sheik I think, wants it for his son for a few years. It's got to be ready by the end of August. Apart from that, it's all been fairly quiet."

"Any word from Natalya?" I asked.

He shook his head. "Not yet. I have a meeting with her tomorrow. I'll know more then."

We finished breakfast, and I went up to the room to change into a bikini and sarong. I threw some sun lotion and my kindle into my bag, along with my phone and sunglasses, and went back down to the pool. I was swimming lengths with Lucy, when I heard my phone ring. I asked Ivan to get it while I swam to the edge. "Claire Plant wants to speak to you," he said, handing me the phone.

"Hi Elle, it's Claire," I said 'hello' back, "just to let you know that we're ready to exchange contracts. All the paperwork's in good order, and the funds are all in place. Do you want me to wait until you're back or go ahead now?"

"If you're happy, then go ahead now," I said, a little plume of excitement rising in my tummy.

"Ok, will do. I'll do the exchange now, and it'll complete before three this afternoon. Congratulations. Are you having a nice time?"

"Lovely thanks. I'm in Tuscany with Lucy right now. Do you want to say hello?" I handed the phone to Lucy who chatted to Claire for a few minutes, before handing it back to me.

"Hi Elle, just to let you know that you exchanged about a minute ago. Would you like me to call you when it's complete? Only I know that you can't exactly go and get the keys."

"No, but can you let the estate agents know for me please, and explain that I'm away?"

"Will do, and I hope you're really happy in your new apartment."

We said our goodbyes, and I ended the call. "I exchanged on the flat, completing this afternoon. I'm so excited," I squealed. Oscar smiled indulgently, and asked the butler to fetch a bottle of champagne. Ivan gave me a hug and a kiss, and Lucy chattered about interior designers that she knew.

We toasted my new flat with champagne. In truth, I wanted to fly home there and then, and just go and sit in my new flat. For the first time in my life, I had somewhere I could truly call home, that didn't belong to the council, or somebody else. I realised at that moment, that I had somewhere I belonged, and somebody I belonged to. It was a heady feeling. All the dreams I'd had, felt as though they were coming true. I thought back to the day I'd moved into James' place, feeling as though I'd 'arrived', with my new job, and sophisticated apartment share. This was ten times better.

"I bet you wish you were at home now, don't you?" Lucy said, accurately reading my thoughts.

"Well, yes. I wouldn't be rude enough to rush off though." I admitted.

"Elle, if you want to go and see to your new flat, I will understand," said Oscar, "I know just how much this means to you. I won't be offended." I looked at him sitting with his arm around Lucy's waist, and realised that not only would he not mind, but he could crack on with shagging her in every possible way, without me to worry about. I was going to be a bit of a gooseberry.

"If you truly don't mind... It does feel as though I'm being rather rude and ungrateful," I murmured.

"Not at all. Fly home with Ivan tonight, Lucy and I will be fine, I promise, and have the rest of the week sorting out your new place." Oscar said, smiling at my excitement. Ivan squeezed my shoulder, and kissed my cheek.

"I can take some time, and we can shop for your new place, plus we need to visit Windsor, organise the clearance there. Saves spending our weekend doing it. We still have all afternoon and evening to enjoy Oscar's beautiful home, and hospitality. We don't leave until eight."

I beamed at the two men that I loved, who both tried their best to ease my passage through life, and felt a surge of gratitude towards them. I spent the afternoon chatting excitedly to Lucy about furniture and interior design, showing her a couple of the magazines I'd bought at Gatwick, with some ideas for colour schemes, and the latest styles of sofas.

We had the most amazing dinner that evening, eating early, outside on the terrace, as the sun began to set. Oscar explained that a lot of the food was grown on the estate itself, by the farmers who leased the land from him. Almost as soon as we had eaten, it was time to go. The guards took care of our bags, and I hugged Lucy, and told her how happy I was for her. When I said goodbye to Oscar, I hugged him hard. "Thank you for everything. You have no idea how much you've done for me. Be good to Lucy yeah?"

"I will, and you have no idea how much you did for me too. I owe you, not the other way round."

"Come on Elle, your new flats waiting," Ivan called out from the car. I hopped in, and waved goodbye as we set off down the winding driveway.

It only took around two hours before we were back in London. Roger was there to meet us, and took us straight back to Ivan's, where Bella and Tania were waiting to greet us, beyond excited that their daddy was home. We sat up for a while, chatting about our holiday, the food at Oscar's place, and the possibility of James and Lynzi becoming an item. By midnight, I was asleep on my feet, and Ivan led me to bed, and slipped in beside me, pulling me into his arms.

"Sleep baby, you have a busy day tomorrow."

I bounced out of bed at half five the next morning, and after a quick cup of tea, used Ivan's home gym to do a workout before he was even up. I was buzzing with excitement at the prospect of walking into my first ever home, in the purest sense of the word, and was antsy and nervous.

Ivan had to go in to work at around half eight, so promised to drop me at the estate agents to get the keys. From there, it was only a two minute walk to St Saviours dock. He would be free around lunchtime, and would come and see it. Depending on his schedule, he would possibly be able to get the afternoon off to take me shopping. If not, Roger would be at my disposal.

I kissed him goodbye before getting out of the car at the estate agents office, and waved as he drove off. I stepped inside, and saw the agent who had taken me for the viewing. "Ms Reynolds, I thought you were away this week. Your solicitor called us yesterday with the news of your completion, but said you weren't expected back."

"Came home early. I was too excited about this to stay away." He smiled indulgently, and went to a little cabinet to retrieve the keys, found a file with the alarm codes, and handed it all to me.

"I'll take you over there, and show you how the alarm works, and where everything is," he said. We chatted about my holiday on the way over, and stopped at the entrance. He showed me the code to get into the foyer, and I introduced myself to the concierge, who was a jolly looking middle aged man called John. We stepped into the lift, and I pressed the button for the top floor.

"Now the code for the alarm is 7731, and you need to tap it into the keypad just inside the front door. All the instruction booklets are there in your welcome pack." My tummy fluttered as I unlocked the door. I stepped inside to a beeping noise, which stopped as soon as I entered my code. I walked into the main room, and immediately saw a folder on the kitchen island. "That's your welcome pack. It tells you how everything works, where all the control boxes are, and how they work. It also has all the guarantees and warranties for the appliances, as well as full instructions. Your contact details for the developer are in there, in case of snaggings. He'll expect you to compile a snagging list, so don't be shy, include anything that's not perfect." We were interrupted by a buzzing sound. "That's the concierge downstairs," he said. I picked up the phone.

"It's John from concierge, there's been a delivery for you."

"Thank you, I'll be right down," I said. I grabbed my keys, and followed the estate agent down in the lift. After thanking him, I went over to the front desk, where John produced a large bouquet of flowers, a vase, and a large Starbucks. "He thinks of everything," I laughed, thanking John for taking them in for me.

Back in the flat, I arranged the flowers in the vase, and placed them on the island. I opened all the windows to get some fresh air in, and wandered from room to room, hugging myself with glee as I planned what would go where. Ivan had given me a tape measure that morning, so I measured up the space, and noted the measurements down as I went along, particularly the size bed that would fit between the built in bedside tables in the master bedroom. I'd already made a list of household basics that I'd need while I was on holiday, such as kitchen stuff, and cleaning equipment, but the flat looked as though it had been recently cleaned. The limestone floors were immaculate. If I'd had furniture, I could have moved in there and then. I stood at the island and drank my Starbucks, while reading through the file. I was astonished to discover it had a built in vacuum system, so I wouldn't have to carry anything more than a hose from room to room, and a safe, which took me a while to find, as it was rather sneakily hidden behind a false wall in between two bookshelves in the study, which slid back to reveal the door. I opened it using the key provided, and checked out the size. It wasn't anywhere near as big as the one under Vlad's bed, but it was fairly capacious. I locked it back up, and slid the cover back.

I checked that the study had a phone line, and made a note to call BT and sort the phone and broadband as soon as possible. I wandered back to the kitchen, and looked in the pantry, trying to visualise how it would look full of food, and examined the laundry room, with its built in washer, separate tumble dryer, and a rather nifty storage rack for the iron and board. My reverie was broken by my phone ringing from the kitchen. I ran in and answered it.

"Hi baby, what's the code to get in please?" Ivan asked.

"2215, and in the lift, press the button for floor twelve," I told him.

"See you in a minute."

I stood at the front door, to welcome him in. He arrived bearing two more Starbucks, and a big smile. "Everything alright at work?" I asked.

"All fine. I think they work better without me there sometimes. More importantly, is everything alright here?" he asked.

"Totally, utterly, brilliant," I said, stepping aside for him to come in. The guards stood outside, and I noticed that Nico had a briefcase chained to his arm. Ivan closed the front door.

"Case full of cash. Thought we'd go shopping. I'm sure you have a list."

"You really do know me too well," I said. I gave Ivan the guided tour, telling him the details I'd found out that morning.

"I think this apartment is nicer than mine, tell me, is there a 'no animals' clause in the lease?"

"Nope, I checked. The girls are fine for sleepovers." He smiled as I said it.

"Good. Now, we need to discuss security. You need to change the alarm code as the estate agents have used it. Nico will look it over to see if it needs upgrading. We can also install CCTV in the foyer outside your front door. Is there a suitable place for a safe?"

"There's one already, come look." I dragged him into the study and showed him the false wall contraption, which he approved of.

"We need to raise the level of the rail round your terrace, and make it bulletproof too. At a push, the girls could jump it at its current height." He wasn't giving up.

"Ok, install whatever security you want. I want you to be comfortable here."

"Good, now, shall we close the windows and go shopping?"

I was reluctant to leave, but locked up carefully, and followed Ivan out to the car. I handed him a spare set of keys, which seemed to make him inordinately happy, and we headed over to the West End, Harrods, to be precise. What followed resembled a trolley dash around the homeware department, as I chose cookware, (which had to work on my fancy induction hob), basic household stuff, a telly and sound system, and a new bed. We looked at sofas, but I wasn't sure about any of them, so decided to wait. We bought bedding, towels, crockery and cutlery. It was the most enormous fun. The smaller stuff was sent straight up to the car, the bigger stuff was being delivered the next morning at nine.

When we finished in Harrods, we went back over to Canary Wharf, and to my surprise, Ivan suggested going to the large Waitrose, to fill up my pantry, and new fridge. We ended up getting the guards to push two trolleys round, as we filled them up with food, drink, and basic household items. "You look like you're having a great time," I said as Ivan picked out laundry tablets and softener.

"I am, remember, I don't get to do this stuff very often, and your excitement is infectious."

We went back to the flat, and the guards lugged everything in. I unpacked while Ivan found the kettle, the cups and the spoons, and made us both a cup of tea. I sorted out the little laundry room, pouring the tabs into a cute little storage box I'd found in Waitrose, and hooking the ironing board and iron into the storage rack. Already it looked more homely.

Ivan filled up the freezer and fridge, and filled the ice maker. "Have you thought about which cupboards you want to use for food, and which for crockery?" I smiled at him. "Ok, what's so funny?" he demanded.

"You. Being domestic. This is just so....normal," I replied. He rolled his eyes, and carried on pulling cups and plates out of the Harrods boxes.

"Food goes in the pantry, crockery in the cupboards." A thought occurred to me, "I thought you were meeting Natalya today?"

"This evening, she's coming over about seven. We can eat once she's gone."

I busied myself arranging the pantry, making it look like something out of a magazine photo shoot. Satisfied, I turned my attention to the kitchen, where Ivan was loading cutlery into a drawer. I stashed the cleaning gear under the sink, and unwrapped my new, fancy, chrome bin, and put a bag in it, before slinging in the used tea bags and wrappings that were piled up on the island.

The last thing Ivan did before we left was to take the cash left in the briefcase, and put it in my safe. I locked back up, and we went over to his place.

Natalya arrived bang on time, and smiled thinly when I was introduced. I followed Ivan and her out onto the terrace, and took a sip of the wine that Ivan poured. "Please be aware that only English should be spoken in front of Elle," Ivan said.

"Of course."

"So, what news do you have for me?"

She shifted in her seat, "Vlad was definitely your father. The DNA proves it beyond doubt. The details of your conception are still sketchy, but I managed to trace a man who was a neighbour of your mothers at the time. He thinks that it was a brief affair, which ended as soon she knew she was expecting. He seemed to think she met your father straight away, possibly passing you off as his. He was named as your father on your birth certificate, of which I purchased a copy." She pulled a file from her bag, and handed it to Ivan. "Inside is the DNA report, your birth certificate, and the report from the neighbour. Is that everything you require?"

He nodded, looking a little shell shocked. "Yes it is, thank you." She finished her wine, and left, no doubt disappointed that she couldn't stay and flirt. *Bitch.*

"Are you ok?" I asked, as soon as she'd gone.

"Yeah, a little shocked, a little sad. Sad for my father that he never had his own child."

"How come they never had any further children?" I asked.

He wrinkled his nose, "I don't know. Most of the families were huge. I suppose it was a little odd there being only me. I never really thought about it before."

"Maybe he was sterile?"

"Possibly. A lot of men suffered illness due to the chemicals they worked with. I'll try and find out if sterility is common."

"If he was, then at least having you was a blessing in his life. Better than being childless with no way of remedying it." I scanned his face for signs of upset.

"I just hope that Vlad's psychopathy wasn't hereditary. I couldn't bear to be like him." He rubbed Bella's ears as he spoke, she looked ecstatic.

"Ivan, you're not a psycho, I promise you, I'd know by now, and I'd be the first to tell you. The worst trait you have is being a bit of a tosser at times, and that's not the same thing by a mile. My mother was a bit of a loser, but I don't think I inherited that trait, now do I?"

"As usual, you have perfect logic my darling. Ya lublu tebia ee hotchu zhenitsia na tebe."

"That's what you said before. What does it mean?" I demanded. He just smiled an enigmatic smile, and went off to dish up some food.

After dinner, he asked what I wanted to do that evening. "We could have a show'n'tell in your pleasure room. I'm clueless about what half the stuff in there is for." He smiled a salacious smile, and led me down the corridor.

I sat on the bed while he explained the various shaped vibrators and butt plugs. He showed me some weighted ball things that were deigned to be worn internally, and also explained his collection of restraints.

"Is that what you like then, having a woman restrained?" I was curious.

"Not particularly, but it seems to be one of those things that some women enjoy, hence all the cuffs and stuff. Personally I like to be caressed, and touched during sex, so usually it's for the woman and not me."

"What else do you like?"

"Pretty much everything we've done really. I like a butt plug, but anal sex is a turn off. I can get turned on by the thought of

176

fucking in public, but I've never actually done it, and I like porn, preferably without anal, and preferably two women. I quite like waxed pussies rather than hairy, and I love my swing. Anything else you want to know?" I shook my head, amused. "So what about you? What floats your boat?" Ivan asked.

"Love your swing too, like the butt plugs and vibrators. Quite like the blindfold. Not keen on being restrained, but loved the titty wank thing you did. Haven't really watched much porn, so can't comment, and have no desire to watch two women at it anyway. We have done it outside, in your pool, remember?" He nodded.

"Well, seeing as we both agree about the swing, I suggest we give it a little workout. I happen to know you're not wearing a bra under that little dress, and it's been driving me crazy all day." He leaned forward and hooked his finger into the top of my dress, and tugged it down, exposing my left breast. He lightly flicked the nipple, then captured it in his hot mouth and sucked. I cried out as a spike of pleasure travelled down to my groin. He freed my right breast, and did the same. I fumbled to undo his trousers, my hands already shaky. He took over, shedding his clothes quickly. I slipped out of my dress and knickers, and stood expectantly by the swing.

"Oh baby, what you do to me," he breathed, gazing at my naked body. He lowered the swing, and helped me in, clipping my hands into the cuffs. "What I'm going to do to you tonight my darling is make you scream."

"I'll scream now if you like, I'm so horny for you," I panted. Just the action of getting in the swing had me dripping in a Pavlovian response.

"Not yet baby. I have a new vibrator that I want to try on you, to see if you like it. It's meant to give you a big orgasm." He pulled out a strange looking contraption. "It's called an 'ultimate O', and I think you might like it," he purred. It was a curious three pronged shape. He switched it on and positioned it so that one prong was directly on my clit, with the other two prongs each side.

"Hmm, that's nice...I like that," I said, relaxing into the sensation. He turned the speed up, and I jumped. "Bloody hell, that's good. Shove your cock in too, before I explode."

He slammed into me, and holding the prong thing in place with one hand, used the other to swing me back and forth onto his cock. *Ohmygodohmygodohmygodshiiiit.*

My entire body began to tremble as the orgasm built up, culminating in an explosion within my body. It felt as though every part of me was either pulsing or trembling, when another orgasm hit, making me scream out. I felt him swell, and let go, holding still for a second, then rubbing out the rest of his climax inside me.

"Babe, you're gonna kill me if you keep doing that to me," I said. He looked smug.

"Thought you might like it. See, I do think of you." I smiled as he helped me down off the swing. I put on a robe, and we went along to the kitchen for a drink.

I sat at the island, and took a gulp of juice. "How come your guards don't show up when I scream?"

"That room is sort of out of bounds. They know that if we're there, that screams aren't sinister."

"So you could murder me in there, and nobody would come?"

"Pretty much, mind you, the opposite would be the case too. You could murder me, and they wouldn't come running."

Chapter 15

Next morning, I did a workout, and got showered and dressed, ready to join Ivan in the car over to Canary Wharf. He dropped me off outside my new flat, and waited as I went into the foyer. I walked into my flat, and immediately felt the hum of excitement again. I switched on the kettle, before depositing my jewellery and cash in my new safe, and sliding back the panel. At a few minutes past nine, John called up to say that my bed and other items had arrived, and he would send then straight up. A couple of burly delivery men carried my new bed into the master bedroom, unwrapped the cellophane, and slid it into position, while two more were busy fixing my new, huge telly onto the wall where I'd shown them I wanted it. They efficiently channelled the cable into the wall, before re plastering it, and explaining that I'd need a little white paint to cover the area once it was dry. They tuned it all in, and showed me how to tune it into my wifi, once it was installed. I thanked them profusely, and tipped them a tenner each as they left, hoping it was enough.

I spent an hour with the interior designer that Ivan had recommended, choosing sofas, curtains, blinds and cushions from various swatches that she brought with her. She had some great ideas, which I loved, and she was busy measuring up, when I caught an item on the news.

Recruitment tycoon found dead in tragic sex game accident

I turned up the sound, and watched as a reporter described the scene in a flat in Canary wharf where Paul Lassiter was discovered after what was thought to be a game of auto-erotic asphyxiation went terribly wrong. I picked up the phone to call Ivan, but he called me before I had a chance to press speed dial.

"Have you heard the news about Lassiter?" I asked.

"Yes, how do you know?"

"New telly. Shocking news isn't it?"

"You did think there was something off about him. Gut instincts are rarely wrong. I gather he was alone. No mention of foul play, well, apart from his own that is."

"I just feel sorry for the poor man," I said, "he clearly had a few issues going on. I found him to be ok though, as a client anyway."

"He was a good recruiter. I wonder what'll happen to his company now? Did he put a contingency in place?"

"Only in so far as everything goes to his sister, who I gather is a nurse. I don't know if we wrote his will, but I can check. The man's barely cold yet though. I'd leave it a few days."

"Hmm, I wouldn't mind buying it. With the way it's structured, it would fit beautifully, and save us a fortune with staffing. Find out as much as you can please?"

"Sure." *I am on holiday you know.*

I cut the call, and phoned Lewis. "Hey Elle, how's Spain?"

"I'm back in London. Long story. Heard about Lassiter?"

"Yes, terrible business. All very sad."

"Can you check our internal systems, see if we hold his will? I'm not at home, so I can't look."

I heard Lewis tapping at his keyboard. "Yes, updated in July this year. Must have done it when you set up the new companies for him. Want me to look at it?"

"Please."

"It looks like he's left everything to his sister, Julie Lassiter, of 64 Cherry Gardens, Bermondsey."

"Ok, when whoever is dealing with it pulls her in, can you let me know please?"

"Sure, will do....you're meant to be on holiday you know."

"Yes I know. See you Monday."

I called Ivan, and told him the news. "Where did you base the company?"

"The Cayman Islands, why?"

"What's the inheritance tax rate there?"

"Zero, same as their corporation tax rate. It's why I based Paul's, and your umbrella companies there."

"I see. Did he transfer his personal assets there?"

"Not that I know of. I only dealt with his companies. I know nothing about his personal assets. Ivan, as I said before, let the poor man get cold before you start trying to buy his company."

"Hmm, well, we'll see what happens."

I cut the call, and went back to dealing with the designer, and getting my sofas, and other furniture ordered.

That night, we discussed Paul's company over dinner. "She may well want rid of it quickly, if she doesn't know how to run it," said Ivan.

"True, but that's her decision to make, plus there may be other interested parties."

"Like who? How many people have the wherewithal to buy a company that size?" he reasoned.

"Alfred Marks? Executive Search? There's a few."

"That have got a hundred mill sitting around? No chance."

"It's worth way more than that," I reminded him.

"Not without Paul, it's not. It's worth what someone will pay. I'd guess she'd be happy with a hundred mill, with no tax to pay on it. I might be wrong, but I doubt it."

"We'll see."

The next day, I went back to James' to do some laundry, and begin packing my things up. I was interrupted by my phone ringing from an unknown number.

"Elle Reynolds speaking."

"Hello, we haven't met, my name's Julie Lassiter. I understand you were my brother's lawyer?"

"Yes, that's correct. I'm really sorry to hear about what happened."

"Yeah well, he was a bit of a screw up. I really need your help. I gather I'm meant to start running his company, and I don't have a clue what to do. Are you free today to see me?"

"I can meet you in my office shortly." I gave her the details, and cut the call. I phoned Ivan on my way over, and let him know.

She looked heartbroken, her eyes had dark circles from crying, and she looked terribly pale. I pressed record on my iPhone.

"I know Paul was well off, and his company's worth a bit, but I don't have a clue about business, and I'm terrified to even go in there," she began to cry. I handed her a tissue, and watched as she blew her nose. I remembered feeling the same sense of terror at the idea of inheriting Retinski.

"Would you like me to introduce you to someone who would like to buy it?" I asked softly.

"Is there someone that would do that?" She gasped.

"Yes, but as your lawyer, I have to counsel you against making snap decisions."

"Oh that decision wouldn't change. As quick as possible please."

"Ok, have you thought about what it's worth, how much you'd want for it?"

"It must be worth at least a few million," she said, naively, "although doesn't the government take 40%?"

"Not in this case, as I transferred all the companies into an umbrella company based in the Cayman Islands."

"I don't have a clue what that means," she said.

"It means no inheritance tax."

"So I'd get the full amount?"

"Yes."

"What do you think I should ask for it?" She put me on the spot.

"It's worth what someone will pay. Now, I can put it out to several companies, and give a deadline for offers of say, a month or so, if you like, or I can put you in touch with someone who has already expressed an interest, and would like a quick sale."

"The faster the better. As long as I get a couple of million, I'll be happy." *Oh little girl, you need looking after.*

"Ok, I'll take you to the interested party, but I'll be getting a colleague to negotiate on your behalf. Is that ok? Only I have a conflict of interest as he's also a client of mine."

"That's great."

I called Ivan to let him know I'd be bringing Julie up to see him, and Lewis would be negotiating on her behalf. He caught on that something was amiss, but said nothing. Lewis and I took her up to Retinski, noticing how intimidated she looked at the fancy offices.

Galina showed us through to the meeting room, and I left Lewis alone with her to discuss strategy. I went to find Ivan.

"Babe, I couldn't shark her, I'd get struck off. You do understand don't you?"

"Of course. Your integrity works both ways, I know that. What's Lewis' opening bid gonna be?"

"The girl wants a few million, please don't rip her off. She's totally clueless. I hope Lewis doesn't go along with her wishes, and only asks for a bit of pocket money. Please open with a decent amount."

"Of course. If we can get this agreed, how fast can you do a sale contract?"

"Close of play today?"

"Ok." He stood up, and let me sit at his desk to begin the contract. I opened a word page, and began to type. Half an hour later, they all returned. Julie looked dazed. "We need champagne," Ivan said to Galina, who scurried off to sort it out. "The sale price is £95 million, and we would like to complete the sale as fast as possible please," said Ivan. *Ok babe, I'll let you off the five mill that you just couldn't resist squeezing. The rest is at least fair.*

"Well done Julie, Lewis," I said. "I'm preparing the documentation now. I'm sure it won't take long, as I set up the companies for him, and know all the details." I typed for a solid hour, printing off pages for Lewis to check and proof as I went. When the last page was done, I printed out a few copies of the entire document, and checked that everything was correct. It had been a hell of a task, and I was exhausted.

Julie and Ivan both signed all the copies, shook hands, and the deal was done. I escorted her back downstairs, and she breathed a sigh of relief. "Thank you so much. I've been suicidal with worry about dealing with it all. I'm just relieved it's all over, and I can grieve Paul in peace."

"I'm sorry about him, I liked him a lot. He was an extremely perceptive and clever man."

I exited the lift at my office, and went to pick up my bag. Lewis followed me in. "You were only just on the right side of ethical there, Elle. If you hadn't declared a conflict of interest, you would have been out on your ear. As it was, your boyfriend got a bargain." His anger was barely suppressed.

"And Pearson Hardwick kept a client. What would you have preferred? A messy administration? Selling to Alfred Marks for the same money, and the work going to Odey and Corbett, their lawyers? She got way beyond what she wanted for it, and the result she wanted. I also happen to know, through my 'conflict of interest' that Ivan wasn't going to pay more than a hundred mill for it, so the price was extremely fair to her."

"That company was worth more than that, and you know it."

"I gave her the choice of putting it up for sale with a deadline for offers, or a quick sale today. It was her choice to do it today, not mine, and if you want the truth, I could have kept quiet, and let Ivan have it for five mill. I didn't, because I do actually have ethics, and she was a clueless little girl, who needed protecting from a certain Russian shark." My voice had risen, there was no way I was letting Lewis get away with accusing me of sharking her.

"Really?" Lewis looked a bit sheepish.

"Yeah really." I played him the recording of my meeting with her. He listened in silence, while I stood with my arms crossed. "Now if it's all the same to you, I'll get back to my holiday."

"Of course, and I apologise for accusing you."

Ivan was late home from work that night, having a vast amount to deal with regarding his latest acquisition. It gave me time to do some packing, and sort out my holiday laundry. Roger picked me up at nine, and took me over to Ivan's place as he was about to get home.

The girls greeted me enthusiastically, and danced around my feet as I looked in the warming drawer to see what we'd been given for dinner. He arrived home five minutes later, looking exhausted. "Hi baby. Sit yourself down, and I'll sort dinner," I teased, pulling on a pair of oven gloves.

"So you're not angry with me?" He asked, looking wary.

"No, should I be?"

"I squeezed her for five mill. I thought you'd hit the roof."

"Don't be daft. You had to get a little bit of sharking in, otherwise you wouldn't have been happy. She only wanted a few mill for it, so she got a good result. Thankfully, I recorded my conversation with her, otherwise I'd be unemployed by now. Lewis really tore into me about you getting a bargain. He did apologise afterwards though." Ivan listened to the recording while we ate.

"Well played baby, got you right off the hook. I looked at Paul's accounts, and I'm happy I got a bloody good deal. She's happy to be out of it, and rich, and you're happy that you won't get struck off. A good day all round." He clinked my glass in a toast.

"It was meant to be my holiday," I muttered.

"I know darling, but I'm taking tomorrow off for you, so it was better to get everything done today. I may get phone calls tomorrow, but at least I won't have to go in."

"What's the plan?"

"Your mum's ashes first, Galina sorted the appointment, then on to Windsor. Boxes and vans have been organised already. How does that sound?"

"That sounds fine. I'd like to keep Friday free though, as I'd like to start moving those boxes of clothes into the flat."

"Of course. I'll let Nico know, and he can arrange a van and some assistance for you."

"Thanks."

We were both tired and tense that night, so made love slowly, and quietly, savouring the variety. Afterwards, the girls snuggled in, and we all dozed off in a group hug.

The next morning dawned a bright and beautiful, sunny day. I did a run on Ivan's machine, before taking a long, hot shower, and dressing in a muted pair of long shorts and a pale grey top. We headed over to Eltham after breakfast, which my stomach threatened to expel the closer we got. We pulled into the car park, and went into the reception. We were told to choose a place, let them know, and someone would come out with the ashes to help us inter them. I had ordered a little plaque with her name on, to mark the spot, so that there'd be a permanent reminder of her. I picked it up, and read her name, marvelling at how little was actually left to remind the world that she'd once existed.

We walked around in silence, Ivan holding my hand. Even his guards kept a respectful distance. I found a sunny spot in the rose garden, beneath a pretty, pink rose bush. Judging by the number of little plaques dotted around, it was quite a popular spot. *She'd like that,* I reasoned, she'd always been quite sociable. Ivan went off to get the man who sorted the ashes, and let him know we were ready.

I was surprised at just how much was there. I don't know what I was expecting, but it seemed like a hell of a lot. The man produced a little shovel, and dug a small hole, before pouring in her ashes. I said goodbye in my head, and handed him the little plaque to stick in the ground, and mark her resting place.

We walked back to the car in silence, Ivan's arm around my shoulder, holding me close to him. No sooner had we got in, than I let out a sob. He slid up the privacy screen, and held me close, letting me cry into his chest.

"Malyshka, let it out, let the tears fall," he murmured, "you'll feel better if you cry for her." I sobbed all the way to the M25, soaking his T-shirt. He didn't seem to mind, and just sat stroking my hair gently, whispering soothing words.

By the time we got to Windsor, I'd stopped crying, and composed myself. We stopped at a Starbucks for some coffee to take with us, and I was grateful for the hot drink to soothe my dry, constricted throat.

At the house, it was all systems go. The house was being rented fully furnished, so all personal items had to be removed before the company doing the inventory could go in. We worked quickly, and methodically, through the house. Boxes were packed, and marked to go to either Ivan's, mine, charity or rubbish. He slung out every item in her sex room, although I was convinced that I saw Nico gaze at it all rather longingly. I found loads more stuff for the girls at work, and only slung out Dascha's underwear. I noticed that a couple of the dodgy paintings had gone from Vlad's bedroom. Ivan explained that he'd had an expert round from the stolen art register while I'd been in Spain, and they were indeed stolen works. The funny thing was that he stood to get a reward for 'finding' them, which was quite ironic.

The last things we tackled were the safes. We piled the cash into boxes, which were loaded into the boot of the Bentley. With everything sorted, the house was locked up, and we headed back to London. We stopped off at my new flat to stack some of the cash in my safe, as it wouldn't fit in Ivan's. I watched as he stuffed it in, and calculated that I must have had at least a few million in there. I locked up again, and we went back to his apartment. I mused about how blasé I'd become about having access to millions. Only six months before, I'd been circumspect about which sandwich I'd buy for lunch, only choosing the cheapest options.

It was still early, so we decided to eat out. We went south of the river to St Katherine's dock, and found a great little Indian restaurant.

"So are you relieved that your mother's ashes have been interred now?" Ivan asked, before shovelling a popadom into his mouth.

"Yeah, glad it's all over. Did you go to Vlad and Dascha's funerals?" They'd been held the week we'd split up.

He nodded, "yes, paid my respects, as it were, said goodbye, although it was more good riddance. There wasn't many people there, even their staff didn't bother." I thought back to my mum's funeral, with the packed chapel, and the neighbours lining Lovell Avenue. At least she'd been well liked, as well as loved. It was a crumb of comfort. He changed the subject, "so when are you planning to move out of James'?"

"Next week. He comes back on Sunday, so I'll probably spend either Sunday or Monday evening there. I'll pretty much have my things moved tomorrow. My new sofas arrive tomorrow, and the curtains and blinds will take a few weeks. I can live there with what I've got though. I have a bed and a telly, so that's fine."

He laughed, "You and your TV, have you ordered sky as well?"

"Not yet, but John downstairs told me I can get cable, which is better, and it's all wired for it already. I need Internet really, for work. I'll give them a call tomorrow."

"Whatever you need, just use the cash in your safe."

"Ivan, I get paid well, I can use my own money, but thanks for the offer."

He sighed, "Elle, that dodgy money can only be used for certain things. Your salary is legit, so you should save or invest it, and use the cash for food, furniture, and fripperies. I can't use it for much, so you might as well help."

"Don't you worry that I'll spend it all?"

"Baby, I'd be delighted. It'd mean you had a good time, which would please me."

"You're very trusting."

He smiled, "I think you're the only person on the planet I truly trust, and that's the truth. You've proved yourself again and again. Ya lublu tebia ee hotchu zhenitsia na tebe."

"You keep saying that, come on, what does it mean?"

He smiled, and blushed, then took a deep breath, "Ok, it means 'I love you, and want you to be my wife."

I stared at him. "Is that a proposal? Or a statement of intent?"

He laughed, "a statement of intent I suppose. I know that you're young and ambitious, so I won't ask you to give that up just yet, I just want you to know how I feel about you, let you know that you're secure."

"Ok, how do I say the same back to you?" He smiled, and patiently tutored me in the Russian for 'I love you too, and want you to be my husband," (at least I hoped that was what I was saying).

We lay in bed that night, after making love, and he whispered, "I have a confession."

I groaned, "go on."

"I bought the apartment below yours, for the guards. I plan to stay over."

"I see."

"I really like your apartment."

"Good."

"You're not angry?"

"No. Should I be?"

"No, it was just a bit presumptuous of me. Expecting to stay over, the girls too."

"I'd be more worried if you didn't. Now go to sleep."

"Yes ma'am."

Next morning, I was at my apartment by eight, as Ivan had an early meeting, and was dropping me off on the way. I had a day of deliveries and workmen ahead, so nipped across to the shop to buy extra milk, knowing I'd be making copious amounts of tea.

I began to unpack, and sort out my clothes, when the designer arrived, she'd done a design for some shelves and rails in the spare bedroom to hold my shoe and bag collections, and needed it me to ok it, before it was ordered.

She was still there when the sofas arrived. I was delighted with them, and proportionally, they were perfect. The delivery men unwrapped and arranged them for me. I clapped my hands in excitement. I'd ordered a large, glass coffee table, which was next to arrive, and be carried in rather gingerly.

A bunch of workmen arrived, brought by Nico, to install double height bulletproof railing around my terrace. I made everyone cups of tea, while they got on. Some bar stools arrived for the kitchen, and outdoor sofas for the terrace. The last delivery of the day was my dining table and chairs. I gave everything a dust over, and stood back to survey my purchases. The flat still looked a little bare, so I decided it needed some plants and pictures. I didn't want to leave the workmen alone in there, so got on with my clothes until they'd gone.

I was still hanging up my work clothes when Ivan arrived to tell me it was nearly six, and time to head down to Sussex. He wandered around the flat, looking at all the new things, and declaring that he loved my taste in furnishings. "I need to get some pictures and plants, that sort of thing. It still looks a little empty," I declared.

"Have you moved everything out of James'?" Ivan asked.

"Yep, all here now, apart from a few work clothes for Monday."

"Besides clothes, you don't have much do you?" He said, eyeing my elderly laptop.

"Not really. When I moved into James' place, I had a couple of bags of clothes, and that was about it. I've never had the money for lots of 'stuff' before. My legal books are at the office, and I've never been one for knickknacks."

He pulled me into a hug. "I want to give you the world baby, surround you with beautiful things, make you happy."

"You make me happy, this...love, makes me happy. I don't need ornaments to do that. Just you, when you're not being a tosser."

He laughed, "I'm improving though? I've not been a tosser for nearly two weeks now."

"Very true, you've done very well. If this carries on, I might even marry you one day."

He kissed me. "You *will* marry me one day. I promised you I'd be the man you fall in love with. I never renege on a promise."

We had a lovely weekend in Sussex. The sun shone, the dogs played, and we cooked together, in between mad sex sessions. A perfect weekend.

I went back to London on Sunday evening to see James. We got a takeaway, and he told me all about his remaining week. He'd made arrangements to see Lynzi the following night, as it had all gone from strength to strength. The big test would be if they could keep it going back home.

I watched his eyes shine as he talked about her, and deduced that he was in love. He hadn't been as happy or loved up with Janine, so I hoped for his sake that this time, it would be the real thing. Becca had had a fling with the German, which had fizzled out the day before they'd gone home, but it had made her happy to at least have a holiday romance, and some decent shags.

"So when do I get an invite round for dinner at your new place?" He asked, knowing I wasn't a great cook.

"Tuesday evening?" I said, hoping I wouldn't be too late home from work that day.

"Done. You're on. Can I bring Lynzi?"

"Of course. It'd be great to see her again. Invite Becca too if you like."

"Now are you planning to serve cheese on toast? Or would you like me to rustle up a lasagne to pop into the oven?"

I punched his arm. "Cheeky bugger....yes please, if you don't mind." We both laughed.

Epilogue

So life moves on apace, and the story unfolded. Fast forward a couple of months, and my not so new flat is looking a lot more homely. Ivan has almost moved in, the girls have a 'dog loo' planted at one end of my terrace, and squeaky toys in their toy box in the lounge. Ivan has grown into his role as a 'good boyfriend', I'm pleased to say, and I've not had to call him a tosser for weeks now.

My work is still manic busy. We gained three banks as new clients after the LIBOR scandal, so I now head up a small team of four lawyers. My work on the board of Beltan also keeps me occupied, ensuring that Ivan stays on the right side of the law, while he's aggressively trying to own the world. The new board is working well, and he's even grudgingly admitted to liking our female finance director, Gail Hayward. I also managed to sign up Conde Nast. Pearson Hardwick is now officially the biggest of the big four law firms in London. Ms Pearson's delighted.

Lewis and I got over our spat regarding the sale of Paul's company. I found out from Lucy that his sister not only got the money from the company tax free, she also got tens of millions he had stashed away in offshore savings accounts. He was indeed, a very strange man. I still read the books he recommended, and to be truthful, I learnt a lot from him.

Talking of Lucy, her and Oscar are going great guns. Lady Golding herself called to thank me for introducing them, and not only has Lucy taken over the typing of the church newsletter, she's also accompanied Lady Golding on several days out in London. Oscar looks permanently happy, and I think it won't be too long before he makes her the next 'Lady Golding'. I know from conversations with Luce that she truly loves him, and I couldn't have wished for more for him. He remains a great friend. His secret will stay safe with me.

James and Lynzi are still stuck like glue to each other, which is really cute to see. She's given up her rental in Rotherhithe, and moved into his apartment. He fusses over her, looking after her when she does the outrageously long hours that junior doctors have to work.

He loved my new apartment, really liked my new, extra large telly, and pops by every now and then to drink coffee, and berate me for my thinness. He's been getting into baking lately, so occasionally drops by with cakes for me to try. I noticed that Lynzi's not looking so skinny these days.

At the moment, I'm planning our first Christmas together, which we'll be spending in Sussex. I'll never forget Ivan's revelation that he'd never really been bought presents before, so I've got a pile of gifts planned, plus some for the girls as well. He knows something's up, as everything still shows on my face, and he doesn't miss a trick. I've promised him a traditional English Christmas this year, and he'll do a Russian one next year.

I'm sure you all expected me to end up with one of the others, but sometimes it's better to travel the more treacherous route. The rewards at the end are often better, and in my case, the best man won.

ABOUT THE AUTHOR

D A Latham is a salon owner, mother of Persian cats, a dog called Ted, and devoted partner to the wonderful Allan.

Other Books by D A Latham

The Beauty and the Blonde

A Very Corporate Affair Book 1

A very Corporate Affair Book 2

The Taming of the Oligarch

The Taming of the Oligarch- A taster

CHAPTER 1

I sat through yet another business lunch, discussing the same boring subjects, with boring, grey men. I'm sure the food was exquisite, as it was one of the top restaurants in Canary Wharf, but I could barely taste it, so low was my mood. *I'm working too hard again,* I thought. I had one more meeting that afternoon, so planned to call it a day afterwards, pick up the girls from my flat, and drive down to Sussex. I also decided to give Penny a ring, see if a shag would cheer me up, although she'd proven a bit tricky to shake off afterwards, when I wanted some solitude. With my mind made up, I concentrated hard on what my lunch companions had to say, trying not to allow my thoughts to drift as they discussed emerging markets, and predictions for the telecoms industry on the African Subcontinent. The truth was that it was tedious beyond belief. Idly, I wondered how these men summoned up so much enthusiasm for the project.

My meeting that afternoon was with a pair of young entrepreneurs whose company was intent on developing an extra-tough coating for the cables used in fibre optics. I'd decided to invest in them, as I could see a use for the product worldwide. They'd struck me as a bit naive about valuations, so I agreed to meet them in their lawyers office to thrash out the final price. I hoped to have it all wrapped up, and contracts signed before the end of the day, so I could leave for Sussex with no outstanding issues.

I checked my appearance in my office bathroom mirror. I made a point of always being immaculately presented, as it tended to intimidate lesser men when I swept in wearing my bespoke suits and expensive shirts. I brushed my teeth and combed my hair, just to be sure. Nico and Roger fell into step behind me as I strode out of the Retinski offices, and down to the Pearson Hardwick ones.

"Good afternoon Mr Porenski, your meeting is scheduled in room 3, can I offer you a drink of anything?" Their receptionist was always unfailingly polite and efficient.

"No thank you. Shall I go straight in?" I asked.

"Certainly. Let me show you through." She trotted along ahead of us, past the secretarial pool, and into the meeting room. The others were already there, including a pretty little blonde girl. Everyone was introduced, and sat down to begin negotiations. I had to stop myself from staring at her, and concentrate on the task at hand, namely squeezing the saps for a bit more equity than they wanted to give. I pushed the negotiations forward at a punishing pace, confident I could lose them all in the detail of the deal. When I was certain that their eyes had glazed, I threw in a percentage figure which I'd inflated, which would give me 10% more of their company than I was paying for. *Like taking candy from a baby,* I mused.

"My colleague has indicated a possible discrepancy with the percentage figure," said their lawyer, "we'd like to request a recess to check the figures."

I shot little Miss Blondie a furious look. *How the hell did she manage to keep up?* She looked like a rabbit caught in the headlights. *Yeah, yeah, so I was sharking baby girl. I'm impressed by you though.*

We all took a break while they recalculated. I knew full well that their figures would be correct, and reconciled myself to gaining just 53% of the company. I observed her closely when they all returned. The over-riding attribute I noted was how healthy she looked. Pretty girls were ten a penny, but Miss Reynolds glowed with good health. Her skin was perfect, and her hair shone. Being attracted to women with clear skin and shiny hair was definitely a throwback to my pauper roots, as poor health and weakness was common, and marked you down further into a life of grinding poverty. My first girlfriend, Irina, had been the only girl in my year at school back in Russia with lovely skin, and nice, clean hair. Miss Reynolds surpassed her in every way, with a superior intellect as the cherry on top.

The rest of the meeting passed quickly, and I was forced to acquiesce gracefully on the subject of the percentage figure. I gave Miss Reynolds a pointed look, but couldn't stop the corners of my mouth twitching, seeing how apprehensive she looked. We agreed to meet again on Monday afternoon, and after the usual pleasantries, I swept out, my guards trailing along behind me.

"I'd like a full background check on Miss Reynolds please, I want to know everything," I barked at Roger, just before I bumped into Oscar standing outside reception. I assumed he had business there, and greeted him warmly, despite the fact I was intensely envious of his position in life. I actually quite liked him, once I'd got over just how easily he'd acquired everything, particularly his castle. He had also inherited his position at the helm of his family bank, and was my banker.

"Hello Ivan, how nice to see you. I trust you're keeping well?" he said in his upper class accent. "Another acquisition?" He asked, nodding towards the glass doors of Pearson Hardwick.

"Yeah, although it proved a little tricky. What about you?"

"Here to see a certain lady I'm pursuing. Quite an impressive young lawyer, just started work there."

"Blonde hair?"

"Yes. The one you just ordered a background check on. I take it you met her then?" Oscar raised his eyebrow.

"Hmm, yes. She just put the kibosh on wrapping the deal today. Called me out on some figures. Just cost me 10% of a tech firm. I wondered who she was."

"She's a lawyer, that's all you need to know. I saw her first, so I'd appreciate it if you stepped aside where she's concerned." Oscar looked impassive, but he wouldn't make a statement like that unless he meant it. I resolved to ask her out for dinner, and discover what had made Oscar lose his usual ultra-detached demeanor. It would be fun to wind him up.

"So, are you taking her out this weekend?" I was curious.

"Hopefully. That's what I'm here for. She certainly knows how to play it cool."

"Oh well, good luck. I'll probably see you Monday. I have some business to take care of with one of your staff. I'll pop by and see how it went." I noticed that Oscar looked a little nervous.

Back home, the girls made a fuss of me, making me smile for the first time since I'd said goodbye to them that morning. They were my saving grace, the reason I took weekends off, and made the drive to Sussex. They forced me to walk through the woods, which did me as much good as them. Those two little spaniels kept me sane, and in return, I kept them safe, loved and well fed. Their unquenchable thirst for fun was the perfect antidote to my rather grey, featureless world spent chasing deals and worshipping the god of money.

I stripped off my suit, and changed into jeans and a thin jersey, ready to begin the process of relaxing. The two spaniels sat on my bed and watched me as I dumped my work clothes in a bag for my housekeeper to dry clean, rolling about for tummy rubs as soon as I was finished.

Each sat on my lap in turn while I fastened their collars and leads, and gave them a kiss on the nose. I packed their portable water dispenser and a rawhide bone each for the journey down, and called Nico to bring the car round.

I called Penny on the way down to Sussex. I figured it was better to see her on Friday night, rather than Saturday, in case she insisted on staying the night. My Sundays were sacred, even more so after getting rid of Dascha, my poisonous ex-girlfriend, I'd vowed never to spend Sundays with anyone who wasn't canine. Penny had sounded pathetically grateful that I'd called, and was delighted to be invited over for what was in effect just a booty call. I'd have to think of a creative excuse to get rid of her afterwards.

She turned up that evening wearing a short, tight dress, clearly thinking she looked alluring. I just thought she looked tarty. I didn't even bother to offer her anything to eat, I just got straight into the shagging. She was one of those insatiable women who wanted it every way it was possible. She begged me to fuck her up the arse, which I declined with a grimace.

Her particular kink was to be tied up. I happily obliged, relatively pleased that her cold, clammy hands wouldn't be running over my skin. On the one occasion I'd fucked her with her hands free, she'd scraped her acrylic nails painfully down my back, which had made me wince, and lose my erection. I was definitely not into pain with sex.

I was grinding away, trying to feel something, anything, when the image of Ms Reynolds inexplicably popped into my head. I closed my eyes, and let myself fantasise about fucking her, instead of Penny, who was yelling her imminent orgasm.

Hmm, silky warm skin against mine, those baby blue eyes filled with lust, begging me to fuck her hard and fast. Her soft little hands caressing my cock, as she wraps those pretty, plump lips around it...

I came with a shout, pumping Penny full of the cum Miss Reynolds should have laid claim to. Without the fantasy I'd allowed myself, I seriously doubted that I'd have been able to come at all. For a fleeting moment, I felt a little ashamed of myself, then shook it off, and turned my attention to getting rid of the limpet-like woman in my spare bedroom. I disposed of the condom in the bathroom, and pulled on a robe. Returning to the bedroom, I took a deep breath. "I have a load of phone calls scheduled for overnight, time differences, you know. It would be better to have Roger take you home," I said, not really caring whether she thought I was a bastard or not. She pouted slightly.

"Means we'll miss out on some morning action," she countered.

"I know, but I have meetings from early tomorrow, and need to leave here by seven at the latest," I lied smoothly. I just wanted her gone, so I could scoff some food cuddled up in my own bed with my girls, and watch some TV. She got out of bed reluctantly, and began to get dressed. I pulled out my phone and called Roger.

When she'd gone, I fixed a tray of snacks, and climbed into bed. Bella and Tania snuggled in, and I watched the news, sharing a packet of cheese straws with the greedy little spaniels. I mused about my naughty fantasy involving Miss Reynolds, and wondered how she'd seeped into my subconscious so quickly. I looked at the clock, and hoped that Oscar wasn't shagging her at that moment. *Jammy bastard gets everything he wants.* The thought of him having the delectable Miss Reynolds grated on me, almost as much as his money, castle and private bank did.

On a personal level, I quite liked him, and enjoyed his company. I could see why women would be drawn to him. On a business level, he was as sharp as his father had been. The late Lord Golding had been complicit in the raping of Russian natural resources, with the help of the oligarchs and the politicians. He had been in cahoots with Vlad, my was-to-be father in law, and the pair of them had set me up to take control of Russia's telecoms industry back in '99. Oscar was one of the few people who knew exactly what had gone on, and it was in all of our interests that it remain concealed.

The next morning, I woke up early, and slid out of bed quietly, so as not to disturb the sleeping spaniels. I cooked some sausages for us all, putting mine in a sandwich, and slathering on a generous helping of ketchup. The smell must have woken the girls, and the pair of them came skidding in, sliding to a halt in front of me, with winsome smiles on their faces. Laughing at them, I cut up their breakfast, and let it cool slightly before putting the bowls down on the floor, only to see the contents inhaled within 30 seconds.

"I don't know why you do that, you should make the most of it," I admonished, as they looked at me expectantly, hoping for more. They knew I always held back a sausage or two for later. I took them straight out into the woods, knowing that they'd need the loo.

Walking through the tree lined paths, I pondered my past week. All the meetings had seemed to blur together, except one. I'd had a few significant wins, namely driving down some staffing costs by outsourcing some call centre work to India, and a significant loss, which was having a certain little lawyer keep up with me during that deal.

As a rule, I never went for intellectual women. I had an image to keep up, so tended to value a woman's looks ahead of her brains. Clever women rarely seemed to take care of themselves as well as airheads, so generally didn't appear on my radar. Thinking about it, I'd never been out with a woman who possessed a degree, let alone one in law. I doubted that Oscar had either. All of his exes had been tall, willowy blondes, usually with a braying voice, and an inbuilt snobbery.

I tended to go for tall, slim brunettes, although my relationship with Dascha had seriously put me off that particular type. I'd also vowed to stick to English or American women, and never ever succumb to a Russian woman's charms again.

I set off after lunch, having appointments with both my tailor and hairdresser in the West End. Bespoke suits were a weakness of mine, and I judged them to be worth the extra time it took with fittings. After my haircut, and a massage, I shopped a little, buying some new underwear, some shirts, and new collars for the girls in the pet department, also picking up new squeaky toys, as they'd destroyed the last ones quite thoroughly.

I arrived back in Sussex around 7, and, after eating, went into my study to check my emails. Straightaway I saw the one from my security company, containing the background check on Miss Reynolds. I ignored the rest of my emails, and opened it.

Background information requested by Ivan Porenski

Name: Elle Reynolds

Address: 14A, 176 Jamaica Wharf, Coriander Street, London E14 2FT

Previous Address: 14b Lovell Avenue, Welling, Kent, DA16 4AH

Mobile Number: 07956 567895

National Insurance number: NR66 01 88 E

Bank Account: NatWest Bank, Welling branch, account number: 26597856

Balance: £3100.34

No other bank or savings accounts found.

Debt: None

D.O.B: 21/10/1988

Mother: Deborah Reynolds 15/3/1967

Father: Unknown (not listed on birth certificate)

Education: Fosters primary school, Upper Wickham Lane, Welling

Bexley Grammar School, Danson Lane, Welling 12GCSEs, 4AS levels, 3A levels. All achieved with A* grades

Cambridge University (achieved first class honours degree in law, highest marks in her year group) Full bursary grant received.

Joined Pearson Hardwick immediately after her year of law practitioners course, taken at Cambridge.

Work History: July 2009-sept 2009 waitress at The Nags Head restaurant, Welling

Sept 2009- June 2011 part time waitress at The Crown Carvery, Porrit road, Cambridge.

June 2011- current Pearson Hardwick law practitioners, corporate law division, Canary Wharf.

Previous Relationships: December 2010- May 2011 Niall Duffy

August 2011- November 2011 Craig Lutey

Property owned: Nil

Social Networks: None

Sexual Orientation: Heterosexual

Sexual proclivities: None known

Criminal Record: none found

Driving Licence: none

Passport: British

I must have read through the report at least ten times. If anything, it made Miss Reynolds even more of a mystery. I printed it out to peruse later, and turned my attention to the rest of my emails, grimacing at a company report on costings for new cabling through downtown Moscow. I then spent a little time researching the information regarding Ms Reynolds. Satisfied that I'd dealt with everything, I switched off my computer.

I lay in the bath that evening, ruminating on that report. *Elle, hmm, the name suits her.* I'd google-earthed Lovell Avenue, discovering that it was a fairly grotty maisonette in South London. Her schools had been state run too. *Miss Reynolds hasn't come from money. In fact, I think she comes from poverty. No wonder she's a closed book. I bet Golding doesn't know. Wonder why they couldn't find all her boyfriends though, that's a bit strange.*

The fact that I was thinking about her so much surprised me. As a rule, women flung themselves at me, and I took my pick. I got bored fairly quickly, took them out for a final shopping trip, then sent them on their way. I didn't usually *think* about them. They were just...there, even Dascha, who was about the nearest I'd got to a relationship, even though it had been largely platonic, thanks to her horrific sexual preferences. She'd been into the BDSM scene in a big way, so we'd agreed early on that we were sexually incompatible, and that our relationship would be an open one, with both of us free to seek sex elsewhere. Even without the sex aspect, I'd disliked her intensely, and could barely be in the same room as her. Great introduction to relationships.

Most women seemed to be happy with a few good shags and a shopping trip or two, and appeared to be quite sanguine about being ditched. A couple had been a bit clingy, but my extensive security arrangements had stopped them becoming a problem. I decided to find out more about Elle Reynolds from Oscar on Monday.

I dressed carefully on Monday morning, conscious that I'd be seeing Elle again that afternoon. I dealt with about a million emails, then caught the lift down to Goldings bank for a meeting at half twelve to move some money into the main Retinski account to cover some acquisitions. I preferred to do it in person, as the web of companies was fairly complex, and required careful oversight. I'd dealt with Mrs Restorick for quite a long time, so she greeted me warmly, and set about enacting my requirements. As I fully expected to complete my deal with the cabling company that afternoon, she set up a new account, and a vast line of credit, ready for my takeover.

I bumped into Oscar on my way out, and, at his insistence, joined him for a coffee in his office. "How was your date with Miss Reynolds?" I asked, trying not to sound too interested.

He pulled a face. "The date was great, then she refused a shag, sent me home, and stormed off at breakfast the next day when I came on a bit strong. Ignored me ever since. She's certainly a feisty one." He looked annoyed.

If I could have punched the air at that moment without him seeing, I would've done. "So she's still a single woman?" I asked.

"Yeah, but I doubt if you'll get anywhere with her. I happen to know she wouldn't date the opposing side. Besides, I think she's a little too ladylike for you Ivan. Let's face it, if she's the first woman to say no to me, she's hardly going to drop her knickers for you now is she?"

"Well, I am better looking than you, Osc, so you never know." We both laughed, but inside I was thrilled. *What is it about her?* "All I can say is may the best man win." I threw down the gauntlet. Probably not a wise move to declare my interest, but I figured that Oscar would back off, having been turned down by her. I certainly didn't expect him to pursue Miss Reynolds, as it would be extremely out of character. He expected women to fall at his feet, and regarded them as playthings. *Rather like me,* the unwelcome thought popped into my head.

"I shall enjoy hearing all about how she turned you down flat," said Oscar, with a slight sneer. *We'll see about that,* I thought. At that moment, I was determined to have Elle Reynolds, if nothing else just to piss Golding off, and wipe the sneer from his face.

"She won't turn me down. I shall dazzle her with my Russian charm," I announced. Oscar started laughing.

"Russian charm? First time I've heard those two words in the same sentence. I haven't given up yet, so calm yourself down, you're up against some stiff competition, and I have a title and a castle up my sleeve." *Yes, yes, I know, you jammy bastard. And I'm just the Podunk with a lot of money, I get it.*

"That as may be, but you've been turned down and ignored. You're already a busted flush, leaves the field wide open my friend," I pointed out. Oscar scowled, which pleased me enormously. "Plus of course, I'm seeing her in..." I looked at my watch, "fifteen minutes."

I arrived at the Pearson Hardwick offices at precisely two o'clock, and was shown straight into the meeting room. I let my lawyer do the talking, and used the opportunity to get a good look at Miss Reynolds. I watched as she sorted some papers, her little blouse draping provocatively over what looked like a perfect pair of C cup breasts. I signed the contract, and the deal was done. Everyone got up to leave, so I seized my opportunity.

"Miss Reynolds, I would like to speak to you alone please." I asked her, fixing her with an intense stare. She looked apprehensive.

"Sure," she said, "here ok?" I nodded, and waited for the rest of the men to leave, before striding over to the door and closing it.

"You are very impressive for such a young woman," I said. Not my most original opener, I admit, but I thought it would flatter her. She didn't look particularly flattered.

"Thanks.......is that all?" She said, a hint of sarcasm in her voice.

"No. You intrigue me Miss Reynolds. Do I intrigue you?"

"Mr Porenski, it's not something I've given any thought to. Now is there anything else? I have a full schedule to be getting back to." *Oh I haven't finished yet, prepare yourself...*

"Would you have dinner with me tonight?" I looked at her expectantly. I fully expected her to smile gratefully, behave all coy, and say yes immediately. Women loved my pretty face, and deep, Russian accent.

"No, I'm sorry but I'm busy." *WHAT? Did she just say no? Maybe she's gay?*

"Oscar was a fool to let you slip away from him. I wouldn't

make the same mistake. Now, Elle, take a good, long look at me, and tell me if you see a man who takes no for an answer." *Women just....never say no to me.*

"No means no. I have no idea what Oscar did or didn't tell you, but when I say no I mean it. Do yourself a favour, and accept it gracefully." She said it quite forcefully, and looked a bit annoyed. She grabbed her files, and stormed out of the room. I stood rooted to the spot in shock. *She really is quite magnificent,* I thought.

I didn't see her as I left, and went back to my office to sulk. Galina put a coffee down in front of me, and barely even flinched as I growled at her to leave me alone. She really was worth her weight in gold. Very few secretaries would put up with my moods the way that she did. Half an hour later, Oscar called. "Hello Ivan, just thought I'd find out how your meeting went."

"It went well thank you. Contracts are all signed, and the deal concluded."

"That's not what I meant, and you know it. What did Elle say? Presuming you mustered up the courage to ask her out, that is."

"Of course I did, but she turned me down flat. Were you aware that she's a lesbian?" I heard Oscar chuckle down the phone.

"She's no lesbian Ivan. Guess she's still hung up on me. Hmm, she's quite the ladylike little thing." *Yeah she is, and she's way too good for you, you spoilt brat.* I changed the subject to that weekend. Oscar's family seat was about 10 miles from my weekend house, so we often met up if neither of us had anything going on. We arranged to have dinner Saturday evening, providing that neither of us had anything more exciting come up.

It probably sounds a bit boring, two thirty something bachelors spending their Saturday evenings in the depths of Sussex, but the truth was that both of us were a little jaded with the constant womanising and carousing of London life. We'd both spent our twenties being playboys, sampling the best that London had to offer. Oscar had ended up a junkie, and I'd had a breakdown. Both events had been hushed up, and kept out of the papers, but they were always there, reminding both Oscar and I that peace and solitude were a necessary antidote to the excesses of our business lives. In my own case, I'd worked almost twenty hours a day, to both build the business, and avoid Dascha, and the sense of failure I felt around her. I'd squeezed women into my mad schedule, almost as appointments. It had been a terrible way to live.

As with everything in my life, the stars had aligned to save me. The poisonous ex had tried to kill my dog, and gave me a superb excuse to finally kick her out and send her back to her father, who, as an animal lover, had accepted that she'd done a terrible thing. My breakdown happened shortly afterwards, which I was able to keep secret from both blabber mouth Dascha, and her psychopath father, who would have used it against me. So here I was, six months later, the calmest and happiest I'd ever been, except...I was a little...lonely.

For the next few days, I tried to forget about Elle, and concentrate on business. I was offloading a small company I'd purchased ten years ago for buttons, to Vodafone for eighty five mil. It had definitely proved to be a superb investment in more ways than one, as the technologies it had developed had cut our infrastructure costs by millions as well. My in-house team were handling the sale, with Pearson Hardwick handling the purchase for Vodafone.

I worked my way methodically through all the figures, satisfying myself that we'd left no stone unturned, and had fully disclosed every patent, asset, and liability so that nothing could possibly come back to bite us. I also knew that Vodafone were desperate for the technologies that had been developed, so the price was a touch on the high side to reflect its value.

Figures were my thing, the area in which I excelled. I prided myself on being able to keep up with, and outwit, the best accountants. I'd been taught basic maths back home in Moscow, but it hadn't been until I'd got to the UK, that I'd fully explored my aptitude. Two years of studying accountancy at night school had revealed a talent that I never knew I had.

My only break from working on that deal was a meeting at Elle's offices to map out the timings involved with transferring the company. I felt a pang of disappointment that she wasn't present. I'd been looking forward to seeing her more than I cared to admit. During the meeting, I wrote out a note for her, adding my phone number, just in case she changed her mind, or regretted turning me down. I dropped it into her office on my way out, again disappointed that she wasn't there. She was fast turning into a bit of an addiction, like crack for the soul. Given that she hadn't shown the slightest interest in me, she was a habit I needed to break.

I entertained some business associates that evening, taking them out to the Dorchester grill, and on to Whisky Mist. They were fellow Russians, which meant I could relax a little. I understood them, they understood me, and we had plenty in common. One of them, Karl, was what would commonly be described as a pussyhound, unable to keep it in his pants for any length of time. Fortunately his wife allowed his behavior, thanks to an unlimited credit card, and his blind eye to her preference for the ladies as well.

"So Ivan, who're you shagging these days?" He asked.

"Only some actress, but if I'm honest, she's starting to irritate me. I need to fix up a shopping trip." I admitted. Karl nodded, understanding immediately what I meant. Our other companion, Mika, was a little older, and was loved up with his current lady, a model called Katrina. I noticed he kept looking at his watch, as if was dying to get back to her.

"Mika, if you want to go, we won't be offended," I said.

"Yes we bloody will," countered Karl, "one night out with the boys shouldn't be a problem."

"Ivan can wingman for you tonight," Mika said, "I've got better at home than there is in here."

I looked around, to see the place stuffed full of pretty girls, some throwing glances our way and preening. "Yeah, I'm up for it tonight. I could do with some fun," I told them. Karl looked delighted. With business dealt with during dinner, we were looking forward to some drinking and womanising. With all our security seated on the table next to us, it didn't matter how pissed we got, we all knew we'd get scraped up and delivered home safely, and any girls would be dropped off if need be.

Mika said his goodbyes, and left us to it. "Pussywhipped," declared Karl, "he'll learn."

"Learn what?" I asked.

"Women. They break your heart if you let them. Far better to keep them at dicks length."

"I fully intend to," I laughed. *Apart from Miss Reynolds that is.* I noticed a girl at the bar who looked a little like Elle, with long, fair hair, and similar tits. *I could pretend it's her.* I smiled my best, most dazzling smile, and indicated that she should come over and join us. She smiled back, and grabbed her friend to point us out. The pair of them sashayed over.

"Would you like to join us for a drink?" I said.

"Ooh, lovely, could I have some champagne please?" The Elle lookalike said, before pulling up a chair. Karl ordered another bottle of Krug from the hovering waiter.

"What's your name?" I asked.

"Amy, and my friend is Tracey. What's yours?" *You don't recognise me?*

"Ivan, and this is Karl. I've not seen you in here before." *That's because I've only been here a couple of times, but you don't need to know that.*

"First time here. It's really packed isn't it? How did you manage to get a table?" *They recognised me, dumb girl.*

I shrugged, "just lucky I guess." I noticed Karl smiling at Tracey, like a lion smiling at the zebra he was about to devour.

"I love your accent, where are you from?" Amy asked.

"Russia, Moscow to be exact."

"I thought Russians talked like 'zat', 'zey vont a wodka'," she giggled.

"I took English lessons," I explained, amused at her impression of a Podunk.

"Enunciate the 'wuh' sound, Ivan, your lips should form a kiss," explained Ms Bishop in our English class. I practiced constantly, asking the staff at the home to correct any mistakes I made with my grammar or pronunciation. I was determined to be able to say 'the' like a Londoner, and be able to keep up with any conversation in English, without being left behind. A bit of an accent was ok, sexy even, but sounding like the vampire in a cheesy horror film wasn't, so I worked hard.

Another bottle of Krug later, the two girls were giggly and clearly up for anything. We ended up booking rooms at the Dorchester, under the premise of carrying on the party. They appeared too stupid to notice that we took them into separate rooms.

Amy turned out to be a surprisingly good shag, and a bit of a tiger between the sheets. She got a couple of orgasms, and I was able to indulge my fantasy that I was shagging Ms Reynolds, thanks to some low lighting and a bit of imagination. When we'd finished, I took her number, and arranged a car home for her. I was after all, a gentleman.

Made in the USA
San Bernardino, CA
22 January 2016